Acclaim for Michael Nava's

LAY YOUR SLEEPING HEAD

This new iteration of Michael Nava's *The Little Death* is such a different book I could not remember which Henry Rios novel I was re-reading. *Lay Your Sleeping Head* is both sexier and starker than its original, which, in comparison almost seems like the outline of the novel that Nava has given us now. A much deeper and more personal introduction to Henry Rios--from his alcoholism to his passionate nights with Hugh Paris-- this is both a poetic character study of the first queer Chicano lawyer in Latin@ letters and a mystery with a mission that uses the noir genre to expose family secrets such as incest, depression, and addiction, as well as the rampant homophobia of both mainstream and Latin@ culture. The most surprising part of this new edition is the 13-part Author's Note at the end. By learning more about the abuses and inequalities the author experienced in his family life, as well as the homophobic attitudes and policies of his coming out years in the 1970's, intersecting with racial bigotry, internalized hatred, and stultifying isolation, we understand why Nava had to create a character like Henry Rios, dedicated to social justice and committed to healing from his own demons. If you're a young queer of color just discovering the Henry Rios novels, this book will fill you with recognition, this book is your own "affirming flame" (with nods to W.H. Auden).

Alicia Gaspar de Alba, Professor of Chicana/o Studies and Chair of LGBTQ Studies at UCLA, author of *Desert Blood: The Juárez Murders*

LAY YOUR SLEEPING HEAD

LAY YOUR SLEEPING HEAD
A HENRY RIOS MYSTERY

Michael Nava

foreword by
Michael Hames-García, Ph.D.

Kórima Press

The poems quoted in this novel are used with the permission of Joan
Larkin. My deepest thanks to her. They are: "The Offering," "My Body,"
and "Breathing You In" from the collection *My Body: New and Selected
Poems* (Hanging Loose Press, 2007).

The quotations attributed to Grover Linden's memoirs are taken from
Andrew Carnegie's book, *The Gospel of Wealth*, now out of copyright.

Author photograph: David Quintanilla

Cover and Book Design: Lorenzo Herrera y Lozano

Published by Kórima Press
San Francisco, CA
www.korimapress.com

ISBN: 978-1-945521-00-3

A version of this novel was previously published as

The Little Death

for Bill

CONTENTS

FOREWORD

Lay Your Sleeping Head is not *The Little Death*. *The Little Death* is a good read and a promising first novel. *Lay Your Sleeping Head* is something most novelists spend a lifetime trying to produce. Selfishly, I'm glad that Michael Nava waited to revisit and rewrite his first novel, because it means I get to read *Lay Your Sleeping Head* for the first time now. I was in my early twenties when I first heard about Nava's work. I'm now in middle age, partially disabled, more familiar with addiction and illness than anyone should be, and far better prepared to appreciate the imperfect humanness of Nava's characters. I'm tempted to read *Lay Your Sleeping Head* in the ways that I approached Nava's work ten or twenty years ago: as a novel about identity, about race, gender, class, disability, and sexuality. As I read the manuscript, though, I begin to see that its core is concerned with something else. Fundamentally, what Nava has gives us in these pages is a forceful meditation on inequality and the value of those lives society considers disposable. It doesn't seem right to call *Lay Your Sleeping Head* "gay fiction" (despite some excellent sex scenes that weren't in the original) or even "detective fiction" (despite a thrilling legal mystery). As a contribution to American letters, this new novel puts me in mind of books like Ann Petry's *The Street*, Richard Wright's *Native Son*, and John Steinbeck's *Grapes of Wrath*.

In some ways, it remains a novel of the 1980s. In other, more important, ways, it is a novel of now, with much to say about the meth epidemic in the gay community, and more unexpectedly perhaps, about the police state that the United States has become in the decades since Reagan's presidency. The spirit of justice that motivates protagonist Henry Rios to take on the system like a queer, brown Bernie Sanders is the spirit that understands how this system is rigged against his clients, especially those whom Chicana feminist Gloria Anzladúa in *Borderlands/La Frontera: The New Mestiza* calls "los atrevesados": "the squint-eyed, the perverse, the queer, the troublesome, the mongrel, the mulato, the half-breed, the halfdead; in short, those who cross over, pass over, or go through the confines of the 'normal.'" Nava's protagonist, Henry Rios, more prosaic than Anzaldúa, might simply call them the marginalized or the downtrodden.

As I write this foreword, the U.S. political establishment is touting the fact that unemployment rate is around five percent, roughly the same as in Britain and down significantly from its peak of 10% in 2010. Yet, the Bureau of Labor Statistics website tells us that the percentage of those between the ages of 16 and 64 in the United States who are "not in the labor force" is 30%, which is twice that of Britain. These are not people who are underemployed, retired, working part time, or looking for work. They are jobless and not seeking jobs. If you add the unemployed to this number, you have *just over a third* of the nation's labor force not working. Yet the economy is growing, and those of us who benefit enjoy organic donuts that practically melt on one's tongue. We wash them down with seasonal craft beers on tap. We "share" the experience with friends across the globe using a cellphone app whose algorithms give it all more critical analysis than we do. But there are shantytowns everywhere today. Our city planners keep them just out of sight so that we don't get indigestion after our donuts and beer. But we know they are there, waiting for us if we fall through the cracks. In addition to the fear, there is anger in the air today. Confrontations between far left and far right youth turn bloody on the streets of Chicago and Sacramento. The police reveal Klan robes under their body armor in Baltimore, Ferguson, and Oakland. So-called "mass shootings" take place on a daily basis across the nation, taking the lives of school children, dancers, and moviegoers.

It is often at moments of extreme inequality and urgent crisis that the noir genre gains in popularity. Dashiell Hammett published *The Maltese Falcon* in 1929 at the dawn of The Great Depression, and Roman Polanski's *Chinatown* premiered in 1974 at the height of a global recession. I thus find now an appropriate time to revisit Nava's Henry Rios novels. Noir protagonists often operate outside of and antagonistically toward the official array of police, courts, and prisons. This positioning helps them see that "the system" is mostly set up to protect the interests of the wealthy and powerful. So our noir heroes and heroines do what the police won't: they confront the criminal cartels, the vast conspiracies, and the unofficial networks that hold the lives of the powerless to be without value. By the very nature of this confrontation, they rarely succeed in bringing the system to its knees. They and their fans must find solace in what partial justice their perseverance enables them to achieve.

The best noir endings thus nearly always leave me feeling melancholy. When grinding inequality and conspiracies of the powerful seem insurmountable, however, witnessing the integrity and commitment to justice of a man like Henry Rios reminds me that I am not alone. I take comfort in knowing that he starts out as a drunk who has never had a romantic relationship. I couldn't stand to have Superman rescue me. He's too good, too clean, too perfect. I need a hero as fucked up as I am. I know Henry wouldn't judge me or pity me. Maybe he could even love me. And it's inspiring to think that even someone as broken and fucked up as Henry can consistently stand up for what he knows is right. To hint at a moment of poignancy in *Lay Your Sleeping Head*, sometimes all we have is footnote four of United States v. Carolene Products. In other words, sometimes, when winning seems out of reach, all we have is our ability to resist injustice and the conviction that we do not struggle alone.

Michael Hames-García, Ph.D.
Eugene, Oregon

LAY
YOUR
SLEEPING
HEAD

Lay your sleeping head, my love,
Human on my faithless arm;
Time and fevers burn away
Individual beauty from
Thoughtful children, and the grave
Proves the child ephemeral:
But in my arms till break of day
Let the living creature lie,
Mortal, guilty, but to me
The entirely beautiful.

W.H. Auden
Lullaby

The man who dies rich dies disgraced.

Andrew Carnegie

ONE

I stood in the sally port until the steel door lurched back with a clang and then stepped into the jail. A sign ordered prisoners to proceed no further; an emphatic STOP was scrawled beneath the printed message. I looked up at the mirror above the sign where I saw a slender, olive-skinned, dark-haired man in a wrinkled seersucker suit. I adjusted the knot in my tie. A television camera recorded the gesture in the booking room where a bank of screens monitored every quarter of the jail.

It was six-thirty a.m., but in the windowless labyrinth of cells and offices in the basement of Linden's City Hall, perpetually lit with buzzing fluorescent lights, it could have been midnight. Only mealtimes and the change of guards communicated the passage of time to the inmates. I had often thought the hardest part of doing time was that time stood still; serving a sentence must feel like scaling a mountain made of glass.

I stepped out of the way of a trustie who raced by carrying trays of food. Breakfast that morning, the first Monday of June, 1982, was oatmeal, canned fruit cocktail, toast, milk, and Sanka— inmates were not allowed caffeine because it was a stimulant.

Ironic considering the other stimulants that made their way into the jail; you could get almost any drug here. Jones stepped into the hall from the kitchen and acknowledged me with an abrupt nod. He had done his hair up in cornrows and his apron was splattered with oatmeal. On the outside, Jones was a short-order cook and a low level drug dealer. I'd represented him after his last bust. In exchange for snitching on some higher ups, I got him a plea, a reduced sentence, and a guarantee he could serve it in county jail instead of state prison where his life expectancy would have been about that of a soap bubble. Unlike the prisons, the jail population was either transient or made up of inmates serving short sentences for relatively minor offenses. The deputy sheriffs who ran the place weren't as tightly wound as prison guards and you didn't see inmates sleeping in the halls or six to a cell because of overcrowding. Jail was easy time compared to the hard time at places like Folsom or San Quentin and a lot safer for a snitch like Jones. Still, county had the familiar institutional stink of all places of incarceration, a complex odor of ammonia, unwashed bodies, latrines, dirty linen, and cigarette smoke compounded by bad ventilation and mingled with a sexual musk, a distinctive genital smell. The walls were painted in listless pastels, faded greens, and washed-out blues like a depressed child's coloring book, and were grimy and scuffed. The linoleum floor, however, was spotless. The trusties mopped it at all hours of the day and night. Busy work, I suppose.

Everyone in the Public Defender's office had to take the jail rotation. Unlike my colleagues, I didn't mind it. If, as my law school teachers had insisted, the law was a temple, it was a temple built on human misery and jails were the cornerstones. It was salutary to have to encounter the misery on a regular basis because otherwise it became too easy to believe that trials were a contest between lawyers to see who was the craftiest. It was good to be reminded that when I lost a case someone paid a price beyond my wounded pride. Not that I was in particular need of that memo at the moment.

A few months earlier, I'd lost a death penalty case where, *rara avis*, my client was innocent. Not generally innocent, of course— he had been in an out of juvie hall, jails, and prison since he was 15—but innocent of the murder charge. After the jury returned its guilty verdict, I snapped. When the judge asked the usual, "Would you like to have the jury polled, Mr. Rios?" I jumped to my feet and shouted, "This isn't a jury, it's a lynch mob." He warned me, "Sit down, counsel, or I'll find you in contempt." I unloaded on him. "You could never hold me in more contempt than I hold you, you reactionary hack. You've been biased against my client from day one . . ." I continued in that vein until the bailiff dragged me out of the courtroom and into the holding cell. Eventually, I was released, lectured, held in contempt, fined a thousand dollars, and relieved as my client's lawyer. When word got around the criminal defense bar about my rampage, I received congratulatory calls but not from my boss, the Public Defender himself.

A death penalty trial is really two trials, the guilt phase where the jury decides whether the defendant committed the charged murder, and the penalty phase where the same jury decides whether to sentence him to death or life without parole. My outburst came at the end of the guilt phase. This meant another deputy public defender would have to be appointed to the case, get up to speed, and argue for my client's life in front of the same jury I'd called a lynch mob.

"I should just fucking fire you," Mike Burton told me, savagely rubbing his temples. The PD was a big man, an ex-cop in fact who had his own awakening about the criminal law system after he watched his partner beat a confession out of a suspect in the days before *Miranda*. "The only reason I'm not is that if Eloy does get death, at least you've handed us grounds for appeal." He glared at me. "Ineffective assistance of counsel."

I squinted at him, my head throbbing with a hangover headache. "What do you want me to say, Mike? I screwed up."

"You've been ten years on the job, Henry, and you're a damn good lawyer. What the fuck, kid?"

I shrugged like a surly teenager. "Eloy's innocent. The jury didn't care, they wanted blood. It got to me."

"It gets to me every fucking day of every fucking week," he snapped. "But when I want to go off on someone, I remind myself, oh, yeah, it's not about me. It's about the client, first, last, and always. That's the golden fucking rule around here and you broke it. You got some hard thinking to do, too, my friend. You can do it in Linden. I'm transferring you."

Linden. A sleepy suburb thirty minutes south of San Francisco that owed its existence to the great university of the same name where I'd been both an undergrad and a law student. I still lived in the town, in the same apartment I'd moved into when I was studying for the bar exam. I'd worked briefly at the PD's Linden office while waiting for the bar results, but as soon as I passed I had transferred to the main office in San Jose where the action was. The big cases, the best lawyers. Linden was the PD's Siberia, where errant lawyers were exiled and broken down veterans put out to pasture. Not exactly the homecoming I had had in mind when I'd set out ten years earlier to change the hard heart of the world.

I'd been at the Linden office for ten months and, as ordered, I'd done a lot of thinking. My courtroom outburst had been the culmination of years of frustration with the criminal law system of justice but that was only part of it. The other part? That had come out of some deeper place, an empty place where my life should have been. I was a lawyer and, like Mike said, a good one. I gave a hundred and ten percent to my clients. For a long time, that was enough to keep me out of my head. At some point, though, after I turned thirty, the disturbing feelings and intrusive memories I had avoided since I'd left home for college had begun to emerge in my mind like bloated corpses rising to the surface of a lake. Flashes of anger, moments of heart-pounding anxiety, a loneliness that clawed at my chest accompanied memories of my raging father, of a childhood that felt like imprisonment and of the boy whose friendship tortured me because I wanted to be more than his friend. These things tugged at me constantly, demanding some kind of resolution. I thought I had long since resolved them when I left home and came out as a gay man. I had no other answers except to work harder and drink more but they would not be silenced by work or drowned by alcohol. I had reached a point of quiet but persistent desperation. Something in my life had to change, that much I knew, but I didn't know what or how or where it would come from. In the meantime, I sucked it up and went about my daily routines.

My jailhouse office was a small room with gray walls tucked away at the end of a corridor, furnished with a prison table and chairs. I picked up the arrest reports and booking sheets from the previous night. Vagrants, drunk drivers, bar fights—Linden was not Al Capone's Chicago. The only potential felony was an auto burglary. The two suspects had been caught breaking into cars in the parking lot of a Mexican restaurant on El Camino, the town's main drag. They were Chicanos in their early twenties with just enough by way of rap sheets to appeal to a judge's hanging instinct. I gathered the papers together and went into the booking office where Deputy Novack was reading the sports page from the *San Francisco Chronicle*.

"Good morning, Henry," he drawled. Novack was pale, pudgy, and baby-faced. Recently, he'd grown a wispy little moustache that floated apologetically above a mouth set in a perpetual smirk. He treated me with the same lazy contempt with which he treated all civilians, not holding the fact that I was a lawyer against me. This made us almost friends.

"Deputy," I replied. "What's the good word?"

"We had ourselves a little bit of excitement here last night," he said, folding his paper. "Los Altos brought in a drunk—that's what they thought he was, anyway—and it took three of us to subdue him."

"What was he on?"

"Found a couple of sherms on him when we finally got him stripped and housed, so I'm guessing PCP."

"I didn't see an arrest report for him."

"We couldn't book him until he came down enough to talk."

"Where's he at now?"

"In the queens' tank. Guy's a fag."

I bridled but said neutrally, "Been ten years since the Legislature repealed the sodomy law."

"Yeah, and now the buttfuckers parade down Market Street," he said. He handed me the arrest and booking reports. "Here's the guy's paperwork."

The suspect's name was Hugh Paris; five-foot eight, blond hair, blue eyes, 26 years old. New York license. He declined to give a local address or answer questions about his employment or his family. No rap sheet. I studied his booking photo. His hair was like a coxcomb, his eyes were dazed, and he was ghostly white. Blond, white boys are not my usual type but Hugh Paris was beautiful. I closed the file before Novack could notice how intently I was looking at the photo.

"How do you know he's gay?" I asked.

"They picked him up outside of that fag bar in Cupertino."

I nodded. The bar was called The Office and its matchbooks were inscribed, "If anyone asks, tell them you were at The Office." It drew a mixed crowd of gay guys, but was more preppy than anything else, not the kind of place where you'd expect to find someone high on a poor folks' drug like PCP. Nor did Hugh Paris look like a typical PCP user; I'd have guessed white wine and maybe a little pot on the weekend.

"Charged with being under the influence of PCP, possession of PCP, resisting arrest, and battery on an officer. Geez, did the arresting officer go through the penal code at random?"

Novack shrugged. "If that's what it says, that's what he did."

"Any officers injured?"

"By that cream puff?"

"Doctor take a look at him to see if he was under the influence?"

"Nope."

"Did he submit to a urine test?"

"Refused."

"So all you've really got is possession."

"Well," Novack said, "I guess that's between you and the DA. Are you going to want to see the guy?"

"Yeah," I replied, "but first I'll want to talk to these two," and I read him the names of the burglars.

My burglars were bored but cooperative. Repeat offenders were the easiest to deal with, treating their lawyers with something akin to professional courtesy. All these guys wanted was a deal, a short jail stint and, as one of them said, "to get back to work." I knew he wasn't talking about his dishwashing job. When I told people I was a criminal defense lawyer, I often got a variant of "But how can you help let criminals back on the street?" in response. To which, depending on my mood and level of intoxication, I might give a serious answer or blow them off with "Repeat offenders keep me in business." I did enjoy yanking the chain of the respectable; respectability being, in my mind, vastly overrated.

After I finished with them, I walked back to the booking office and poured myself a cup of Novack's vile, but caffeinated, brew. I flipped him a quarter and asked to see Hugh Paris.

The deputy brought him into my office in handcuffs and a pair of oversized jail blues that fell from his shoulders and covered the tops of his bare feet. My first thought was, five-eight. Not likely. He was five-six, maybe five-seven in shoes. His eyes were focused and his color had returned, but his hair still stuck out from the top and sides of his head. The deputy shoved him into the chair across from me and left the room.

"Mr. Paris," I said. "I'm Henry Rios, from the Public Defender's office. How are you feeling this morning?"

He frowned, as if how he felt should be obvious. He raised his cuffed hands.

"Are these really necessary?" His voice was soft and slightly sibilant.

"Security measure. The deputies insist."

"You're bigger than me," he pointed out. "I couldn't hurt you if I wanted to. Which," he added with a small smile, "I don't. I just want to get out of here."

I summoned the deputy and told him to remove the handcuffs.

"Better?" I asked, after the deputy left us.

"Much," he said.

He rubbed his wrists and smoothed his hair, buttoned the top buttons of the jail jumpsuit, and pulled himself up in the chair. He smiled, revealing a set of expensively maintained teeth. The small gestures restored his dignity and turned him back into a person instead of a prisoner; a really attractive person.

"What am I doing here?" he asked conversationally.

"You were arrested last night at The Office," I replied. I read him the charges.

"Gee, I had some kind of night, didn't I?" he said. "Too bad I don't remember it. I can tell you though, Henry, I didn't do any drugs."

I'd been called many things by the men who'd sat in Hugh's chair, but never by my first name as if we were a couple of pals chatting over a drink. That showed a level of self-assurance I associated with the rich boys I'd gone to school with. That and his nice teeth made me wonder, who is this guy?

"You sure about that?"

He shrugged. "I split a joint in the parking lot with a friend. After that, it all gets kind of cloudy."

"What's the last thing you do remember?"

"I was at the bar having a drink," he said. "I must have gone outside because I remember street lights. And then I woke up here. Where are my shoes, by the way?"

"What about the sherms the cops found on you?"

"The what?"

"You don't know what a sherm is?"

He frowned. "If you'd told me there was going to be a quiz, I would've studied. No, I don't know what a sherm is."

"Sherman's is a brand of cigarettes that are dipped into PCP. That's usually how it's sold."

He shook his head. "I don't smoke at all and I've never used PCP."

"You said you split a joint with someone before you went into the bar. Who was he?"

He appraised me for a moment before he answered. "He was a trick, Henry. He said his name was Brad."

"Did you meet him at the Office?"

He shook his head. "We hooked up at a bathhouse in the city last week and he called me out the blue and asked me to meet him at the bar. I had a good enough time with him to make the drive."

"Do you have a way of reaching this guy?"

"I might have his number somewhere," he said, then asked, lightly, "How much trouble am I in?"

"You're looking at misdemeanor use and possession. Not too serious unless you've got a record somewhere else. Do you?"

"Opiate possession in New York," he said. "Oh, and a couple of solicitation arrests but no convictions. Don't look so shocked, Henry. I can't be your first junkie whore."

"They're not usually white and male," I said.

"What can I say, darling," he replied with hard haughtiness. "I'm an overachiever."

He looked like a trust fund baby and sounded like a street queen; Hugh Paris had me flummoxed.

"I'm not a current user, Henry," he said, reverting to his soft tone. "I've been clean for nine months. That's why I told you no drugs. Well, pot, but that doesn't really count, does it?" He gave me a dazzling smile. "I mean, I bet even upstanding lawyers smoke a joint now and then."

And now he was flirting with me. I pushed his booking photo across the table. "You were high on more than pot last night."

He studied the photo. "God, I look terrible." He raised his head, his blue eyes wide and sincere. "Honestly, Henry, I didn't touch anything last night but grass and a glass of bad chardonnay."

"The joint could have been dipped in PCP without you knowing," I said.

"Why would Brad do that?" he said. "He didn't have to drug me to get laid, I was ready to give it up." He jerked back in the chair and said, "Oh, fuck."

"What?"

"Nothing," he said, but it was clear something disturbing had occurred to him.

"You remember something about last night. What is it?"

"I think I was set up."

"Are you saying this guy, Brad, drugged you intentionally and planted the PCP on you? I thought he was just a guy you'd tricked with."

He looked scared, then angry, but said nothing.

"Hugh? What's going on?"

"I need to make a call," he said.

"When we're done," I said. "Are you going to tell me what happened last night?"

"You wouldn't understand," he said, regretfully.

"If you don't talk to me, you'll sit in jail until they arraign you this afternoon. Since you refused to give a local address, you'll probably be remanded and rot here until they remember to give you a trial. Is that what you want?"

"Don't worry about me, darling," he said, lightly. "I've been in worse scrapes. I just need to make that call to fix it."

"Okay," I said. "Have it your way. I guess we're done here."

"Wait," he said. His eyes locked into mine, searching, it seemed, and then having found what he was looking for, he said, "You're gay."

"That's not relevant," I replied.

"I suspected you might be when I started talking about bathhouses and tricks and you didn't look like you wanted to retch, like a straight guy would, but then you don't sound or act like one of us. Except when you look at me."

"I didn't mean to make you uncomfortable," I said, abashed.

He laughed. "Uncomfortable? You didn't notice I'm looking back? If we were anywhere else I would've jumped you ten minutes ago."

I grinned. "Good thing the camera in this room doesn't record sound, too."

"I've never met a gay lawyer before," he said. "Are you in the closet at work?"

I could have ended the interview but his tone suggested more than mere curiosity. I recognized that tone; it was a signal from one lonely traveler to another. We moved through a world so inescapably and aggressively straight that coming across another gay man in an unexpected circumstance was like stumbling into a refuge where, for a moment, it was possible to lower our shields and breathe.

"I'm out to my employers," I said, "but not my clients."

"Why not tell them?"

"It's not necessary for me to do my job and some of them might have a problem with it. I need for them to trust me."

"By lying about who you are?"

"I'm sure I don't have to explain to you how complicated being gay can be."

"You're right," he said. "I'm sorry. Are there a lot of gay lawyers?"

"Hard to say. I assume most of us are still in the closet, but there's a small group up in the city that started a gay and lesbian bar association. I've been to a couple of their meetings, but I'm not much of a joiner."

"Do you have anyone, Henry?" he asked after a moment.

"You mean, like a boyfriend? No."

He grinned. "That's hard to believe."

"My job keeps me busy," I said. It was my automatic response.

"And alone," he said quietly.

The words seemed to echo in the little, gray-walled room. It was just talk, I told myself. He hadn't meant anything much by it, certainly he couldn't have known how deeply those words cut at the moment.

"Do you have anyone, Hugh?"

He shook his head. "God, no. Who'd have me?"

"You're from New York?"

"From here originally," he said. "I came back to take care of some things. Family things."

"I see," I said. "I wish you luck."

We caught each other's eyes again and then he said, "You think when you come out, your life will be less lonely, but it isn't. You can find guys for sex. That's easy. Sex is how gay guys shake hands. Don't get me wrong, Henry, I'm not knocking sex. But it costs so much to come out, you'd think there'd be something more at the end of it than another guy's dick. My problem is, I never figured out what that something more is."

"To be loved?" I suggested.

Hugh said, "I'm not sure anyone could love me. I've been such a fuck-up. I'm trying to put my life back together. I got off junk. That's a start."

"Until last night," I said.

"I told you, Henry, that wasn't intentional. I was set up."

"I'd like to get you out of here if I can. Tell me what happened and let me help you."

"I appreciate that," he said. "I really do. But last night was part of a long, long story. You wouldn't believe me even if I told you."

"Try me."

He shook his head. "I wish we hadn't met like this."

I took my business card out of my pocket, turned it over, wrote my home phone. "Here. Call me anytime."

He took the card, looked at it. "For legal advice?"

"For whatever you need," I replied.

After that, there was nothing left to say but neither of us moved or looked away. His lips were slightly parted. A blue vein beat in his pale neck. The hard overhead light picked out the darker strands of gold in his pale hair. Something about this soft-voiced, mysterious, pretty little man slipped past my defenses and reminded me that desire was the uncomplicated moment when two people look into each other's eyes and each one thinks, "Yes, you." I saw the assent in his eyes and I knew he saw it in mine, but we were sitting in a gray room in a jail on opposite sides of a table that separated lawyer from inmate. He had refused the only help I could offer and now he was on his own. Still, I could not restrain myself from reaching across the table and taking his hand. He was startled, but then he threaded his delicate fingers into mine and we sat there for a moment holding hands.

"You're sweet," he said, tightening his grip.

"Not usually," I replied.

Then I remembered the camera in the corner, and Novack sitting in the booking office, and let go of him.

"Last chance," I said. "Let me help you, Hugh."

"You have," he replied.

I shrugged and called the guard in to take him back to his cell and went off to see about getting him his phone call.

Outside it was a bright, balmy morning. A fresh, warm wind lifted the tops of the palm trees that lined the streets and sunlight glittered on the pavement. I put on my sunglasses and headed toward California Avenue to meet my friend, Aaron Gold, for our standing breakfast date. A couple of kids cycled by with day packs strapped to their shoulders. The Southern Pacific commuter, bound for San Francisco, rumbled by. I felt a flash of restlessness as it passed and thought, Hugh Paris. That's all, just his name, but those three syllables packed some unexpected regret. I was thirty-three years old, had been out since I was a freshman in college, and I had never had a boyfriend. Just the occasional one-night stand when I needed to scratch the itch. Those times were farther and farther apart; the itch was still there, but tussling with yet another stranger for a couple of minutes of release no longer appealed to me. Being gay had become more a principle than a practice, a political stand like being a socialist or in favor of legalizing pot. In my day to day life, it hardly figured at all. But that moment in the jail with Hugh had brought back the naked longing I remembered from when I had first come out as a seventeen year old, intoxicated and terrified by the beauty and possibilities of other men. I told myself, you need to get laid, but that was a lie. Hugh had stirred up more in me than the ache of sexual loneliness. I tossed the feeling on the pile of feelings that had accumulated inside me like a tower of unread books that would someday come crashing down and bury me.

"Hey, Henry!" Gold bustled toward me, his intelligent, simian face balled into a squint against the sunlight. He was my height, a hair below six feet, almost as dark as me—"we're Sephardic, not Ashkenazi," he had explained to me when we were law school roommates, comparing skin color—and getting a little thick around the waist.

"Morning, Aaron."

He tilted his chin at the window of the pet store when my ruminations had stopped me. "Thinking about getting a dog?"

"No, just waiting for you to buy me breakfast."

"You always stick me with the check," he complained.

"On your salary, you can afford it," I replied. In his tailored suit, Gold looked sleek and prosperous from his polished shoes and manicured nails to the fifty-dollar haircut that subdued his curly, black hair.

"At least you're a cheap date," he said. "Eggs over easy, bacon, and whole wheat toast." He took me by the elbow and led me across the street into the restaurant where all the waitresses knew him by name. We found a table at the back, ordered breakfast, and drank our first cups of coffee in silence.

I met Gold my first day of law school in a seminar called *Western Theories of Justice*. The professor, an affable man given to bow ties, began the class with the etymology of the word justice. "It comes from the Latin," he said, "*jus* meaning right or law. That ambiguity is the subject of this course. Is justice simply the creation of man-made laws and, therefore subject to change as laws evolve or is it a universal right that transcends human law, an ideal toward which human law struggles? Let me give you an example, capital punishment. For centuries, western law has held that certain crimes are so abhorrent justice requires taking the life of the criminal. However, another strain of western thought is that all killing, except in the most limited circumstances of self-defense, is immoral, whether committed by the individual or the state, and therefore capital punishment is inherently unjust. One view is what we might call utilitarian or pragmatic, the other idealistic. Where do you stand?"

Gold raised his hand and launched into a spirited defense of the death penalty. I raised my hand and challenged his defense, point by point. We continued to argue in the hallway after class was over, then over beers at a student hangout, and we had been arguing ever since. Gold presented himself as the hard-headed pragmatist and considered me an ivory tower idealist. That may have been true in law school, but our years in practice as actual lawyers had softened his edges and hardened mine. We were each other's sounding boards and best friends, even though he'd never completely reconciled himself to my being gay. There was something in his Jewish upbringing, a touch of Leviticus maybe, that made him recoil at the thought of two men together.

"But you're a *mensch*," he told me, "How can you be ... like that?"

"You'll have to work that one out for yourself, Gold," I told him. He was still trying to.

Now, as we waited for our food, he was saying, "Run into anyone I know at the jail?"

"You don't go to county jail for SEC violations," I replied. "They put you in some country club federal prison."

"Actually," he said, "that's what I wanted to talk to you about."

"Your rich, scofflaw clients?"

"No, your future. My firm wants to bring on an associate with a criminal law background. I've circulated your name. People are impressed."

"Why would your firm dirty its hands with criminal practice?"

Gold put his coffee cup down and said, "You were joking about SEC violations, but you're right, Henry. A lot of these regulatory statutes come with criminal penalties and right now we have to farm out that work. That's lost revenue for the firm. It makes sense to have a small criminal law department. We'd start you as a fifth-year associate, at sixty thousand a year."

"Not interested."

Gold said, "Look, if it's the money, that's just starting pay. In two years, if everything works out, you'll make partner and be pulling down six figures."

"It's not the money, Gold, it's your client pool." I said, reflecting that the sum he named was double my present wage.

"What's wrong with my clients?" he asked sharply.

"I didn't go to law school so I could represent rich people."

"What, you don't think rich people are entitled to the same defense as poor people?"

"Yeah, but strangely, you never hear much public outcry over the quality of legal representation of the rich."

"Goddamn, Henry, what do you want?" he asked, his voice rising. "The rosy warm glow that comes from doing good? It's not like you're representing Nelson Mandela now. Your clients are street trash."

"I'd rather work for them than the country club clones you represent."

"Oh, it's that gay thing again, isn't it?" he said, flatly, dropping his voice. "You like to think of yourself as Mister Outsider. Give me your poor, your deviant, your huddled psychos. Is that really who you identify with?"

"I identify with people who can't catch a break. Your people write the breaks, and always in their favor."

"You know what your problem is, Henry? You have a persecution complex."

"No, I'm actually persecuted. And, by the way, this from a Jew?"

"Fuck you, it's not the same."

"You know who Hitler sent off to the camps with the Jews? Homosexuals."

"Shut up, Henry," he said, "before we get into a real fight."

I set my fork down and glanced out the window at the luminous summer light. Gold and I had a variation of this conversation nearly every time we talked and the only thing it accomplished was to get us angry at each other.

"Ah, forget it, Gold. My choices are my choices. What do you care?"

"Because, lately, you don't seem very happy with them."

"And you're so happy with your twelve-hour days and your six-day weeks?"

"Sure, life's a cabaret, old chum." He held up his empty coffee cup. After the waitress left, he said, "Right now, it's all about billable hours. I'll worry about happy after I make partner."

Our food came and we ate in silence.

"Forget about the job offer," he muttered through a mouthful of Denver omelet. "You're right, you and the firm wouldn't be a good fit. How was your morning in the dungeon?"

I found myself telling him about Hugh Paris, leaving out the part where we came out to each other and held hands like teenage sweethearts.

"Hugh Paris," he said. "That's a pretty fancy name for jail scum."

"He wasn't jail scum," I said. "He had self-confidence, good manners, and a lot of expensive orthodontics."

Without looking up, Gold said, "So, *nu,* he was cute."

"I can't believe you said that."

"Hey, I'm mellowing. You wanna be careful about hitting on clients, Henry. Do the words conflict of interest mean ring a bell?"

"Screw you," I said, glad we were back on teasing terms. "I'm not representing or dating him. I just, I don't know. I see a lot of people in trouble. Now and then, one of them really gets to me."

"You are such a fucking bleeding heart," he said as he reached for the check.

It was just before nine when I got to the PD's office on the fourth floor of city hall. The reception room was already crammed with clients and their families holding the thick packets of court papers criminal defendants generate as they go through the system. Our receptionist was late again, so they swarmed me when I walked in. I answered as many questions as I could. Finally, I made it past them and through the door that separated attorneys from clients into a narrow corridor, made narrower by file cabinets pushed up against the walls. There was nowhere else for them in our overcrowded offices. I walked past my office to the lounge for a final coffee fix.

Frances Kelly, the supervising attorney, sat at a table with the daily legal journal spread out in front of her. A cigarette burned between her fingers. She lifted it to her lipsticked lips just as the ash fell, sprinkling the lapel of her navy jacket. I almost turned around and walked out before she saw me. She'd been after me for days for a heart-to-heart talk that I figured could only bring bad news. Too late, she saw me.

"Did you know Roger Chaney?" she asked me.

"Not well," I answered, filling a Styrofoam cup. "He was leaving the office just as I was coming in."

"Excellent lawyer," she said. "He and I trained together, shared an office. He helped me prepare for my first trial."

"Is there something about him in the journal?" I asked, sitting at the table across from her. She crushed her cigarette into a cheap glass ashtray and lit another.

"Yes. He's being arraigned today in federal court in San Francisco," she said. "Charged with conspiracy to distribute cocaine."

"What?" I asked, incredulously. "I thought you were going to tell me he'd been appointed to the bench."

"With Roger, it could've gone either way." She put the paper down and looked at me. "He was brilliant but reckless. I walked in on him doing a line of coke on his desk one morning, just before he was going to start a multi-defendant murder trial. Do you know what he told me?"

"No idea."

"Lock the door."

She rose heavily, an elegant fat woman in a linen suit with black hair and beautiful, clear eyes, and ambled to the coffee maker. She poured herself a cup and asked, "You have a minute to talk, Henry?"

It wasn't so much a question as an order.

"Sure," I said.

I followed her into her office, the only one with a window. Outside, a thin layer of smog rose in the direction of San Jose, but the view to the brown hills surrounding the university was clear as they rolled beyond the palm trees and red tile roofs.

Frances was saying, "You know, what we do is very tough work. If you can't find a way of leaving it in the office at the end of the day, it can eat away at you. Now, me, I have a husband, a daughter, and a rose garden. Not much but I wouldn't risk any of it. Those things keep me grounded. They give me something to go home to."

I stirred uncomfortably in my chair. "Why are you telling me this?"

"I can smell the booze on your breath some mornings when you come in," she said. "I worry about one of my lawyers who has nothing better to go home to than a bottle."

I felt myself flush with anger and shame. "I've never come to work drunk."

"That's a pretty low bar," she said. "Wouldn't you agree?"

"Are you trying to fire me, because if you are, I want my union rep."

"Fire you?" she said, shaking her head. "You're one of my best lawyers. I'm trying to figure out how to help you. I think you should consider taking some time off and going into treatment."

"Treatment? For what?"

"For your drinking," she said. "I talked to Mike and he agrees. Your health insurance will cover—"

"You talked to Mike about my drinking?" I said angrily. "You had no right to do that. If it doesn't affect my job, it's none of your goddamn business. And, by the way, I'm not an alcoholic if that's what you're implying."

She sighed. "Listen to me, Henry, do you think you're the first lawyer I've supervised with a drinking problem? I can see the signs. I know the pattern. Right now, it's just hangovers. Pretty soon, you'll be calling in sick. Eventually, you will start showing up under the influence. Here and in the courtroom. I'm offering you a chance to nip it in the bud before you get into serious trouble."

"And if I don't? Then what?"

"Then I'll watch you self-destruct and at some point in the process, you'll give me cause to fire you."

I stood up. "I'm not a drunk," I said and walked out of her office, slamming the door behind me.

I went into my office, shut the door, and sat down at my desk. There was a pile of cases to review for arraignment and a list of clients to call and advise about the status of their cases. I had a half-dozen motions to draft and as many discovery requests to complete. Oh, and a trial set to start on Friday. I opened the first file but I was too enraged at Frances to focus on the words. I couldn't believe she thought I was an alcoholic. Of course I wasn't. I defended alcoholics and I wasn't anything like them. I got up and went into the bathroom and splashed cold water on my face to take the edge off my anger.

Drinking was not the problem, life was the problem. I had graduated from college when I was twenty, from law school when I was twenty-three, and I was handling death penalty cases before I was thirty. The forward momentum that had propelled me from one achievement to the next had stalled and left me treading water and doubting myself. Left me holding a bag of bad feelings, dissatisfaction, agitation, and depression. Was it any wonder I needed a fucking drink now and then? I went back to my office. Outside in the corridor, I heard the babble of voices as my colleagues interviewed clients and witnesses or hurried off to court shouting last-minute questions about a legal issue or a particular judge's temperament. I felt the excitement but did not share it. My law school professors said law was a temple. What it had been for me, though, was a religion. The religion of righteousness where the voiceless were heard and sometimes answered. I was their voice. But, as with all religions, belief was entirely a matter of faith. Faith that what I was doing mattered. Faith that it was right. I had lost my faith when the jury came back and convicted Eloy Garza of a murder he had not committed. I was like a priest who held the host and saw only a piece of dry bread, who lifted the chalice and smelled only cheap wine.

I rolled a piece of paper into my typewriter and started typing.

"Henry? Why aren't you in court?" Frances asked when I slipped into her office. "You have arraignments."

"Beth's covering for me," I said. "I had to talk to you. I'm sorry about earlier. I know you meant well."

She narrowed her eyes. "Okay," she said. "Apology accepted. Is there something else?"

"Yes," I said. I handed her the letter I had written.

"What is this?" she asked, then started reading. She looked up, shocked. "You're resigning?"

"Effective immediately," I said. "I already called San Jose and told Mike."

She shook her head and puffed disapprovingly. "This is ridiculous, Henry. You're going to walk away from your clients, from your career. For what?"

"For something else."

"This is bad, Henry," she said. "Very bad. You really need help."

I stood up. "Thank you for everything, Frances. Good-bye."

I went back to my office and cleaned out my desk. Some of the other lawyers drifted in, stood around nervously, and said a few well-intended words. By three o'clock I'd done nearly everything I needed to do to extricate myself from my job. Just before I left I called down to the jail to find out about Hugh Paris. The deputy told me the DA had called earlier and said he wasn't going to file any charges. Hugh had been released. I gathered up my personal papers, threw them into a box, and went home.

TWO

A movement in the shrubs outside my bedroom window woke me. I glanced at the alarm clock: 3:18. The soft shuffle of footsteps on the sidewalk was followed by a quick rap at the front door. I pulled on a pair of pants and felt my way through the darkness to the living room. I stood at the door and listened. There was another knock, louder, and more urgent. I looked through the peephole. Hugh Paris stood shivering in the dark. I was startled but not surprised. Maybe because I'd thought of him so often in the past few weeks, it was as if I'd finally conjured him up. A breeze blew his hair across his forehead. I opened the door.

"Hugh?"

"Don't turn on the porch light," he said. "I think I'm being followed."

"Come in." He slipped through the door and I closed it softly behind him.

Followed? Was he high? I guided him to my desk and switched on the reading lamp to get a good look at him. His eyes were clear and alert. He was wearing jeans and a black T-shirt; I scanned his arms for signs of track marks. The ones I saw were old and healed.

"I'm not high," he said, watching me. "But I could use a drink."

"Sure thing," I said.

I went into the kitchen and poured a couple of shots of Jack Daniel's. When I returned to the living room he was poking around the stack of orange crates that held my books and music. The last time I'd seen him, the oversized jail jumpsuit had concealed his body. The form fitting jeans and T-shirt revealed a slender but muscled frame; a gymnast's physique. I was appropriately appreciative.

"Here you go," I said.

He turned and took a glass from me. "*Prost*," he said, touching his glass to mine. Smiling slightly, he openly appraised my body. "Not that I'm complaining, but when I pictured you naked, I saw a hairy chest."

"It's the Indian blood," I said. "What are you doing here, Hugh?"

"You gave me your card, remember, told me to call you day or night, for whatever I needed."

He set his glass down on the coffee table, took mine from me, and set it beside his. He stepped forward into my arms, tipped his face upward, and we kissed. His tongue slid lazily into my mouth and I savored his taste and the warmth of his hard, little body against mine. I licked that elegant neck and cupped his hard little butt. His fingers worked the buttons of my 501s and grazed the tip of my cock. With a last, lewd kiss, he dropped to his knees. I reached down, hooked my arms around his armpits, and lifted him to his feet.

"Stop," I said.

"You want me to stop? I'm famous for my blow jobs, baby."

"Sit down," I said, directing him to the couch. I buttoned up my jeans and sat down beside him. "I gave you my card weeks ago. If all you wanted was sex, you could've called me anytime. I would have come running. Instead, you show up at my apartment in the dead of night telling me you're being followed. You're not obviously high, so what's up?"

When he picked up his drink, I caught the glint of his watch. It was very thin and silvery but not silver. Platinum. Watches like that went along with trust funds, prep schools, and names ending with Roman numerals.

"I'm sorry I didn't call. I really wanted to. I felt, you know, that we connected."

"Me, too," I said. "I tried to find you. Looked you up in the phone book, had a friend at DMV run your name. I even went to The Office a couple of times thinking maybe you'd show up."

"I'm not easy to find," he said. "Precautions."

"Against what?"

"I told you I came back from New York to deal with some family things and they've been getting pretty heavy. I got a scare tonight. I needed to find a safe place. I thought of you."

"You need to fill in some blanks for me."

"I don't want to mix you up in my drama."

"You already have. So let's hear it."

He picked up his glass and took a slug. "I come from money."

"I guessed that from the watch."

He glanced at the watch. "Good eye," he said. "Vintage Patek Philippe. It was my dad's. I managed to hang on to it through—everything."

"Everything meaning junk."

"Everything," he said empathically. "Including junk. But like I told you at the jail, I'm clean now."

"I'm glad you kicked, Hugh. Go on."

"My family has a lot of money. My grandfather controls most of it through a family trust. While I was out there using, the only thing I cared about was that he give me enough to maintain. Eventually, he cut me off. I had to find other ways to take care of myself. After I got clean, I began to look into the trust. All I wanted to know was what was mine, but I discovered some things about how my grandfather got control of the money. Criminal things."

"Like what, diverting funds? Embezzlement?"

"Murder," he said.

"What?"

"He had people killed. That's how he got control of the money."

I had heard enough incredible stories from interviewing clients that I knew to keep a game face, ask leading questions and wait until they tripped themselves up.

"Who do you think he had killed?" I asked.

"My grandmother and my uncle," he replied.

"Why them?"

"It was my grandmother's money. She was going to divorce him. He killed them to prevent it."

"What does this have to do with you being followed?"

"He knows I'm on to him," Hugh said. "I felt like someone was following me tonight. I freaked out. The city didn't feel safe, so I came here."

"What do you think your grandfather's going to do to you?"

"If he can't scare me off, he'll kill me, too, Henry."

I finished my drink and said, neutrally, "Your grandfather wants to kill you. Really?"

He frowned. "You think I'm crazy, don't you?"

"Put yourself in my position. In the middle of the night, a guy you met once shows up at your house and tells you he's being stalked by his grandfather who's some kind of serial killer. What would you think?"

"See," he said angrily. "That's why I didn't say anything to you at the jail."

"How did you get out of jail?" I asked him. "Who did you call?"

"My great-uncle John, my grandmother's brother. He has some influence down here."

"I'll say he does. I heard the DA dropped all the charges," I said. "Does your great-uncle know about your allegations against your grandfather?"

Hugh shrugged. "I told him. He thinks . . . He thinks I'm angry about how the old man's treated me."

"He doesn't believe you," I said.

"I have evidence," Hugh said.

"Then you should take it to the police," I said. "There's no statute of limitations on murder and if your grandfather is cheating you out of money that belongs to you, I can refer you to a good civil lawyer."

He stood up. "I'm sorry I bothered you, Henry. I'll be leaving now."

I grabbed his hand. "Wait. This is what I think, Hugh. You come from money but you ended up on the streets shooting junk and now you're clean. While you were out there, your grandfather cut you off and you're angry about that. Maybe he was practicing tough love or maybe he's an asshole, I don't know. I do know that depending on how long you used, it might be awhile before your head clears up completely. In the meantime, I'd be very careful about accusing people of being murderers."

"You've got me all figured out, don't you?" he said with a small smile.

"I'm just trying to make sense of what you've told me."

He looked at me. "You want me to go?"

I shook my head. "I want you to take your clothes off."

He smiled. "If you still want me to stay after what I told you, you're as crazy as I am."

"I haven't stopped thinking about you since we met."

He pulled his shirt over his head and tossed it to the floor, kicked his shoes off, unbuttoned his pants, pushed them to his feet and stepped out of them. He hooked his fingers into the waistband of his briefs and slipped them off. He stepped between my legs. This time when he sank to his knees, I didn't stop him.

I woke up alone and watched the shadow of the tree outside the window sway across the wall. The only noises were the clock ticking and the wind. The sheets and blankets were kicked back and over the foot of the bed. A wadded-up towel lay crumpled on the floor among Hugh's scattered clothes. The detritus of passion.

I could still taste him in my mouth, ripe, meaty, musky. Armpits, anus, cock. My stomach was glazed with his semen, the sheets were stained with mine. Like everything else about him, sex was compelling and off-kilter. What started as the standard one-night-stand groping and negotiations quickly became something more serious.

"Use me," he told me, when I had tumbled him to his back and parted his legs. "That's how I like it."

There was always that moment when I was grappling naked with another man that our bodies veered toward violence; it was part of the excitement of the encounter that these tough, male bodies capable of inflicting injury on each other would, instead, become instruments of pleasure. The line could be very fine. Now I looked into Hugh's eyes, dark with emotions I could not decipher, inviting me to cross that line, to hurt him. I couldn't deny that some part of me was urged to give him what he wanted because I wanted it too. To hurt him as a surrogate for all the men who had hurt me with their rejection and contempt. But he wasn't one of those men. He was a man like me who, having suffered the same rejection and contempt, wrongly believed he deserved the worst.

"Come on, Henry," he said. "You can do anything you want to me."

I lay down beside him, pulled him into my arms and kissed his forehead. He was startled but then he relaxed into my arms and let me hold him. I pulled the blankets over us, stroked his hair, and let him fall asleep in my arms.

Just before dawn, his tongue parted my lips and slipped into my mouth, waking me. His small, muscled body rested on mine, his hard-on trapped between our bellies. My hands drifted to the small of his back, to his butt, as we washed the sourness of sleep out of each other's mouths. Now I was hard, too. He slipped his hand between us and gently tugged our cocks together. It had been months since another guy had touched me but his hand squeezing the bulbs of our cocks together was all it took to set my nerve endings on fire. I let my fingers slip between his ass cheeks, pressed his hole with my index finger and slipped it in. He broke our kiss and lifted his head slightly so we could see each other.

He stroked my cock and said, "You're big."

"If you don't stop that, you're going to make me come."

"Just doing this?"

"It's been awhile since I had sex. It won't take much."

He let go of my cock. "In that case. Lube?"

"In the drawer in the bed stand," I said.

He rolled off of me, opened the drawer and removed the tube of KY Jelly. He straddled my thighs, squeezed a gob on his finger and his hand disappeared behind his body. He smirked as he coated his hole with the lube. I reached up and traced the ridged muscles of his belly with my fingertips.

"You are so beautiful."

"You are, Henry."

He squeezed another thick drop of lube on his fingers and slowly spread it up and down my shaft. I squirmed beneath the cold jelly and his fingers.

"I'm going to ride you," he said. "That okay?"

I managed a weak, "Uh-huh."

He lifted his thighs, scooted up my body, positioned my cock against his hole and then, mouth slightly ajar, his eyes locked on mine, slowly lowered himself. The tight muscle gave way, stretching to take me in.

"Oh, fuck," I whispered, as the cock penetrated the sticky heat of his anus. A rush of blood prickled my chest and belly; my groin pulsed sweetness.

Hugh's mouth was an O, his eyes clouded with pleasure. For a moment, he remained motionless, his butt on my thighs, his hands on my chest. Then, he began to move up and down on my cock, slowly fucking himself on me. I thrust upward in response.

"No," he said. "Let me take care of you."

I nodded and lay back. Expertly, he impaled himself on me, varying the speed and depth of the strokes, tightening and relaxing his hold around my cock as he did. He watched me, smiling when I moaned, shaking his head when I couldn't help thrusting. Translucent threads of precum spilled from his cock to my belly. I reached for it, massaged the head with the stickiness. Gently, he moved my hand away. "This is all about you," he said. I surrendered and lay back, closed my eyes and slipped into the swamp of sensations, smells and sounds of sex; his butt rising and falling on my sweaty thighs, the bursts of breath and involuntary moans, the fire in my engorged cock responding to the heat and friction as he pounded himself on me. When I stuttered, "I'm coming," he slowed the pace, squeezing my cock with his hole, and when I came, it wasn't in a hot gush, but a slow flood that curled my toes.

When the last pulse of my semen emptied into his gut, he grabbed his cock. A few rapid strokes brought an arc of cum that splattered my chest and chin. Slowly, he disengaged from himself me. "Lie still," he said and went into the bathroom. I heard the water running, and then he returned with a wash cloth and a towel.

Delicately, he washed his come off me and then washed and dried my genitals.

He tossed the towel and washcloth on a chair and settled back in the bed beside me. "How was that?" he asked.

"I don't think I've ever come that hard. Was it good for you?"

He smiled. "This was about you."

"I wanted it to be about us," I said.

He looked away. "I barely remember what it's like to have sex I'm not getting paid for."

"I'm not one of your johns," I said.

"I didn't mean it that way," he said. "I was trying to explain that for me sex has been a way of getting what I need, not how I express," he paused, searching for the word. "Affection."

"We don't have to fuck again until you want to," I said.

He turned his face to me. "You mean that, don't you?"

"Yeah, of course."

"No guy has ever not wanted something from me," he said.

"I didn't say I didn't want something from you," I said. "It just isn't sex."

He lay his head on my chest. "What do you want, Henry?"

I put my arms around him. "This."

After a moment he said, "You seem so confident I wouldn't have guessed that you're lonely, too."

"Now you know," I said.

He came back into the room, wearing an old robe of mine that was too big for him. He sat at the edge of the bed. "You're awake."

"I'm glad you're still here. I was afraid you might have left."

"I like being here," he said.

He climbed into bed. On his chest above his heart was a tattoo of a peach, beautifully rendered and colored, ringed by Chinese characters. I had noticed it as soon as he had undressed but had been too preoccupied with other things to ask him about it.

"What is this tattoo?" I asked, touching it.

"It's for protection," he said.

"I don't understand."

"When I was nine, my dad took me to a tattoo parlor in Amsterdam and had it done. He said it would protect me against evil." He ran his fingertip across the tattoo. "My dad was pretty sick by then and he didn't always make a lot of sense, but I would do anything for him."

"Why were you in Amsterdam?"

"My parents were pretty footloose," he said. "It was the sixties, they were like hippies. We lived in communes, on an ashram and one winter in a castle in Scotland. God, that place was freezing cold."

"Who took care of you?"

"Dad, when he could. My mother, when she was sober. Sometimes I had a nanny, but I spent a lot of time on my own." He shrugged. "It wasn't bad."

"What do the Chinese characters say?"

He looked at the tattoo. "You know, I had no idea until this one time in New York I was with this Chinese john from Hong Kong and I asked him. He said it says, 'Heaven protects the innocent.' "

"What was wrong with your dad?"

"I don't want to talk about that now," he said. He stroked my cock. "I want you to fuck me."

"Are you sure that's what you want?"

"Oh, yes, I'm absolutely sure."

All my questions went out of my head.

Afterwards, we lay beside each other. Hugh asked me, "Have you always known you're gay?"

"Yes," I said. "You?"

He squeezed my hand. "I knew I was different than other boys but not why until someone showed me."

"Showed you? How?"

He let go of my hand. "He raped me when I was ten."

I started to speak but he pressed his finger to my lips.

"Don't," he said. "Don't ask me any questions. Don't say you're sorry it happened. Let it go."

"Have you let it go?"

"I said, no questions."

I pulled him on top of me and held him. His heart beat against mine. He tipped his chin and I kissed him gently.

"You're sweet," he said.

"You called me that at the jail." I said. "I'm not, you know."

He laughed and rolled on his back. "Yes, you are. You look tough and you talk tough but you're a soft touch. You learn these things when you're on the street. Call it junkie's intuition. Don't get pissed, Henry. Here, lay your head on my chest."

His heartbeat pulsed in my ear. "Hard to imagine you on the street, Hugh."

"Like I said, sometimes the family cut me off and you know how much a habit costs. A pretty blond boy can make a lot of money on his back." The street hardness slipped back into his voice. "Not every guy was as reluctant as you were to hurt me. I charged extra for that."

"Why did you use?"

"To get well," he said. "That's what we say when we need a fix. I need to get well. Like life is the disease and junk is the cure."

"Then why get clean?"

"The cure became worse than the disease. It always does, whether it's junk or speed or alcohol." He combed his fingers through my hair. "It's Tuesday, shouldn't you be getting ready for work?"

"I quit," I said.

His fingers paused. "You did? Why?"

"I stopped believing that what I was doing made enough difference to keep doing it."

"What will you do now?"

"I don't know," I said. I looked at him. "Get to know you better."

"You know, Henry, I'm not really like you."

"What does that mean?"

"I'm not another man with a boy inside of him waiting for the kiss that ends his loneliness and takes away his pain. Junk took away my pain, but in exchange it turned me into a liar and a thief and whore. You shouldn't trust me."

"You're clean now," I said.

"You know what they say about old habits. They die hard. I don't want to hurt you."

"Let me worry about that."

"I have to go," he said. He slid off the bed and went into the living room. After a moment, I followed him and found him rooting among the pile of our clothes for his underwear and pants. I sat down on the couch and watched him dress.

"Was it something I said?"

"I have a meeting in the city this afternoon with someone who doesn't like to be kept waiting."

"Okay," I said, skeptically. "Call me later?"

He pulled his shirt over his head, tucked it into his jeans. He came over and kissed me and said, "Thank you, Henry," and then he slipped out the door.

A week passed. Two. I slept late, went for long runs, read some of those books I'd always promised myself I'd read, ate a lot of eggs because that's all I knew how to cook, drank myself to sleep more often than was good for me. I didn't expect to hear from Hugh again, but that didn't mean my heart didn't flutter every time I walked into my apartment and the answering machine light was flickering. Half those calls were from Gold who had heard I'd quit the PD's office and wanted the story. I finally agreed to meet him for a drink.

Barney's was a yuppie bar for the freshly minted graduates of the university who missed their frat houses. The walls, floors and ceiling were planks of oak with a dark, shiny varnish. A rail along the top of the walls held a collection of beer bottles while the walls were decorated with neon signs, license plates and stolen traffic signs. There were dark booths and ugly tables and the floor was covered in peanut shells. Young guys in suits—lawyers, stockbrokers, bankers—or in khakis and crewnecks and button-down shirts parked their worked-out butts on the bar stools and drank expensive scotch and imported beers, mindlessly cheering whatever sporting event was on the TV above the bar. I never saw a woman in the place. Gold knew I loathed the place which is why he chose it. He was already in a booth working on a Jameson on the rocks and cracking peanuts when I arrived.

I slid into the booth and said, "You know, Gold, there are never any women in this bar. Doesn't that seem a little gay to you?"

He smirked. "You wish."

"No, really, all we need is a disco ball and Gloria Gaynor on the jukebox singing *I Will Survive* and we'd be in business."

"Yeah, I don't know what any of that means," Gold said. "I don't speak gay." He flagged down a waiter, ordered a refill of his Jameson's and a Jack Daniel's for me. When the drinks came, he tapped my glass with his and said, "So I heard you quit the PD. Mazel tov. You were wasting your time there."

"When did you become such a reactionary? I seem to remember back in law school you called yourself a socialist."

"Everyone was something in law school. Socialist, feminist. Gay. Call it youthful experimentation."

"It was more than that for some of us."

"Whatever," he said, brushing peanut shells to the floor. "My folks were honest-to-God socialists. My dad lost his job teaching at Cal State LA because he wouldn't sign their loyalty oath and ended up working on an assembly line at a Ford factory to keep us fed."

"Principles come with a price," I said. "I'd be proud of him if he were my dad."

"You wouldn't feel that way if you'd seen what that did to him. Broke him down, made him old before his time, and what did his principles change? Not a fucking thing. Money still rules the world." He poked around the peanut bowl for the last couple of peanuts. "I am in need of sustenance. Hey, waiter. Another round and an order of potato skins. Why did you quit, Henry?"

"The system is gamed against my clients. I was just one more stop in the conveyor belt that dumped them with all the other garbage."

"Your clients were guilty," he said. "What were you supposed to do? Pull a Perry Mason and get some witness to break down on the stand and confess?"

"Not all my clients were guilty," I said, remembering Eloy Garza. "And the ones who were, what were they really guilty of? Desperation. Poverty. Being the wrong color and the wrong class. The entire criminal law system has one goal, to protect the haves from the have-nots."

"Now who's the socialist," he said, as the waiter set a plate of fried potato skins on the table and carried off our empty glasses. "Hmm, bacon, the forbidden fruit of Jews. Seriously, Henry, you had to know you couldn't change the world by doing criminal defense."

"I wasn't trying to change the world. I was trying to get justice."

"Well, we both know from first year law school how unrealistic your idea of justice is," he said. "What are you going to do now?"

"I don't know. I didn't think I'd need a Plan B. Hey, Gold, do I drink too much?"

"We both drink too much," he said. "It's a good man's weakness."

I touched his glass with mine. "I'll drink to that. I saw Hugh Paris again."

"Hugh Paris? That gay guy you talked to in the jail?"

"He showed up at my place a couple of weeks ago."

Gold stared. "Don't tell me you—"

"Yeah, I slept with him."

"A client, Henry!"

"He was never a client. It's fine."

"Fine? Whether he's a client or not, he's a criminal, Henry. You're having sex with criminals."

"He's not a criminal," I said. "He wasn't even charged."

"Don't split hairs, counselor. You have to know how this looks."

"Tell me something, Aaron," I said, helping myself to a potato skin. "How old were you when you had your first girlfriend? Fifteen? Sixteen?"

He grinned over the top of his glass. "Sixteen."

"You remember her name?"

"Deb," he replied. "Debbie Abramov."

"I bet you held Debbie's hand when you walked her to algebra and made out with her in the rec room or whatever and you pinned a corsage on her and took her to the junior prom and all the other boys and girls said what a cute couple. Did you fuck her, Aaron?"

"I think you've had one too many, my friend," he said.

"Humor me, Gold. Did you lose your virginity to her?"

"Yeah. So what?"

"Because that, counselor," I said, feeling the booze now, "was how you learned the proper order of things. First love, then sex." I picked up my drink, swirled the whiskey, tasted it. "My Debbie was a boy named Mark. I was his best friend. He was a lot more than that to me. I wanted to hold his hand in the hallways between classes, hang out with him in the senior quad after school, feel each other up in the back seat of his crappy car. I wanted to make love to him. If I had so much as hinted any of that to him, he would have been disgusted with me. So I kept those feelings to myself. The first time I had sex was in a bathroom at the university when another freshman gave me a blow job in one of the stalls."

"I could have gone all my life without hearing this," Gold muttered.

I reached across the table, grabbed a fistful of his jacket and dragged him toward me. "If I have to hear about the size and shape of the tits of every *shiksa* you lust after and how what you really want is to meet a nice Jewish girl and settle down, you can hear me out for once."

"Let go of me," Gold said quietly. I released him. He straightened his jacket, and sipped his drink. "So, you're saying you want to take this Hugh Paris to the junior prom?"

I laughed. "Fuck you," I said. "Yeah, something like."

"Counselor, I think that ship has sailed."

"Yeah, you're right. Anyway, Hugh isn't really prom material."

"You're not going to see him again, are you?" Gold asked.

"I don't think so," I said. "I'm pretty sure it was a one-night stand."

"Good," Gold said. "That's good."

I woke up the next morning inhaling the fumes of the previous night's liquor: Gold and I had closed down the bar arguing whether Reagan was as stupid as he seemed or if it was an act that concealed his political genius. "He's an asshole either way," I said on the sidewalk after we'd been 86'd. "I saw 'im once," Gold countered. "Purple hair! Total dye job. Shows up brown on TV."

I got myself into the bathroom, puked, rinsed my mouth and splashed my face with cold water. In the kitchen I swallowed four aspirin, brewed a pot of coffee and scalded my tongue on my first cup. I took my second cup to the couch where I sat in my boxers as someone tightened a thin wire around my temples and reminisced fondly about my twenties when I could close down a bar and show up for my 8 o'clock Contracts class no worse for the wear. The aspirin wasn't working, the coffee wasn't working; drastic measures were in order. I went back into the bedroom and pulled on my running clothes. I gulped the last of the coffee, went outside, stretched creakily, and then set off at a slow pace toward the university.

Summer was a wistful time of year in Linden, when the great engine of the university was stilled. I knew those summers well from the ones I had spent there, as an undergrad and then a law student. The summer after my freshman year I went home to the small Central Valley town where I'd been raised. I worked construction alongside my *macho* father who teased me brutally about being a college boy and mocked me for still being a virgin. (I was a virgin only by his definition, not that I dared correct him.) The other guys on the crew, *mexicanos* like him, took up the cudgel and bullied me mercilessly. I could have endured that but when they started putting me in dangerous situations, I bailed and hitchhiked back to Linden where a sympathetic professor let me sleep on her couch until school started. I never went home again. Holidays I stayed in the dorms; summers I rented a room in town and worked at whatever job I could find. Those undergrad summers were lovely and long and lonely. I biked around the vast, empty campus, exploring its obscure corners and hidden niches. For all that, the university never felt like home to me. I was grateful it had taken me in but I had more in common with the maids who cleaned my dorm room than my classmates.

I ran through the quiet town and reached the university entrance gates, stopped, and threw up again. Before me was the mile-long prospect of University Drive, marked on either side by a row of Queen Palms that lifted their shaggy heads against the pastel sky. On either side was the Arboretum, a forest of trees from every continent, a carefully designed wilderness that had once housed the stud ranch of the university's founder, the nineteenth century magnate, Grover Linden. Glittering at the far end of Palm Drive was the gilt mosaic of Jesus that decorated the front of the immense chapel at the center of the Old Quad, a collection of somber buildings, arches and covered arcades fashioned out of buff-colored sandstone and roofed with red tiles; the university's original hub.

I gathered myself and ran briskly down the drive, remembering the story of how, when he was told by his architect that it would cost no less than ten million dollars to build his university, Grover Linden turned to his wife and said, "I think we can manage that, don't you, mother?" Like the fortunes of most of his fellow robber barons, his was blood money, made over the corpses of the miners who perished in his mines and the Chinese workers who died constructing his railroads and the suicidal farmers ruined by his financial speculations. Some maintained the university was Linden's atonement, like Andrew Carnegie's libraries or Alfred Nobel's peace prize. I'd always thought it was a monument to the self-regard of the man who was buried in the woods in a mausoleum guarded by sphinxes.

I stumbled up the steps and beneath an archway into the expansive courtyard of the Old Quad. Grover Linden hand-picked and legendarily hen-pecked the architects who built his university, demanding opulence and solemnity on a vast scale. What they had accomplished in the Old Quad was a gloomy magnificence that never failed to remind me of the presidential palace of a banana republic. Along the north and south ends of the courtyard were arched corridors and buildings characterized by roughly hewn stone walls, cavernous door openings and deep window reveals. These buildings housed the departments of English and History where I had spent much of my undergraduate years in capacious classrooms distracted by the carnal scent of freshly cut grass drifting in through the nineteenth century windows. Anchoring the quad was the Romanesque pile of stone called Memorial Church. Its glory was the golden mosaic of Jesus that covered much of its façade; a blond, blue-eyed and distinctly Nordic appearing Jesus who looked more like a young titan of industry than the prince of peace. Hard to imagine him healing lepers and consorting with whores.

I jogged through the quad, where a busload of Japanese tourists wandered around taking pictures, and past a small subterranean stone building. Steps led down into a marble chamber, the infamous men's toilet where, at seventeen, another freshman pulled into one of its commodious stalls and demonstrated that a blow job involved no actual blowing. Heading toward the foothills behind the campus, I ran past one of the old dormitories, a sprawling Mission-style edifice built around the lovely courtyard, where an Argentine engineering student had completed my sexual initiation on a narrow bed in his monastic dorm room. He was a grad student, older and more experienced and a patient teacher after I told him the entire sum of my experience was the sloppy blow job in the bathroom. Ricardo. He was the first boy I kissed. I remember the shock of amazement and pleasure when he slipped his tongue into my mouth. I remember how puzzled I was when he told me to kneel on the bed between his legs and then lifted them to my shoulders. He reached over, took my rigid cock and began to guide me inside him. My body shook with excitement and disbelief—he was really going to let me do this to him? At the moment of penetration, I looked into his gray-green eyes and everything inside of me assented. Yes, this was what I had been waiting for, to make love to another boy and to feel his flesh close around mine.

The memory quickened my pace as I reached the edge of campus, crossed the road and reached the rolling, oak-tree covered hills behind the school. I entered through an open gate and sprinted up a hill crowned by a radio telescope that everyone called the Dish. The grass on the hillside was dried to its summer gold, and in the near distance cows grazed. Singularly or in groves, the oaks spread their broad canopies of dusty leaves. Fields and oak trees—this was the landscape I had grown up with in the Central Valley; this was my California. I slowed to a stop at the top of the Dish and caught my breath. My clothes were soaked with sweat, and my hangover had been replaced by endorphin-induced euphoria. The morning had heated up and I stripped off my T-shirt. In the northern distance I saw the white buildings, bridges and spires of the city of San Francisco beneath a crayoned blue sky.

When I was a boy, San Francisco seemed like Oz—the magical city of domes and towers at the end of the earth. I had my first experience of the place in high school when some of my friends got cars. On weekends we'd make the ninety-mile drive from our stifling valley town for free concerts in Golden Gate Park, or to join the moratoriums against the war in Vietnam or to hang out on Haight Street, the fading epicenter of the counterculture where a baggie of pot went for ten dollars and a topless girl stood on the corner of Haight and Asbury selling the *Berkeley Barb*.

Even then, though, despite my excitement at being in the big city, something about the place unsettled me. The often vaporous gray air could turn abruptly into a cloak of wet, white, bone-chilling fog. When I walked its old Victorian neighborhoods, what I noticed most was how the light seldom fell directly, but dropped from angles, darkening the corners of things. I would look up at the eaves of a house expecting to see a gargoyle instead of the intricate but innocent woodwork. The city was filled with such shadows as if it were a living thing with secrets and troubled memories.

Standing beneath the Dish and looking at the city, guileless and serene beneath the crayon sky, I thought about Hugh and the thought became tangled with my memories of the boy on his knees in the toilet stall and Ricardo, naked on his back, eyes fluttering, as I entered him. Why this trip down memory lane and what did it have to do with Hugh Paris? A voice in my head hinted, *They were all your firsts.* My firsts—first sexual encounter, first time making love—what did that leave? The same voice suggested, *first time in love?*

"That's ridiculous," I said aloud. "I barely know the guy. I'll probably never see him again."

But now the thought was in my head, and running as hard and fast as I could through the foothills and back to my apartment, I could not dislodge it.

When I returned home, my neighbor Karen, a red-haired medical student at the university, was knocking at my door.

"Oh," she said, seeing me. "Here, this letter got put in my mailbox by mistake."

I took the envelope from her. My name and address in unfamiliar handwriting, postmarked from San Francisco. No return address.

"Um, thanks," I said.

"Secret admirer?" she asked, smiling.

I smiled back. "That would be a first."

THREE

Querido Henry,

Is that the correct salutation? I took a semester of Spanish in prep school but I don't remember much of what I learned. I think querido means beloved but if it doesn't that's what I wanted to say. I was never much of a student. Never much of anything, really. Another junkie with a gilt-edged name called me a "wastrel." We were up in a shooting gallery in Harlem waiting for our connection, exchanging life stories. "You're a wastrel," he said, when I finished mine. I had to look up the word. It means someone who is good for nothing, who has wasted his potential. Old-fashioned word, the kind of word my great-great-grandfather might have used if he had met me. That guy—the guy who called me a wastrel—he overdosed and died. Not that time, but later. I've overdosed, too, more than once, but I survived. I wasn't always happy that I did.

There was another time back in New York when I'd run out of money and needed a fix. You know what that feels like? Your whole body is throbbing and aching and your mind is running like a hamster on a wheel and your skin crawls and you're one breath away from a panic

*attack. I was walking around the Village, desperate for money, and I
remembered the piers. I don't know if you know New York, but there are
some abandoned piers on the Hudson at the edge of the Village where all
the gay guys cruise. Some of them were hustlers and I thought maybe
I could turn a quick trick. It was the dead of winter, Henry, the piers
were deserted. I wandered around, freezing and sick from withdrawal.
Finally, I walked to the edge of a pier and looked at the river and thought,
I should jump in; it was so cold I knew I'd be dead in minutes. But then
some guy tapped me on the shoulder, big guy, middle-aged, not a clone,
some closeted blue-collar worker wanting to get off. He handed me
twenty dollars and I let him fuck me, standing against a rotting wall in a
dark corner of a pier. It was so cold we didn't undress. He unzipped and
I pulled down my pants and briefs, just enough to give him access. He
slammed me against the wall and came in ten grunts, then left me there,
the money for the fix in my pocket, his come running down my thigh.*

*This is who I was—a wastrel, a junkie, a whore. I'm trying to be
a different person now, I want to be a different person, but it's hard to
resist getting pulled back into that black hole inside of me that nothing
ever filled except opiates. When we were in your bed, I looked into your
eyes. I saw myself in them and I felt forgiven. I know that doesn't make
any sense. How could you forgive me for things you didn't know I'd
done? Why would you forgive me if you did know? But the feeling was so
powerful, I thought it must be real and not just my imagination. Then,
afterwards, when you said you wanted to know me, I panicked. I knew
if you did know me, knew everything about me, you wouldn't look at me
with those eyes again. So I ran away.*

*I haven't been able to stop thinking about you, Henry. I want to
see you again but I can't unless you know who I am. Now you do. Here
is my phone number. If, after you have read this, you still want to, please
call me. Also, because I wasn't always a junkie whore, here is a picture of
me before any of that started. I am 15 in this picture. I was confused and
sad but a good kid. Someone who might have grown up to be a good man.
I want to think I still can.*

Love,

    Hugh

I took the Polaroid from the envelope. Pictured were two boys standing against a brick wall, identically dressed in blue blazers, baggy gray trousers, white shirts and rep ties, striped green and yellow and blue. They wore straw boaters, straight out of the 1920s. A costume party? No, he'd mentioned prep school. That explained it. One of the boys was maybe seventeen or eighteen, dark-haired, broad shouldered, his face already settling into its adult lines and angles. He had his arm protectively around the other boy who was shorter, slighter and paler. Fifteen? Hugh looked twelve, his features soft, delicate and unformed; the face of a beautiful child. I turned the photo over. Someone had written, *"Grant and me"* and a date ten years earlier.

I dialed the number he had given me.

"Hello," he said.

"I got your letter," I told him. "I'm waiting for you."

"I'll be there in an hour," he said.

"You can ask me five questions," Hugh said.

We were back in my bed, the sheet beneath us twisted and damp, the top tangled at our feet. He was on his side, his head cradled in his arm, regarding me with his sky-blue eyes. I slowly ran my hand along his naked body, from shoulder to flank, letting its warmth and smoothness suffuse my fingers, my palm. I lifted my hand to his face and he kissed it.

"Just five?" I told him I wanted to know more about his past. "You do remember I'm a lawyer. Asking questions is my job. It's how I get to the truth."

"I'm not hiding anything, I'm trying to start a new life." He pressed my hand to his chest, above his heart. "Five questions for now."

I nodded. "Who was the man who raped you when you were a child?" I asked quietly.

"I don't want to talk about that," he said.

"Five questions," I reminded him. "And no secrets between us."

"My grandfather," he said.

He looked at me warily, expecting, it seemed, that my judgment would fall on him rather than the man who had perpetrated this horror. I stroked his face and said, "Men who do that to children should be locked up and the key thrown away. Where were your parents?"

"My dad died when I was ten. My mother fell apart and left me with my grandparents. I lived with them until I was sent to Boston to prep school."

"No brothers or sisters?"

"No," he said. "It's just me."

"Do you have any other family?"

"My great-uncle," he said. "He's the one who arranged for me to go to prep school when I was fourteen. I think he suspected what my grandfather was doing to me."

Doing to me. His grandfather had raped him more than once. That explained his hatred of his grandfather and it made a lot more sense than the implausible story he had told me about the man murdering his wife and son. It also explained why, driven by the desire for revenge, Hugh had concocted that story. And it may even have explained why he believed his grandfather was following him because, in a way, Hugh was being followed, if not literally, then shadowed by the horror the old man had inflicted on him.

He glanced at me. "What are you thinking?" I heard the worry in his voice.

"Someone should have been there to protect you."

"I survived," he said. "And I'm here with you. That's what matters, isn't it? You have one more question. Not so heavy, okay?"

"Who is the other boy in the picture you sent me."

He smiled. "Are you jealous?"

"Should I be?"

"That's six questions," he said. "His name is Grant Hancock. Uncle John is friends with his father and when I went back east to school, Mister Hancock asked Grant to watch out for me."

"From the way he had his arm around you in the picture, I'd say he took his job seriously."

"You are jealous," he said, grinning. The grin faded and he said softly. "He was a good friend. I owe him amends."

"For what?"

"That's question seven," he said. "Anyway, now it's my turn. Where are you from?"

"I grew up in a little town in the Central Valley called Los Robles, about a hundred miles northeast of here."

"What about your family?"

"My father died of a heart attack when he was fifty-eight, my mom died a few years later. Breast cancer. I have one sister, older. We're not close."

"It doesn't sound like you were close to any of them, Henry."

"I'm going to count that as a question," I said. "The answer is no. I got away as soon as I could."

"Why?"

"My father knew about me before I did," I said. "Knew I was a *joto*—they probably didn't teach that word in your Spanish class, it means faggot—and thought he could beat it out of me." His hand tightened sympathetically around mine. "I survived too, Hugh."

"That must've been hard."

"Don't ask me how, but I knew he was wrong," I replied. "Not wrong about who I was, but wrong to try to change me, wrong to believe there was something defective about me."

"My grandfather told me it was unnatural for a boy to be as pretty as me," he said, quietly. "Like that justified what he did to me."

"We were what they feared or hated in themselves," I said. "It had nothing to do with us. You have one more question."

He was so quiet so long I thought he'd dozed off but then he asked, "Have you ever been in love?"

"No," I said, "but there's a first time for everything."

He was quiet again, but I knew he was awake and thinking.

"We had to take a Classics course at my prep school," he said. "I don't remember anything about it but this one story about the first human beings. They were created with four arms and four legs and two faces and joined together like Siamese twins, men and women, women and women, and men and men. The gods worried the humans were becoming too powerful so they split them in two, condemning them to spend their lives looking for their missing half."

"How will we know if we've found our missing half?"

"Our bodies would fit together," he said.

He eased his body onto mine, I put my arms around him and he sank into me.

My idea of eating out involved a picnic table, a hamburger and a beer at a student hangout in the foothills above the university, so I was surprised at the plush booths, starched white tablecloths and flickering tea lights at the restaurant Hugh had suggested for dinner.

"I've lived here since I was eighteen and never knew about this place," I said, after the waiter handed us oversized, calligraphed menus and departed. "How did you find it?"

"I lived in Westborough," he said, naming a wood-sheltered enclave of old money northwest of the university. "We came here sometimes."

"We?"

"My grandparents. No, it's okay, Henry. They're not here." He applied himself to the menu.

I kept forgetting he came from money and then some quirk or gesture would remind me we had been raised in very different circumstances. Now, for example, even reading the menu he kept his elbows off the table and he hadn't been startled by the arsenal of cutlery aimed at our dinner plates. I was no barbarian—I kept my mouth shut when I chewed and buttered my bread one bite-sized piece at a time—but when the only other brown faces in the restaurant belonged to the busboys, I couldn't help feeling out of place.

"I think I'll have the lamb," he said. "What about—Henry, are you all right?"

"Rich people make me nervous."

His gaze swept the room. "They should," he replied. "Most of them are sharks. Do you want to go somewhere else?"

I shook my head. "Swear you won't let me pick up the wrong fork."

The food was excellent and the wine he'd ordered, a red with a French label, was liquid seduction on my tongue. He told me to order *tarte tatin* for dessert. The waiter set the plate down before me with a small flourish. I glanced at it, then Hugh and said, "Apple pie?"

"Try it."

I cut a piece, with the correct fork, and put it in my mouth. "Oh, my God," I said. "This is what the serpent gave Eve in the garden."

"Nice to know a little caramelized sugar and pastry dough can lead you into sin," he replied, smiling.

"That smile is what led me into sin," I replied. "And believe me I'd follow it anywhere."

He picked up his wine glass and swirled the wine but didn't taste it. "This thing that's happening between us," he said, watching the dark liquid dribble down the inside of the glass. "It's not just about sex, is it?"

I put my fork down. "You know it's not."

He drank some wine, as if to give himself courage. "But I don't," he said, "because nothing like this has ever happened to me before. Sex, yes, I could write the book about sex. There's nothing I haven't done. I know what guys see when they look at me, Henry. A hunky, little, blond twink, the kid brother, the boy next door, the hot ass you can't wait to fuck. That was fine, it's how I made money for the next fix when heroin was the only boyfriend I cared about. But I need to know. What do you see when you look at me?"

"The boy in the picture?" I replied. "The one you said could have grown up to be a good man? I see the good man. Kind, smart, decent. Okay, and beautiful, but I can't help seeing that because you are."

"The first time I came to your place you thought I was crazy."

"The first time you came to my place I barely knew you."

"You know me now?"

"Getting there," I said. I smiled. "Here, have some apple pie."

When the bill came, discreetly tucked into a wallet made from the hide of some endangered species, he took it before I could reach out my hand and said, "I'm paying," in a tone that defied argument.

"Thank you," I said. I watched him pull a couple of hundred dollar bills from the sheaf of hundreds in his wallet as if he were paying for a burger at McDonald's.

Back in bed. Fresh sheets. I was lying on my belly, head buried in my arms, listening to Hugh take a leak; even the splash of his piss hitting the water was sexy to me. I heard muffled footsteps on the carpet and then he was lying on top of me, his cheek pressed against my hair. His scent was as complex as the flavors of the wine at dinner; I wanted him to saturate me in it. His cock twitched tentatively against my butt. I smiled. His cock was as pretty as the rest of him; his genitals could have been carved on a statue of a Greek ephebe. With each breath, his belly expanded against my back. He flattened his feet against my calves, reminding me how much smaller he was than me. His long hair brushed against my neck.

"Have you ever bottomed, Henry?" he asked me in the silty voice I had come to recognize as his sex voice.

"Back in college a couple of times, when a guy wanted to flip," I replied, my voice muffled by the pillow pressed against my face.

His cock twitched again. "Did you like it?

I shrugged against his chest. "I never got past, 'ow, that hurts, take it out.' "

"Those guys didn't know what they were doing," he said. He reached down and stroked my butt. "You've got a great ass, Henry. It's so muscly."

"Running up hills will do that," I said, my own cock beginning to stir as I wondered where this conversation was going.

He slipped his legs between my thighs, forcing them apart. His cock, now hard, grazed the crack between my ass cheeks. He dragged his cock slowly up and down, then stopped and pressed its head against my hole. I made a noise I had never heard myself make before, a kind of whimper.

"That feel good?" he asked.

I managed a barely audible, "Uh-huh."

He laid his cheek against mine and whispered, "Can I fuck you, Henry?"

I moved my head to meet his eyes. They were bright with want. I remembered our conversation about how sex for him had been about getting money or a fix, and not about pleasure or affection. This time, it was all about that for him.

"Yes," I said. "Fuck me, baby."

"Okay, daddy, roll over on your back?"

I raised an eyebrow. "Daddy?"

"Shh, this is my fantasy."

He knelt between my outstretched legs, squeezing lube on his cock from the almost empty bottle. A little of the lube trickled down my thigh; he'd been generous with it. He began to stroke himself. In the dim room, the lamplight cast a nimbus around him. He looked both wild and completely in charge. I was so hard it hurt.

"God, you look gorgeous," he said. "I don't understand why more guys haven't tried to fuck you."

"You know how it is," I said. "They look at me and see the Mexican gardener they always fantasized having fuck them."

"Do you give them what they want?" he asked in a low voice, taking my cock in his hand and stroking it against his.

I shuddered. "Yeah, I like being in control."

"But I'm in control now, daddy," he said. He let go of our cocks. "Lift your legs up."

I stretched up my legs and he positioned them on his shoulders. He edged himself forward into me until the tip of his cock was at my hole. He leaned over my body until our chests nearly touched and slipped his tongue into my mouth. I was so intent on the kiss I barely noticed when his cock pushed into me but then—

"Ah," I said, jerking back. "Wait."

He sat back on his haunches, the head of his cock still inside me. "Breathe. Deep breaths. Yeah, like that. I promise I'll make this good for you."

He took the head of my limp cock between his forefinger and his thumb, gently squeezing and rubbing, distracting me from the discomfort until the discomfort faded.

"Okay," I said.

"It feels incredible being inside you," he said, and drove his cock into me one hard inch at a time, stretching me open. I felt like I was being pushed down deeper and deeper into the bed and then the pushing stopped.

"That's it," he said. "I'm all the way in."

He leaned over me again and we kissed. I felt the heft and fullness of his cock in me and started to get hard again.

"I'm going to fuck you now," he whispered. "I'll start slow."

I managed a weak, "Yeah, do that."

At first I felt only the slide of his cock pressuring what I thought was my bladder but as he quickened the pump, I realized it wasn't my bladder but something else he was hitting and with each hit came a spark of pleasure so intense I almost saw it flicker in front of me, like a firefly.

"Fuck," I gasped. "What is that?"

He smiled. "Your prostate." He pressed his hands against my chest hard. "Ready for more?"

"Oh, yeah."

The bed shook beneath us, his hips slid beneath my fingers and he moved in and out of me. He closed his eyes and tossed his head back, spraying me with beads of sweat. He had never looked so naked as he did at that moment, so ecstatic. His breath came in hot, hard bursts. The sparks of pleasure from his cock slamming into me came faster and faster, racing through a circuit that went straight to my cock. I grabbed it and began jerking myself off. Hugh's eyes opened wide and he gasped, "I'm going to come," and then his cock seemed to expand in me and he shuddered. He pulled out and I felt a warm jet of liquid hit my thigh just before I was lost in my own scalding orgasm. Hugh tumbled forward and fell on top of me, sweat and semen sealing our bodies together. The double man, I thought, when I could think again. This was how you found your other half.

We took a long shower together and then, because we didn't get much actual cleaning done, separate showers. Another change of sheets—I was down to my last set—and we crawled into bed.

I yawned. Hugh asked, smirking, "Did I wear you out? Daddy?"

"What's with the daddy thing? I'm not that much older than you."

"It's not about age," he said. "It's about, you know, power, authority."

"So by fucking me, you fucked authority?"

He shook his head. "No, I felt powerful. In control. Does that sound ridiculous?"

"No," I said. "I get it. You want to know that we'll be equals. We will, Hugh, and if you have to fuck me every now and then to make the point, that's okay with me."

He laughed. "I actually prefer bottoming so your butt is safe."

"What if I want to change it up sometimes?"

"Just say the word, daddy," he said.

I woke up to the smells of bacon and coffee and followed them into the kitchen where Hugh was at the stove in a pair of my running shorts and a Linden University T-shirt. He glanced over his shoulder at me and said, "How do you like your eggs?"

"Over easy," I said.

"Okay, over easy it is. Put some bread in the toaster."

"Let me throw some clothes on first."

We ate at the table on the patio I had forgotten was there, watching a hummingbird dart back and forth between a trellis thick with honeysuckle.

"I have to go back into the city," Hugh said.

"Why?"

"Henry, I've worn the same clothes for the last four days."

I looked at him and said, "To be precise, you mostly haven't worn any clothes the last four days and anyway I have an unlimited supply of running shorts and T-shirts."

"There's something I have to do," he said, growing serious. "An errand. It's going to take most of the day but I can be back here tonight."

"Can you tell me what it is?"

He set his cup down. "When I come back, I'll tell you everything. I promise."

"What am I going to do while you're gone?"

He laughed. "I'd start with the laundry. Your sheets are a scandal."

"Screw that, I'm going to frame them."

But I did do the laundry and, when that was dried and folded away, started cleaning the apartment. It had been so long since I'd cleaned, even the vacuum cleaner had a layer of dust on it. I swept, washed, vacuumed and dusted; it was dark when I finished. I inspected the groceries we'd bought to figure out what I could make for dinner with my limited cooking skills. Ground beef. That looked promising. I glanced at my watch. It was 7:30. Hugh hadn't said when he'd be back, only that he'd be back tonight. That covered a lot of ground. He'd left me his number but I was reluctant to call yet. So, I cracked a beer and watched the tail end of a baseball game that had gone into extra innings. The cleaning must have worn me out because when I opened my eyes, the local ten o'clock news was winding up. I glanced at the answering machine. No messages. I dug Hugh's number out of my pocket, picked up the phone and dialed the number. The phone rang off the hook. I hung up. It was almost 11 now.

At midnight, I was worried, by one I was angry and then, a few minutes before two, the phone rang. I hadn't moved off the couch except to get a couple of more beers. I grabbed it.

"Hugh?"

There was confused silence and then a male voice said, "Uh, hi, is your name Henry?"

"That's right, who is this?"

"Listen," he said, lowering his voice. "Do you have a friend named Hugh Paris?"

"Is he all right?"

"Okay," he said. "My name is Leon. I manage the Liberty Baths in the city. We found your friend unconscious in one of the rooms. It looks like he OD'd on something. Do you know what that might be?"

"Heroin," I said, quickly. "Have you called an ambulance?"

"The ambulance is on its way," he said. "He'll probably go to the emergency room at General. Do you know where that is?"

"Yes," I said. "How is he?"

"He's breathing," Leon said. "He should be okay until the ambulance gets here. This area code I called. You're not in the city, are you?"

"I'm down on the Peninsula. I'll head over to General now."

"Yeah, do that. If he's not there, call me and I'll tell you if they took him to another hospital," he said. He gave me his number.

"Thank you. Leon, did he come in alone?"

"Yeah, and he was alone when they found him. I'm sorry about your boyfriend. I hope he's okay."

I hung up, threw on some clothes and headed out.

FOUR

Hugh lived in a nineteenth century cottage on a sketchy street deep in Hayes Valley. Late Victorian, Queen Anne style; wide wooden plank porch and intricate, extraneous wooden carvings and lattices, all of them in an advanced state of decay. I learned about local architecture from a trick who restored Victorians and whose idea of pillow talk was pulling out a pile of blueprints and showing me the differences between Gothic Revival and Eastlake and Italianate and Richardsonian Romanesque—Queen Anne was somewhere in there. I was standing at the uncurtained window watching the fog lurk in the street and half-listening for the howl of the Hound of the Baskervilles. This kind of wet, cold, spooky summer night was everything I disliked about the city. Out of the fog emerged a figure, male, I thought, standing across the street. I couldn't make out much more than his shape, tall and built. He didn't move. Was he watching the house? I saw the bright, brief flare of a match and then he moved on. He'd paused to light a cigarette, that was all, and yet I remained unsettled.

Hugh was in bed, sleeping it off. The rusting pipes gurgled as they digested the bucket of his puke I'd poured down the toilet.

At the ER he swore that evening was the first time he'd used in nine months, as if that was supposed to make me feel better. The fact he'd been clean that long meant his usual fix could have been lethal. Fortunately for Hugh, the guy who'd wandered into his cubicle at Liberty Baths and found him passed out with his lips turning blue was a doctor. Otherwise, he'd be dead. As soon as I got him into bed, I searched the house for his stash and came up empty-handed, so maybe he had been telling the truth about this being his first slip.

"You little fuck," I said softly, but what I felt more than anger, more than anxiety, was sadness and confusion. *This thing happening between us* is what Hugh had called it. Me, I hadn't called it anything, even to myself, but there was at least a recognition. Yes, that was a good way to think about it; a recognition. But what did we recognize in each other? I was an out-of-work, maybe washed up lawyer, with too much time on his hands and too many unanswerable questions on his mind and Hugh was—well, what did he call himself—a wastrel? Old fashioned word. I thought of another old fashioned phrase for a fuck-up: remittance man; someone paid to stay away from his family. Hugh was a remittance man who had wandered home where no one was waiting for him. Maybe all we had recognized was that we were each superfluous. Or was it loneliness? Isolation? Anyway, one thing was certain. He had warned me not to trust him, and now he had demonstrated why I shouldn't. I told myself that as soon as I was certain he was going to be okay, I would leave, but I already knew I wouldn't. I just didn't know why.

I turned away from the window. In the kitchen I poured myself a glass of brandy. The slow, smooth burn of expensive alcohol on my tongue failed to quiet the damning self-assessment rattling around in my head. Was it just my imagination or had booze begun to lose its sedative quality? I finished the glass in a single belt, poured another and drank half of it. This time the slow warmth spread its tendrils in my brain and turned down the racket so I could breathe. I wandered back into the living room and took stock of the odds and ends of furniture—couch, chair, a coffee table, a couple of floor lamps. Not nearly enough to furnish the big, oddly-shaped space, just enough to suggest transience. The walls were covered with a muted but quite ugly floral wallpaper, curling at the edges. Dark squares and circles and rectangles indicated where pictures had once been hung and furniture had been pushed against the wall. The varnish had worn away on much of the wooden floor and the exposed wood was splintering.

A built-in bookshelf that held a couple of dozen books. Old, worn-out paperbacks, Tolkien, Hermann Hesse, *Howl*—a college sophomore's library. *The Joy of Gay Sex* looked to be the newest addition. Next to it was a worn-out copy of *The Little Prince*, the pages almost in tatters. A solitary, skinny volume lay face down on the bottom shelf. I picked it up: *Whirligig: Selected Poems* by Katherine Paris. Hugh's mother? I scanned the table of contents and turned to a poem called "The Lost Child."

> *When they cleaned you and gave you to me,*
> *long legs and fingers, red glow*
> *rising from creased flesh,*
> *eyes already awake, gaze steady,*
> *I shook for three days*
> *in my knot of hospital sheets.*
> *Tears came later—cries, fears, fierce holding.*
> *The ways you'd shake me off.*
> *Your well of rage. Over and over*
> *you bloomed in your separate knowledge.*

Your well of rage. I turned the phrase over in my mind. The phrase was apt from what Hugh had told me about himself; neglected, abused, self-destructive. There was a cauldron of anger boiling in him that he calmed by sticking needles in his arm. What had set him off this time?

"Is that my mother's book?" His voice was flat.

He wore baggy sweatpants, thick wool socks and an old black cable-knit sweater over a black turtleneck. His pale skin was the texture of a parchment or a blown narcissus petal. The blue eyes were still like the sky, but the sky at twilight, the upper reaches fading into black. He had never looked more fragile or more desolate or more beautiful. I wanted to fold him into my arms but instead I handed him the book, still open to the poem I'd been reading.

"*The Lost Child.* She didn't lose me, she gave me away." He pointed with the book to my glass. "Can I have some of that?"

We traded. I turned the book over to the dust jacket photo of the author. She had been airbrushed to an indeterminate age and, because the photo was black and white, her hair could have been blonde or silver. Her face was as symmetrical as Hugh's but the effect was statuary.

He went on a coughing jag. I put the book in the shelf, went over, took the glass before he dropped it and then went into the kitchen and brought him water.

"Drink this," I said.

He put his hand up, coughed a little more, then took the water and sipped it.

"Are you all right?" I asked him.

He slumped into the couch. "You asked me something like that at the jail," he said. "It was a stupid question then and it's a stupid question now."

I stared at him. "So I guess that means you're fine. In that case, I'll be on my way."

"No, please," he said. "I'm sorry. Please. Please don't leave me."

I sat down beside him. He drank his water. I sipped my brandy.

"What the fuck were you thinking, Hugh?" I asked softly.

"I was thinking I was strong enough to do what I had to do. I was wrong."

I waited.

"I went to see my dad," he said.

I was confused. "Your dad's dead."

"That was a lie," he said. "Half-lie. He might as well be dead. He's in an institution, Henry. He's a schizophrenic."

"I'm sorry," I said, "but why didn't you tell me? Why lie?"

He shook his head. "Because I'm afraid I might be like him."

I moved an inch closer to him. "Why would you think that?"

"They say schizophrenia's genetic. Sometimes, I wonder if some of the things I think I remember aren't just delusions, like my dad's. Like maybe my grandfather didn't rape me."

"You think you imagined that?"

"A shrink told me it might be, what was the word, a confabulation." He sprang to his feet and went to the same window where I had stood. "That someone did rape me when I was a kid, but it wasn't my grandfather. That I was blaming him because when my dad went into the hospital and my mom left and I went to live with my grandparents, I was too young to understand and I thought he had taken me away from them." He turned from the window and looked at me, pleadingly. "Do you think that's possible? That I made it up."

"You said you were ten years old when it started," I said. "Old enough to remember. You tell me, was it him?"

He nodded. "Yes. I remember when he shoved his dick into my mouth it tasted like piss and I started to vomit. He pulled my head back and told me if I threw up on him, he'd hurt me. I remember the smell of the cream he used when he fucked me. One of my grandmother's creams. After that, every time I smelled it on her, I felt sick. I remember the next day there was blood on my underwear and I washed it out so no one would see it and ask me what had happened. Fuck, can you believe that? I protected him!"

"Come over here," I said. He came back to the couch and curled up beside me. I put my arm around him. "Your shrink was a quack. You're not making this up. What he did to you was horrible, unforgiveable. It would be easier to believe it hadn't happened than to face that it did. Maybe that's why you doubt your memories."

"You're so sane, Henry," he said.

"You'd be surprised," I said. "What happened when you went to see your dad?"

He sighed. "The last time I saw him, I was nine years old. He went off in a black car without even saying goodbye. No one told me anything except that he had to go to the hospital. I knew something was wrong with him. Half the time he didn't make sense and he had a bizarre fear of Chinese people."

"Really? Do you know why?"

He shook his head. "I asked my mother but she wouldn't tell me. My family's like that, a bottomless pit of secrets. All that matters to them are appearances. Only my dad was different. He was my playmate. Even when I was a baby I remember crawling all over him on the floor, both of us laughing. We'd empty my toy box and play with each toy. When he put me to bed, he would ask me to tell him five words and he would turn them into a story." He paused to keep from breaking down. "In that cold family, he was a warm hug, a goodnight kiss. He called me his—"

"Little prince?"

"How did you know?"

"The book on your shelf," I said. "You must have looked like the boy in book, blonde and blue-eyed."

"That book and my watch are all I have left of him."

"What happened yesterday?"

He closed his eyes for a moment. "I drove to Napa where they've locked him up in a place that looks like Tara from the outside. Appearances, right? Inside? It's just another hospital. Railings along the walls, disinfectant in the air. Reminded me of the jail where we met," he said, smiling a little. "Except it was really, really quiet. Too quiet."

"What do you mean?"

"I've made the rounds of institutions myself," he said. "Jails, rehab, hospitals. They're not quiet places. In that place, you could've heard a pin drop. I figured out why when they brought my dad to me in a wheelchair. He was bloated and lethargic and his hands and face were twitching. I asked the nurse what was wrong with him and he told me it was the side effects of the drugs he was on. They must have the whole place drugged into oblivion."

I nodded. "I've had clients on some of those meds. Haldol, Thorazine. They're like chemotherapy. The treatment is almost as bad as the disease."

"He didn't know who I was," Hugh said. "I tried to jog his memory but he sat there and stared at me and there was nothing in his eyes."

I pulled him closer. "I'm sorry."

"As long as I thought he was alive somewhere, I didn't feel completely alone. But he's gone, Henry."

I held him and let him cry.

"You could have called me," I said quietly.

He sat up, wiped his nose on his sleeve. "I'm not used to having anyone to call. That's funny, isn't it? They're all here now, what's left of my family. Uncle John, my grandfather. Even my mother is coming."

"Coming from where?"

He shook his head. "She lives in Boston but she's going to be at the university this semester. Some kind of writer in residence thing. I haven't seen her since I got out of rehab the last time. I was planning on seeing her. Now, I don't know. Part of me wants to run away from my family for good."

"Maybe that's not such a bad idea," I said. "I ran away from mine."

"And you never think about them?" he asked skeptically. "About your dad who hated you?"

"Okay," I said. "Point taken. What do you want from them?"

"I want them to be different people," he said. "I want to have a different life."

"You can," I said, "starting now. But you can't change them or the past."

He slumped against me and grabbed my hand.

"Hugh," I said, "This story you told me about your grandfather killing people to get his hands on the family money? That isn't true, is it?"

"Doesn't matter," he said. "I can't prove it and without proof, who's going to believe me? You don't. No, you don't have to say anything. I didn't mean to drag you into it in the first place."

"Do you believe he's out to hurt you?"

He shrugged. "I do a pretty good job of hurting myself. I don't want to talk about my grandfather anymore. Everything seemed so clear when I left New York. Now I don't know what's true anymore." He added a miserable, "Henry, I'm sorry I used."

I pulled him back into my arms. "You could have killed yourself, baby."

"I wanted to get out of my head."

I kissed his forehead. "We're both tired, Hugh. Let's get some sleep."

His head was buried in my chest. I heard a muffled, "You're not leaving?"

"No, I'm not leaving. Come on, let's go to bed."

Over his bed was a poster, a black and white photograph of Billie Holiday, head tipped back, mouth forming a perfect O, the famous gardenia in her glossy hair.

"Lady Day," he said. "The queen of junkies."

We stripped to our underwear and crawled into bed, holding each other as much for warmth as anything else. We kissed a little, with more tenderness than passion. I looked into his eyes and saw what it was I had recognized the first time I looked into them, and what he had recognized in mine: courage.

We two boys . . . the phrase came into my head with a memory trace of a summer day at the university sitting on the lawn outside the student center with a book on my lap. I didn't realize I had spoken the words aloud until Hugh repeated them.

He said, " 'We two boys.' What does that mean, Henry?"

"It's from a Walt Whitman poem. 'We two boys forever clinging, one the other never leaving . . .' I don't remember the rest. I'll find it for you."

"A love poem?"

"Yes," I said.

He pressed himself against me. "I've never been in love with anyone before."

"Me, either," I said, and we left it there.

The next morning I found Hugh in the living room in faded red sweatpants, kneeling in a patch of sunlight. He extended his forearms to the floor, then slowly lifted his legs straight up before curving them over his head with slow, deep breaths. His torso quivered as he inhaled, bringing his chest and abdominal muscles into sharp relief. When he exhaled his skin darkened as the blood rushed in a torrent beneath it. He held the pose for ten breaths before he released it and sat on a floor with his back to me.

"What was that?" I asked.

He stood up. "A yoga pose called *bhuja*," he said. "I started yoga in rehab. It really helped calm me down but I haven't been keeping up."

"That looked pretty advanced for someone who's out of practice."

"I danced in college so I was kind of a yoga natural," he said. "I'm freezing."

He stepped into my arms and jammed his hands down the back of my briefs. "Cold hands," I complained. "You look good this morning. How are you feeling?"

"I'm good," he said.

We pressed against each other, getting warm.

"Did you go to Linden University for college?" I asked.

"I need some coffee for that conversation," he said.

In the kitchen, he measured coffee and water into a sleek coffee maker with an Italian name and pressed the on switch.

"I barely graduated from prep school," he said. "Uncle John said he'd get me into Linden, but I didn't want to come home. He found a college in New York, a couple of hours north of the city, that was basically a dumping ground for rich fuck-ups. No mandatory courses, no grades, big emphasis on creativity." The last word was accompanied by air quotation marks. "There were drugs everywhere and everyone was fucking everyone. Students, teachers. I was pretty aimless but I had this friend, a girl, who was a dance major and, I don't know, almost on a dare, she got me to take a beginning dance class." The coffee was ready. He took two mugs from the cupboard and filled them, pushing the sugar bowl across the counter toward me. "There are spoons in the drawer behind you. Anyway, it turned out, I could dance. My body had a kind of physical intelligence that had nothing to do with this." He touched his head. "If someone showed me the steps I could mimic them almost perfectly, but if they tried to explain them, I got bogged down in thinking. There are never enough guy dancers, so I danced. " He sipped his coffee. "When I wasn't getting high, or wandering around Manhattan, I mean."

"Did you try to do anything with dance after you graduated?"

He put his cup down and spread his hands behind him on the counter. "I dropped out without graduating," he said. "Moved to the city. Got it into my head to audition for the Joffrey Ballet School. They laughed me off the stage. That was the end of that."

I sipped the coffee. "Was there anything else you wanted to do?"

"Get high, get fucked, in that order." He put his arm around my waist. "I told you I was a wastrel."

"You're bright and athletic and you can write," I said, thinking about the letter he had written to me. "All the parts are there, they must add up to something."

"I wouldn't know," he said. "The difference between us is that no one ever told me I had to be anything."

"What did you tell yourself?"

"Honestly, I haven't had that conversation yet," he said. He frowned. "Does that bother you?"

"No, it just isn't something I understand. You're right about me. I've always had a plan."

"Did you always know you wanted to be a lawyer?"

"I knew pretty early on I wanted to do something to help people," I said. "Then it became a matter of figuring out the best way to do that. I thought I'd figured it out with the law. Now, I don't know."

"So, you may also need to have a talk with yourself about the future," he said.

"Yeah, but not today. Today, all I want is to be with you."

He laughed. "God, you just say what's on your mind, don't you?"

"It prevents misunderstandings."

"Okay," he said. "Two can play this game. Let's go back to bed and fuck."

"Bed?" I said, incredulously. "When I could bend you over this perfectly good kitchen counter?"

We did eventually make it back to the bedroom where Hugh played me Billie Holiday records he pulled out of an orange crate filled with LPs on an expensive stereo system. No wallpaper here; the walls were painted white or what had been white a couple of decades ago. A brass Victorian lighting fixture with four arms, each holding a bare light bulb, hung above the mattress and box spring where we lay beneath an eiderdown comforter. A dresser, a floor lamp, an electric heater and a roll top desk and chair completed the décor. The desk was quite an object; in the center of the tambour was a medallion with a copper plate depicting Nike, the goddess of Victory. The sides and drawers were decorated with inlaid wood showing lyres and olive branch wreaths; the legs were Corinthian columns.

"Where did you get that desk?" I asked, adjusting my arm beneath his neck.

"Uncle John," he said.

"That his spare?"

He smirked. "You think you're joking but he collects antiques and he's been at it so long, there's no more room in his house so he keeps most of his collection in a warehouse down in South City."

"What does he do, go down and visit once a month so it won't feel neglected?"

"I doubt it," Hugh said. "I think for him the thrill is in the hunt."

"Does he have kids?"

"Uncle John never married. He—" Hugh stopped himself and massaged one of my feet with one of his. "I shouldn't say anything. He belongs to a different generation that didn't discuss private matters."

"Now you have to tell me."

"My great-uncle is an elderly bachelor who collects antiques. Draw your own conclusions." He sat up. "I love this song," he said and began to sing:

I'll be seeing you
In all the old familiar places
That this heart of mine embraces
All day through

I could tell he'd sung this song many times before and he had a nice voice but after a moment he stopped and let Billie Holiday take a solo.

"I'm surprised you like this old mush," I said. "You're what, twenty-five? I'd have figured you for a David Bowie fan."

"Twenty-six," he said, settling back into my arms. "Like I told you, Billie is the queen of the junkies. Seems like half the guys I got high with put *Lady in Satin* on the turntable as soon as we shot up. Does it bother you when I talk about using?"

"No, a lot of my clients were addicts. I never went in for drugs myself. I never saw the attraction. Especially something as hardcore as heroin."

"I took to junk like a duck to water," he said. "The first time I shot up, it was like one of those time-lapse movies where you go from seed to flower in five seconds. For the first time, the world made sense and nothing hurt." He looked at me. "For the last five, six years, I've been high more than I've been clean. That's my normal, not this. I'm sorry, I don't mean to scare you, but that's the truth."

"Could you get used to this?" I asked him. "To reality."

"I want to try. Yesterday was—"

"Yesterday," I said.

After a moment, he said, "The little death."

"What?"

"I knew another junkie who told me the rush was like coming without sex. He called it the little death. I found out later that's what they call an orgasm in France. *La petite mort.* Not just for the way it feels but because they think each ejaculation takes a man one step closer to death."

"Those morbid Catholic countries," I said, "really know how to take the joy out of sex."

He smiled but his eyes were serious. "Each fix takes a junkie closer to death."

I kissed his neck. "No one is dying anytime soon."

"Not me," he said. "What time is it? Two-thirty? I'm starved. Let's go get some lunch or whatever people eat this time of day."

It was a rare sunny summer day in the city. We soon peeled off the outer layers of clothing we were wearing—Hugh a cardigan, me a hooded Linden University sweatshirt from my undergrad days—as we made our way west on Grove Street. We passed a block of Victorians that were identical although this was not immediately obvious because they were in different states of rehabilitation or disrepair. All had slanted Bay windows and rounded cornices that extended above the roof line, giving the street the appearance of a movie set. Imposing columns framed the front doors and above the entrance were small, ornamental balconies. A few had been restored and were beautifully painted, but the others were falling apart; plywood covered windows where panes had been shattered, paint blistered and peeled to reveal the graying wood beneath, and marble steps leading to entrances that were cracked or broken and filthy.

"Slanted Bay Italianates," I said knowingly, pointing them out.

"How did they survive the fire?"

There was only one fire in San Francisco, the one that followed on the heels of the 1906 earthquake.

"The fire line was at Van Ness," I said. "Everything east of there burned."

"Why don't you live in the city?" he asked, taking my hand.

I was startled, and a little nervous—we weren't in the Castro or on Polk Street—but then the fact I had to think twice about holding his hand made me angry.

"Ouch," Hugh said. "You trying to break my fingers?"

"Sorry," I said, loosening my grip. "I don't live here because it's not enough to be an ordinary person in San Francisco. You're expected to turn yourself into a character. I'm not that interesting."

"Oh, but you are," he said. "After New York, San Francisco feels like a toy town. I don't plan to stay here long."

That hurt. "Back to New York?"

"No," he said. "Too many triggers."

It took me a moment to understand what he meant. Drug associations. "Then where?"

"Maybe we can figure that out together," he said softly. "Unless you want to stay on the Peninsula."

"At this point, living there is just force of habit. I can go anywhere."

There was relief in his smile but he said nothing. He didn't have to. We both understood what we'd just said.

We turned north on Divisadero, passing coffee houses, head shops, a yoga studio where Hugh ran in and grabbed a class schedule, a lamp repair shop, an antique store, a pet hospital. Above us the street was crisscrossed with wires, power lines and telephone lines and cables for the buses that made their loud and stately way up and down the street. We stopped at a Mideastern restaurant and shared plates of olives and feta and hummus, stuffed grape leaves and Baba Ganoush with warm pita bread. I watched him dip a piece of bread into a small bowl of olive oil and plop it into his mouth. I wondered how I had ever eaten alone.

After lunch, we walked to Civic Center. We crossed Van Ness at Grove, between the sleek new symphony hall and the opera house and walked along the southern wall of City Hall toward the grassy plaza. Civic Center, with its gray Beaux Arts granite public buildings, could have been the capital of a small nineteenth century Balkan principality. Anchored by City Hall, a domed wedding cake of a building that occupied two square blocks, the Civic Auditorium, public library and the California Supreme Court building enclosed a big plaza where we joined the sprawl of sunbathers, bums, buskers, drug dealers, roller skaters and government workers taking advantage of the unseasonable August warmth.

We found a place beneath one of the plane trees that lined the walkway bisecting the plaza. I sat with my back against the trunk. Hugh lay his head in my lap and closed his eyes.

"What's a sealed document?" he asked lazily.

"What?"

"In a court case," he said. "What does it means when someone says a document has been sealed?"

"It means that, for one reason or another, the document can't be examined by anyone without a court order, unlike most documents which are public. Why are you asking?"

"Last night you asked me if what I told you about my grandfather being a murderer is true. I believe it is, Henry. I've been gathering evidence but some of it is sealed."

"What kind of evidence do you have?"

"Whatever I could find."

"Have you shown it to a lawyer?"

He blinked the sun out of his eyes. "No, I told Uncle John about it, but I haven't shown it to anyone."

"What did your uncle say?"

He frowned. "He told me the day his sister and nephew were killed was one of the worst days of his life, but that it was an accident and I should leave it alone."

"How did they die?"

"In a car crash," he said.

"Was your grandfather in the car?"

"No, he was at home. My Uncle Jeremy – my dad's brother – was driving my grandmother. They were going to Reno where she was going to file for divorce."

"So how was this murder?"

"A witness told the police that someone forced them off the road," he said.

"Did the police investigate his story?"

He shook his head. "No. They said it was an accident."

I stroked his face. "Do you want me to look at your evidence and give you my opinion?"

"I'm afraid to," he said.

"Why?"

"Because if you tell me there's nothing to it, I'm not sure I could drop it and then you really would think I'm crazy."

"Let's worry about that when we get there. Where is this evidence?"

"The desk in my bedroom," he said.

"Okay," I said. "I'll take a look at it sometime." I yawned. "I have to go back to Linden."

"Why?" he asked drowsily.

"This time I'm the one who needs a change of clothes."

"You should just keep some here," he said. "I can keep some of mine at your place."

"Yeah, let's start tonight. You want to drive down with me?"

"Have to meet Grant for dinner," he said.

"Grant Hancock? The other boy in the photograph?"

"He's not a boy anymore," Hugh said. "He's a lawyer, like you. I arranged this a couple of weeks ago and I can't cancel. It's important that I talk to him but I could come down to Linden afterwards."

I couldn't keep the nerves out of my silence. He noticed.

"Henry, I promise."

"Okay," I said. "Do you know about when?"

"Meeting him at eight. I can be there by ten-thirty, eleven." He dug into a pocket. "Here," he said. "It's a key to my place. I made if for you before I—" he shrugged. "Anyway, I want you to have it."

"We can get you a key to my place tomorrow."

"When were you thinking of leaving?"

"Why? Did you have something in mind?"

He got up, dusted off the seat of his pants and extended his hand. "Let's go home," he said.

We ended up in bed again. Sex had been many things for me but never life-giving; that's what this felt like. I fucked him slowly, deliberately, looking into his eyes. He pressed his hand against my chest, a gesture of supplication. *Whatever you want*, I whispered. *Just you*, he said. He came without touching himself, an arc of thick, warm liquid that beaded in his pubic hair like pearls. A moment later, when I came inside of him, a vein of sadness seeped through the pleasure and I thought about the little death.

Later, it took me twenty minutes to get out the door because we could not let each other go for more than a moment before one of us pulled the other back into an embrace. I drove home confounded by happiness and yearning; I had never felt this for anyone. Was it too soon to call it love? What was love anyway? Could two men love each other? The world said anything we called love was a travesty of the real thing. That was a poison fed to us from the moment we became aware we were different and none of us was entirely immune. All of us wrestled with the fear that maybe the world was right, that two men could never be more than their parts and that together they still added up to nothing. What I felt for Hugh told a different story. When we were together, we made something that was more than either had ever been on his own.

The first thing I did when I got home was rummage through my books. I found *Leaves of Grass* wedged between my constitutional law text and a Joseph Hansen mystery. I flipped to the *Calamus* poems—Whitman's paeans to male love—and found what I was looking for.

> *We two boys together clinging,*
> *One the other never leaving,*
> *Up and down the roads going—*
> *North and South excursions making,*
> *Power enjoying—elbows stretching—fingers clutching,*
> *Arm'd and fearless—eating, drinking, sleeping, loving,*
> *No law less than ourselves owning—*
> *sailing, soldiering, thieving, threatening,*
> *Misers, menials, priests alarming—air breathing,*
> *water drinking, on the turf or the sea-beach dancing,*
> *Cities wrenching, ease scorning, statutes mocking,*
> *feebleness chasing,*
> *Fulfilling our foray.*

The phone rang. I picked it up, hoping it was Hugh, but instead of his voice, a frantic Aaron Gold said, "Henry, where have you been?"

"Hey, Gold," I said, putting the Whitman face-down on the coffee table. "Hello to you, too."

"Where are you?" he demanded.

"At home," I said. "What crawled up your shorts?"

"Have you been with that guy, Hugh Paris?" he demanded.

"Yes," I said, warily. "Why is that any of your business?"

"Don't go anywhere. I'll be at your place in fifteen minutes." He hung up.

Fifteen minutes later, he was standing in the living room, asking, "Got any booze?"

"Sit down," I said. I poured him a drink from the Jameson I kept around for him, and poured myself one too.

"Okay," I said, handing him the glass. "Here's your drink. Now what the hell's going on?"

"How much do you know about Hugh Paris?"

"Why are you asking me this?"

"Do you know who his grandfather is?" he asked.

"No idea," I said.

He downed half his drink. "He's Robert Paris, retired federal judge."

"So what?" I said.

"Do you know who his great-great-grandfather is?"

"Stop playing games. We didn't discuss Hugh's family tree."

Aaron chugged the rest of the whiskey, "Grover Linden."

I fell back against the couch. "Are you serious?"

"Serious as a heart attack, chum."

"Fuck," I said. I chugged my drink. "So, that's a surprise. But I still don't see what business any of this is of yours."

"Judge Paris is a client of my firm. So it is my business when my best friend starts shacking up with his mentally deranged grandson."

"Watch your mouth, Gold," I snapped.

"Did he tell you his father's been in a private nuthouse up in Napa for the last fifteen years?"

"I know about his dad," I said. "But Hugh's not crazy."

"No? Read these," he said, tossing the accordion file he'd brought with him on the coffee table.

"What is this?"

"Copies of letters your boyfriend's been writing to his grandfather. They're filled with crazy threats and accusations. Go on, read one of them."

"You should go now," I said.

He got up. "Fine, throw me out, but read the fucking letters, will you? Hugh Paris is seriously bad news, Henry."

After he left, I picked up the file, glancing inside at a sheaf of xeroxed pages. Even the glance confirmed the writing on the top one was Hugh's but I didn't read it. I put the file in a desk drawer and called Hugh. There was no answer.

Eleven. Midnight. One. No answer when I called him. I threw the empty Jameson bottle against the wall. I was drunk but not drunk enough because I was still awake, muttering, "Fuck you, fuck you, fuck you," to no one in particular. Had there even been a dinner with Grant Hancock or was that an excuse for him to score? My guts were sour and twisted up. I finished the bottle. Somewhere in the apartment, I remembered, there was a Valium or two left over from a root canal. I poked around the kitchen cabinets, found the bottle, took the pills and crawled into bed. I dreamed of a Queen Anne cottage with broken floors and when I looked down through the boards I saw nothing but a void.

Someone pounding on my door. A loud male voice. "Police! Is anyone home?"

I pulled on my pants and stumbled across the living room. A sandy-haired young cop stood, fist raised in the air, about to strike another blow to the door. Behind him, a woman cop, smaller, dark-haired, Chicana.

"What is it, officer?" I rasped, not even trying to be civil.

He backed up, took stock of me and said, "Sir, have you been drinking?"

"Yeah, and I'd like to get back to it if you don't mind."

His face colored. *Don't bait the cop*, I thought. His partner stepped between us and said. "Sorry to bother you, sir, but are you Henry Rios?"

She was half a head shorter than me and reminded me of one my girl cousins. "Yes," I said. "How can I help you?"

"We need you to come to the morgue with us to see if you can identify a body."

The bright morning light blurred. "I don't understand."

"The university police found a man in his car this morning. He was dead. His wallet was gone but he had your card on him. We thought he might have been coming to see you."

"Give me ten minutes," I said.

I ran back into the apartment, splashed my face with cold water, rinsed the booze out of my mouth, threw on some clothes. They were standing beside their patrol car, the male cop drumming his fingers on the roof. The woman had a cup of coffee.

"Here," she said, handing it to me. "You need this more than me. It's black, that okay?"

"Thanks. Yeah, that's fine." She opened the back door for me and I got in.

"What kind of car?" I asked as we swept down the quiet streets.

"Little blue BMW coupe," the male cop replied.

"Oh, fuck," I said.

Nice drive, I teased him. Bet that leather back seat can be slippery. We'll have to see about that.

It was a twenty-minute drive to the coroner's office in San Jose. Beyond the generically furnished reception room was a white corridor, antiseptic and silent, lined with gray, numbered doors where autopsies were performed. At the end of the corridor was an unnumbered room; the cooler. A medical examiner was waiting for us and we introduced ourselves. Mr. Rios, Doctor Harris. He told the officers to stay outside to their clear disappointment and let me into the room where three covered gurneys were perfectly aligned.

"Are you ready?" he asked, approaching the table nearest me.

I stopped him. "What can you tell me about his death?"

"University police found him in his car around six and called the Linden police," he said. "Needle in his arm. Old and new track marks. We sent a blood sample out for toxicology but it looks like an overdose."

"They found him at the university?"

"Yessir."

I shook my head. "That doesn't make sense."

"You were expecting someone last night?"

"Yeah, my friend coming down from the city. He never made it."

The medical examiner threw me a curious, rather hard look and I realized what he thought.

"I don't use drugs," I told him. "That's not why he was coming down and he would know better than to show up high."

"Well," he said, skeptically, "maybe it's not the same person. Are you ready?"

I nodded.

"There's a sink behind you if you have to—" he said, and pulled back the sheet.

I felt all the breath leave my body in a sharp, high-pitched yap, the sound a wounded animal makes. I turned away and pressed my head to the wall, struggling for air.

The medical examiner came up behind me. "Mr. Rios, can you tell me who this young man is?"

I nodded, not trusting my voice. He gave me a moment.

"The sooner we know, the sooner we can inform his family."

I'm his family, I thought. "His name is Hugh Paris," I said.

"Do you know who his next of kin would be?"

I turned back and walked to the table. The beautiful body was pale and still. I waited for him to breathe, but no breath came. There were bruises on his chest, light discolorations. A fresh needle mark on his right arm, just below the bend in his elbow. His eyes were closed. Next of kin? His grandfather? No. Uncle John? I had never learned his last name, was it Paris? Linden?

"His mother, Katherine Paris," I said. "She's teaching at the university."

"Thank you," he said, making a note. "Until I can confirm the cause of death, the police are treating it as suspicious. They'll want a statement from you." He drew the sheet over Hugh's body. "It's such a shame. He was so young. Thank you, Mister Rios. I'm sorry for your loss."

I left the room and walked into the corridor where the two young cops were waiting to drive me home. They were giggling over something but when the girl took a look at me, the smile leaked from her face.

FIVE

Someone opened the front door, came into the apartment and shouted "Henry!" I tossed aside the pillow covering my head, rolled out of bed and staggered, naked, into the living room where I found the manager of the apartment complex and Aaron surveying the wreckage.

Aaron said, "Put some clothes on, man."

"Fuck you," I said. "You're in my house."

The manager said, "Uh, I think I'll leave you guys to it," and hurried out the door.

"What are you doing here, Gold?"

"I heard about your friend," he said. Then, almost pleading, "Henry, please, put something on."

I considered saying no because he was so obviously distressed at seeing me naked, but I was beginning to feel foolish.

"Whatever," I said, and left him standing there while I went back into the bedroom.

I had not left my apartment in five days except when, on day two, I made a liquor run. On day three, I'd stopped having any feelings, so that was all right. By day four, no amount of alcohol could get me drunk and the feelings started to seep in again. I took the last remaining valium and went back to sleep. That was—what?—twelve hours ago? I took a long piss and decided a shower might wash away the stink of booze sweating from my pores. Gold could wait. Or not. I didn't much care one way or the other.

I made it into the shower, turned on the hot water full blast, and let it scorch me until I couldn't bear it. Then I turned on the cold and stood in the stream of warm water, weeping. As I dried myself and got dressed, I heard Gold muttering in the other room, and the clink of glass and metal as he cleared away empty bottles and cans of half-eaten ravioli and creamed corn.

I found him at the sink, washing glasses.

"What are you doing?"

"Cleaning up," he said.

"Leave it. What do you want?"

He dried the glass in his hand on a paper towel. "I heard about your friend. I'm sorry."

"His name was Hugh."

"Yeah, about Hugh."

"Okay," I said, turning my back to him. "Condolences accepted. Let yourself out."

He grabbed my shoulder. "Henry," he said. "You're scaring me."

I shrugged off his hand, went into the living room, fell onto the couch. "What are you talking about?"

He sat beside me. "Look at yourself. You're a wreck. I'm really worried about you."

I saw the worry in his eyes and etched in the furrows across his forehead. My anger evaporated. He was my friend, maybe my only one.

I shrugged. "I'll be all right."

"What can I do?"

"Pour me a drink."

He said, gently, "I think you've had enough for now."

"Yeah, you're probably right. Maybe some coffee."

"Sure," he said.

A few minutes later we were sitting outside where I'd last sat with Hugh. It was a hot day, too warm for coffee but I guzzled it anyway.

"You put a lot of sugar in this," I said.

"You need the calories. You have anything to eat besides Chef Boyardee?"

"I'll order a pizza or something later," I said. "Not really hungry right now."

"So? Wanna talk about it?"

"Do you really want to hear about?"

"I'm your friend, Henry."

The internal conversation that had been going on in my head since the coroner pulled down the sheet on Hugh's body poured out of me, "You grow up and everyone around tells you how it's supposed to be, how it's gonna be, but then, for you, it's different. The question is, how different? And now I know. It isn't different at all. People fall in love. People, Gold. Men with women, women with women, men with men. People."

"That's how it was with you and Hugh?"

I choked back a wave of grief with a clipped, "Yes."

"I'm really sorry."

I watched a hummingbird dart through the air, a blur of blue and green. I saw his body laid out in the morgue.

"It doesn't make sense, Aaron."

"What's that, Henry?"

"He was on his way here and he knew how I felt about drugs. He wouldn't have shown up strung out. That's the part I don't understand."

After a moment, Aaron said, "My cousin's a coke addict. Drug addicts use drugs. They can't help it."

"If he was going to use, he would've done it in the city and stayed there," I sipped my coffee. "Something's not right."

"I know it must be hard to accept, Henry, if you cared for him, but there's nothing you can do for him now."

"I'm still a lawyer," I said. "I know how to ask questions. I need to be asking some."

Gold looked dismayed. "Henry, whatever you find out will only make it worse."

"You don't know that," I said. "Anyway, as painful as the truth might be, it can't be any worse than what I've been imagining. I'd like to be able to sleep without having to knock myself out with booze."

"Here's some unsolicited advice from an old friend," Gold said. "Grieve and move on, Henry. Don't wallow in this."

"You really don't understand, Aaron. One minute I'm holding him in my arms and the next minute the coroner's pulling back the sheet on his body. He was twenty-six years old. Grieve? No, I'm fucking furious. I want to know why he had to die."

"Okay," Gold said, "all I'm saying is if you start asking questions, you might not like the answers." He got up. "What do you want on your pizza?"

We ate pizza, watched a baseball game on TV, and then Gold sacked out on the couch. Only the next morning, after I promised him to stay off the booze, did he go home. I tried to pull myself together with a long run. I steered clear of the campus, not yet prepared to be anywhere near the scene of Hugh's death.

Instead, I ran through Linden, beneath the canopies formed by the branches of the great oaks that lined the older streets dominated by rambling houses Grover Linden had built for the first faculty members. Solid nineteenth century residences that looked like little Tudor country houses or rose-covered Mitteleuropa cottages or turreted Newport-style mini-mansions. Grover Linden came from upstate New York, one of the tens of thousands young men drawn to California by the Gold Rush of 1849 and after he struck it rich—in railroads, not mines—he looked east and to Europe for his idea of civilization. A full-length portrait by John Singer Sargent hung in the entrance of the administration building that showed Linden standing at a table covered with blueprints of his university. Solid, massive man, body encased in a black suit, intelligent countenance, bearded like an Old Testament prophet, receding hairline, blue eyes. Blue eyes. Hugh's blue eyes. I was still trying to put my head around Hugh's ancestry. From robber baron to the gentle gay man in four generations? Comparable to the evolution of dinosaurs to birds. I quickened my pace, trying to exhaust body and mind, both of them aching for my friend.

I ran south, away from the old town to the 1950s suburbs of cookie-cutter ranch houses that students rented during the school year. Gold and I, and a couple of other friends, had lived in one of these flat-roofed, thin-walled tract houses our last year of law school. Strange year. All of us had job offers by Thanksgiving and we were running out the clock to graduation, the bar exam, and what we laughably called "real life." I spent a lot of time in San Francisco that year, in the bars and bathhouses, scratching an itch with this boy or that one. Waiting for my life to begin. Until I'd met Hugh, I hadn't realized I was still waiting.

I urged my body on, trying to quiet the questions. Was he on his way to see me? Or to make a drug connection? Why didn't he call when he was leaving the city? How had he ended up on campus? Deeper and more painful doubts assailed me. Hugh had warned me not to trust him. Had I only seen what I wanted to? Did I know him at all? Was it as simple as what Gold had said—drug addicts use drugs? Those questions I couldn't answer but someone, somewhere had answers to the others. I just had to figure out who to ask.

One of the unanswered calls on my message machine was from a robbery/homicide detective with the Linden Police Department named Sam Torres asking me to come in and make a statement about Hugh's death. Maybe if I answered his questions, he could answer some of mine. I called and made an appointment to come in the next day. In the meantime, I cleaned my apartment, bought some food, limited myself to a couple of weak drinks, watched another baseball game, tossed and turned half the night until sheer exhaustion closed my eyes and, for a few hours, shut off my head.

The Linden Police Department's building looked like a 1960s bank building, straight, simple lines, constructed from glass and concrete, fronted by planters overflowing with seasonal flowers. Not homey, exactly, but not unfriendly either. The kind of place you wouldn't be afraid to enter. But once you got past the pansies and impatiens and forget-me-nots and entered the building, the martial atmosphere asserted itself in the blue uniforms, rigid bearing and barely concealed bellicosity of the cops. The thing about cops I had learned as a defense lawyer is that they regarded all civilians as potential criminals which begged the question of who exactly they served and protected. The short answer was situational; they protected whoever they perceived to be the victim, but that could change from one second to the next. The long answer was, like a lot of bureaucrats, they mostly protected and served themselves and their own interests. The difference was, unlike other bureaucrats, they carried guns. As a rule, I did not like cops.

Sam Torres was proving no exception. Detectives sat at the usual government-issued metal desks in a bull pit behind the reception area. Torres was a bland looking man, shaped like a Chicano snowman with a round face, big belly and twiggy limbs. Thinning hair, blank features except for his eyes which held the typical cop wariness. He interviewed me at his desk while the woman detective one desk over listened in while pretending to do paperwork.

The interview started out *pro forma*. He asked how I knew the "deceased," when I'd last seen him, what I knew about his drug use. Then two things piqued his interest, neither unfortunately having to do with Hugh's death.

He suddenly recalled my name from another context.

"Rios," he said more to himself than me. "Wait, aren't you a PD?"

"I was," I said. "I'm not with the office anymore."

"Go private?"

"No," I said. "Taking some time off."

He smirked. "Uh-huh, getting dirtbags off finally get to you?"

"I was serving and protecting, Detective, just like you."

With a narrow look he said, "Yeah, right."

He'd made me as the enemy.

A little later, going over his notes, he said, "So, according to you, the deceased was driving down from the city to your place?"

"Yes."

"Why?"

"Why? We were friends. He was visiting."

"Uh-huh. He was planning to drive back later?"

"No," I said.

"Staying at your place?" he asked.

"That's right."

"You said you'd been at his residence in the city the night before."

"Yes."

"You spent the night at his place, he was gonna spend the night at your place." A light began to go off for him. "Tell me again what the deceased to you was?"

"A friend."

"What kind of friend?" he asked. "Casual friend, best friend, butt buddy?"

I thought, *"no, he did not just say that,"* but from the pained expression of the woman detective I realized I had heard him correctly.

"What did you just say?" I asked him slowly.

He smirked again. "I asked you what your relationship was with the deceased."

"No, the last thing you said."

He gave a little shrug. "Don't remember. Anyway, the investigation's closed."

"What do you mean closed?"

"The coroner says your friend," he pronounced the word snidely, "overdosed. Nothing you told me adds anything."

"I told you he was coming to see me and he wouldn't have shown up high."

"Yeah, that's what you told me," he said. "Looks like you're wrong." He closed his notebook. "Thanks a lot for coming in."

I stared at him but before I could say anything, the woman detective was at my side. "Come on," she said. "I'll walk you out."

I heard the warning in her voice.

"Sure," I said. "Get me out of here."

I had expected her to leave me at the front desk but she went outside with me and as I was about to walk down the steps to the street, she said, "I want to talk to you about your friend."

She was as tall as me and slender. Her dark blue dress was tailored so austerely I thought it was a uniform at first. Her sandy hair was in a short, unfussy cut and she wore no makeup. I got the impression she worked hard at making herself look plain but her face radiated intelligence. She took my measure with luminous gray eyes.

"I'm Terry Ormes," she said.

"Henry Rios," I replied. "What do want to talk about?"

"You think Hugh Paris was killed, don't you?"

My encounter with Torres left me wary about Linden cops. "Your partner says it was an overdose."

"He's not my partner," she said, "and I think he's wrong."

"What do you think happened to Hugh?"

She pressed her lips together and shook her head slightly. "I'm not sure, but I don't think it was a simple overdose." She indicated a Denny's across the street. "You have time for a cup of coffee?"

"I have nothing but time."

"Let me clock out," she said, "and I'll meet you there. Five minutes."

I nodded and we went off in opposite directions.

Five minutes later she slid into the orange vinyl booth. The waitress came by, smiled at her and said, "Coffee and Danish."

"Thanks, Mary." She looked at me. "You having anything?"

"Yeah, I'll have the same."

When the waitress left, she said, "So, tell me why you think your friend was killed."

"It's your party," I replied. "You go first."

"Okay," she said. "I was first detective on the scene. Your friend was sitting behind the wheel of the car with a needle in his arm. The rest of his works and a baggy with residue were on the passenger seat." She looked at me, frowned. "You okay?"

"Yeah," I said, trying to shake the picture out of my head.

"Then Torres got there. He's senior so it became his case but I thought I'd poke around anyway. I saw some things that bothered me."

The waitress returned with the coffee and pastries, set them down, scribbled a check, tore it and set it on the table.

Ormes said, "Thanks, Mary," and applied herself to putting cream and sugar in her coffee.

"You saw some things that bothered you," I pressed.

"Hmm." She sipped coffee, put the cup down. "The passenger's side windshield was cracked from the inside. The glove compartment was dented. One of the tail lights was broken. Maybe they were like that before. Do you know?"

"I was in his car a couple of days earlier," I said. "It was immaculate. He loved that thing. No cracked windshield or dented glove compartment. Definitely no broken tail light."

"Was that the last time he drove it, when you were in it?"

"Yes, as far I know he didn't drive it again until that last night."

"As far as you know," she said, not skeptically but factually. "There was something else that looked out of place."

"What was that?"

She shook her head. "Footprints leading away from the car. Not your friend's and not the university cops. They pulled up in front."

"Someone walking away from the car," I said.

"Possibly," she allowed. "The car was off road, in the woods not far from the crypt. That part of campus is overgrown and the ground is always damp and covered with leaves, twigs, like that. The footsteps looked recent to me. Of course, someone could have stumbled onto the car before the campus cops got there, freaked out and taken off without reporting it."

"That's true," I admitted. The woods were a known spot for every juvenile miscreant in a twenty-mile radius. High school kids came there to drink, smoke pot and have sex. Since it was summer and school was out, the woods were probably busier than usual. Finding a dead body in a car in the middle of the night would have sent some stoned kid running.

"The ground was also disturbed around the car," Ormes was saying. "From the passenger's side, around the back, to the driver's side."

"So, what did you think?"

"Drag marks, maybe," she said. "But before I could take a closer look, the paramedics had arrived and walked all around the car. Whatever I thought I saw was gone." She broke off a piece of her pastry. "Your turn."

"Before I tell you, I need to know, do you share Torres's prejudices?"

She stopped chewing, swallowed, and took a sip of coffee. "Henry, right? Henry, I'm a thirty-three year old unmarried female cop. I can't begin to count how many times I've been called 'lesbo' and 'dyke,' and I'm not talking behind my back. Which is funny because it's my dress designer sister who's the gay one in our family. That answer your question?"

"I had to be sure. Hugh was my lover. It hadn't been that long but long enough for me to know that he would never have shot up before coming to my place knowing how I felt about his drug use. He'd relapsed a few days earlier and we talked it through. Plus, he'd been clean the nine months before that and he'd almost overdosed when he used again. So, one, he wasn't going to use and two, even if he had, he wouldn't have used enough to overdose, not after what he'd just been through."

"Except," she said, "if he had miscalculated once, he could have miscalculated again."

Grudgingly, I conceded. "Yeah, I guess that's possible. But you don't think it was an overdose."

"I think," she said, carefully, "there are questions that should have been asked and answered before this got written up as accidental death. How was the tail light broken? If he was the only person in the car that night, who cracked the windshield and dented the glove compartment on the passenger side? Were there drag marks around the car? Did someone walk away from the car?"

"Bruises," I said.

"What?"

"I identified Hugh's body. There were bruises on his chest. I know for a fact they weren't there that afternoon when I left him. Is there an autopsy report yet?"

"I don't think so," she said. "But I'll make sure I get a copy. See if there's anything else about the body that wasn't there the last time you saw him."

The image of the medical examiner cutting into Hugh's body was like a jab to my solar plexus.

"Hey, Henry." The sympathy in her eyes forced me to look away.

"For a minute there," I said, "it was like any other case I've worked on. Piece together the evidence, test it, and come up with a theory about what happened and who did it. Then I remembered, this isn't someone else's life. It's mine."

"This is rough on you. I'm sorry."

"I have to know what happened to him."

She nodded. "So do I." After a moment, she continued. "You know, the biggest problem here isn't that the evidence is all circumstantial and can all be explained away. It's that there's no motive. Who would want to hurt your friend, Henry?"

The first night he showed up at my apartment, Hugh had told me two stories about his grandfather. The first story was that his grandfather had killed his wife and brother-in-law to get control of the family fortune. The second story was that his grandfather had raped him. In both versions, Hugh said he had returned to confront and expose his grandfather. I went with the one I believed was true.

"Hugh told me he had returned to California to confront his grandfather because he'd raped him when he was a boy."

A layperson might have been shocked, but all she asked was, "Did you believe him?"

"Yes," I said. "Absolutely."

"If it happened when he was a kid, the statute of limitations would have run out by now."

I saw what she meant. Even if Hugh's grandfather had raped him, he was no longer subject to criminal prosecution, so what motive would he have had to take such drastic action to silence Hugh?

"His grandfather is a retired federal judge," I said. "Hugh's ancestor was Grover Linden."

Now she reacted. "Linden as in Linden?"

"Yes."

"Wow," she said. "Now that would be a scandal."

"Exactly," I said.

"Had Hugh confronted his grandfather?"

I thought about the file of unread letters in my desk. "I think so."

"How was Hugh going to expose him? Go the newspapers, write a book, what?"

"I don't know," I said.

"You know what's amazing about this story?"

"All of it?" I suggested.

"Yeah, there's that, but also Grover Linden's great-something grandson is discovered dead on the university campus and there's almost nothing in the papers."

I hadn't been reading the papers while I was on my drinking binge. "Really?"

"Half a column in the *Linden Gazette*," she said. "Nothing in the San Francisco papers. Not on the local TV news. That's strange."

"His last name is Paris, not Linden. Maybe no one made the connection."

"In this town, someone would have made the connection," she said, then added, darkly, "Maybe someone did and put a lid on it."

"His grandfather?" I suggested. "Or maybe his mother. She's teaching at the university this semester."

She nodded. "Lot of loose ends in this case. They might not add up to anything different than accidental overdose."

"I know," I said. "But let's tie them up. What next?"

"Like Torres said, as far as the department is concerned, the case is closed," she said. "I can't go around interviewing people like his mother or his grandfather, but I can retrace our investigation, review the physical evidence, talk to the medical examiner, and see what comes up. You're a civilian, you can talk to anyone you want. Find out what you can about what Hugh was planning to do with this information about his grandfather and how much his grandfather knew about it."

"Yeah, it makes sense to divide the investigation up like that."

She finished her coffee. "It's not an official investigation, Henry. Right now, we're just asking questions. So don't get yourself into any jams you can't get yourself out of because I won't be able to help you."

"Don't worry about me," I said. "I can take care of myself."

Hugh's cottage was dark, the narrow street empty, and the fog was drifting in as I sat in my car working up the nerve to enter the house. I had a key, given to me by the owner, so I wouldn't be trespassing. The ambush I feared was from my own feelings. I'd brought a pint of liquid courage with me. I downed a slug, got out of my car and made my way up the steps and into the house. Hugh's scent lingered in the frigid air as I moved through the front room into the bedroom. The scent was even stronger there. I switched on the bedside lamp. The unmade bed still held the imprints of our bodies. I touched the sheets. They were cold.

Everything in the house was as chilly as a mausoleum. I reminded myself of why I'd come, went over to the ridiculously ornate desk and rolled up the top. The surface was covered with piles of papers, the evidence he said he'd gathered that proved his grandfather was a murderer. I hadn't believed him, but now he was dead under suspicious circumstances. I had to consider the possibility he had been telling the truth.

I glanced at the papers. Xeroxed copies of newspaper articles and police reports pertaining to a car accident twenty years earlier. The wills of Christina Smith Paris and Jeremy Paris. A thick, red-bound book with its face turned down. I turned the book over and, to my surprise, recognized it as a copy of the trusts and estates case book I had used in law school, authored by my professor, John Henry Howard. I went through the desk drawers and in one of them found three composition books. I opened the first and recognized Hugh's handwriting. The other two were the same. I went into the closet and found a small suitcase. I stuffed the papers, the journals and Professor Howard's case book into it. I looked around the room to see if there was anything else of interest and I saw, propped against the wall, *Lady in Satin*. I grabbed the album and threw it in the suitcase, too. On my way out, I detoured to the bookshelf, found *The Little Prince* and added it to the contents of the suitcase. I cracked open the front door, checked the street to make sure it was empty, and hurried out of the cottage to my car. There was a stop sign at the end of the street. As I waited at it, I happened to glance back at Hugh's cottage in the rear view mirror. Two men were climbing the steps to the entrance. They were too far away for me to see their faces as one of them unlocked the door and they went into the cottage.

Step Eight, made a list of all persons we had harmed, and became willing to make amends to them all.

There was a column of names beneath the sentence. The first one was *Grant Hancock*.

Hugh had begun the journals when he entered the drug treatment facility in New York where he got clean. Evidently, part of the program was based on the twelve steps of Alcoholics Anonymous. I knew about AA because attending AA meetings was a standard condition of probation for my clients who had been convicted of alcohol-related offenses. I had never actually read AA's twelve steps, much less an account of someone attempting to live in his life in accordance with them until I started reading Hugh's journals. I had picked them out of the piles of papers I had taken from his cottage for the simple reason that I wanted to hear his voice again, even if only his written voice.

Today they took us to an outside AA meeting on the upper west side at a big fancy church probably built by one of Grover's friends. The meeting was in the basement, of course. No matter how fancy the church, the basements are always the same. Windowless, scuffed up walls, cheap folding chairs, smelling like stale coffee and mothballs. All sorts of weird things were tucked away in the corners, rolled up flags, choir robes, Xmas decorations. It was my first time out of the house since I detoxed and I was feeling really shaky. Paranoid. Two girls walked in behind me and they were talking and laughing. I just knew they were laughing at me. I felt like I was made out of glass and if I took one wrong step, I would shatter. My hands were shaking so hard I couldn't hold the Styrofoam cup of crappy AA coffee and spilled it all over my hands. I wanted to cry. A guy saw me, took the cup, gave me a napkin to clean up. He took me to a chair. "Sit here," he said. He sat beside me with my coffee. "I'll hold it for you until you can hold it yourself." I nodded. I couldn't talk. Then the meeting started. The speaker was a woman in her fifties, maybe, really nice clothes, nice hair, good makeup. She looked like the house mother for a sorority. Then she told her story. She was a junkie, too, back in the 60s. Strung out and whoring herself for a fix. She was laughing, like it had all been a joke, but I knew she was telling the truth. Then she talked about how she got clean and sober. I was dying, she said, I could feel my body dying, shutting down and that was okay with me. I had nothing to live for anyway. Why not die? Then one day, one shitty day just like all the other shitty days before it, I was lying in my bed trying to think of a reason to get up and I heard someone say, oh, God, I am so tired of all this. Help me. I looked around the room but I was alone. Then I realized I was the one who had spoken, I said it again. Oh, God, I am so tired of all this. Help me. Then I started crying, crying and crying until there was nothing left, not a tear left. I called my brother, who was the last person left who hadn't written me off and I told him, please, help me, I don't want to die.

That's when I started crying. The guy with my coffee put his arm around me. That made me cry even harder. I looked at him and said, "I don't want to die, either." He said, "I know, son. None of us do. That's why we're here."

"Oh, Hugh," I thought and closed the journal. I went out for a walk. Twilight suffused the sky with pinks and gray. Above them, the first stars flickered in the darker blue. Bird song filled the air. He said he wanted to live. He had trudged up from Hell clinging to the hope of a different life. No way he had killed himself. No way.

When I returned home, I put the journals aside and read through the police reports from the CHP regarding the fatal car accident fifteen years earlier that had killed Christina Smith Paris and Jeremy Paris, Hugh's grandmother and uncle. According to the CHP, Jeremy Paris was heading east on Interstate 80 through the Sierra Nevadas in the far left lane at dusk a few days before Thanksgiving. The road was icy, traffic was light and there had been a snowstorm earlier in the week. About twenty miles outside of Truckee, Jeremy Paris lost control of his car and went through the center divider. The car skidded across four lanes of westbound traffic, causing a pile-up as other cars jammed on their brakes to avoid hitting the vehicle before it drove off the road where it slammed into a tree. Christina Smith was dead when the police arrived. Jeremy Paris died at the scene.

A witness named Warren Hansen, who had been behind Jeremy Paris's car, claimed the Paris car was racing another car in the next lane and they were both speeding. He said just before the accident the second car bumped the side of the Paris car. The report noted Hansen was HBD, cop talk for had been drinking. Hansen's statements were duly noted and dismissed. The cop who took the report concluded that Jeremy Paris had simply lost control of his car as he sped down the icy roads at dusk.

A clipping from a Sacramento newspaper basically repeated the CHP report, adding that an inquest had been conducted and the deaths had been ruled accidental.

This is what Hugh had on his grandfather? I read the reports again, and then again. What was Hugh thinking? That his grandfather had run the car off the road? It was, at most, a case of road rage and only if Hansen's account was believable. Obviously the cop who had talked to him on the scene didn't think it was.

Did Hugh find something the cops had missed? I flipped through everything he had collected about the accident. Nothing.

I started to go through Christina Smith Paris's will. It was very long and detailed with pages and pages of addenda but the bottom line was clear enough. Other than charitable and individual bequests, her estate was divided among her two sons, Jeremy and Nicholas. Okay, that was interesting. Christina had left nothing to her husband. That wasn't necessarily significant since he would have inherited their community property. Maybe she figured that was enough. Jeremy, who was unmarried when he died, left his estate in trust to his nephew, Hugh.

I had reached a dead end with the documents. It was time to start talking to people. I would begin with the last person who had seen Hugh alive, the first person on his list of those to whom he owed an apology, the other boy in the picture Hugh had sent to me: Grant Hancock.

SIX

The next morning I went to the county law library and looked up Grant Hancock's entry in Martindale Hubbell, the directory of every lawyer in the country. His full name was Grant Graham Hancock, Jr., B.A. *summa cum laude*, English, from Linden University. Looking at the dates, I realized he would have been a freshman at the university when I was a senior. J.D. from Boalt with honors. I wondered why UC Berkeley instead of Linden for law school. Following graduation from Boalt he had clerked for— the name of the judge stopped me short. The Hon. Robert W. Paris, District Court Judge for the Northern District of California, Hugh's grandfather. When the clerkship ended, he went to work as a litigation associate for, Madison and Dewey, a white-shoe law firm in San Francisco that had been around in one form or another for a hundred years. Precisely the kind of firm I would have expected someone named Grant Graham Hancock, Jr. to have gone to work for. Then, a surprise. After two years at Menzies, he left and went to work for Rosenthal, Dixon, Goldman and Woods, an upstart firm known for its partners' liberal politics and the firm's emphasis on *pro bono* work. For someone with Hancock's pedigree to have gone from Menzies to Rosenthal was like a rich kid who ran off with the circus. Then, under *Associations,* another surprise. Along with the usual yuppie bar and civic organizations, Grant Hancock listed the San Francisco Lawyers for Individual Freedom and Empowerment. Better known under its acronym, LIFE was the city's gay and lesbian bar association.

"Mr. Hancock's office."

"Yes, my name is Henry Rios, I'm a lawyer down in Linden. May I speak to Mr. Hancock?"

"May I tell him what this about?"

"A personal matter involving a mutual friend, Hugh Paris."

"One moment."

A deep male voice said, "Hello, this is Grant Hancock. Who am I speaking to?"

"Mr. Hancock, my name is Henry Rios. I'm a friend of Hugh Paris."

There was a pause. "I see. Is Hugh okay?"

The pause was on my end. "I'm sorry, I thought you knew."

"Knew what?"

"I'm very sorry to have to tell you but Hugh is dead."

A long pause. "What did you say your name was?"

"Henry Rios."

"I'm going to have to call you back. Give me your number."

I gave him my number. He hung up.

Twenty minutes later he called back. "Can you come up to the city tonight?"

"Yes."

"My place at nine."

Grant Hancock lived in a high-rise near the Embarcadero Center. I parked on the street and approached the blue awning that marked the entrance of the building. A burly doorman in a blue blazer and gray flannel trousers stood just inside the double glass doors. It was an odd neighborhood for a luxury high-rise. There were no other residential buildings around, only deserted offices and shuttered stores. That, and the proximity of a sketchy looking, poorly lit park explained the slight bulge beneath the doorman's jacket where he strapped his holster. It also explained why the doorman looked more bodyguard than someone hired simply to hold open the door and accept packages. I identified myself to him and he called up to Grant Hancock. A moment later I boarded a wood-paneled elevator that whisked me soundlessly to the top floor.

I rang the bell to apartment four. The broad-shouldered boy in Hugh's picture had become a broad-shouldered man. Beneath a mop of tousled, dark brown hair, he had a square jawed, sensible face and a big, athletic body. He was wearing navy suit trousers and a pearl-colored dress shirt. The top three buttons of his shirt were undone, revealing a thatch of chest hair. Put him in a pair of dark-framed glasses and you had Clark Kent.

Although the doorman had announced me, Hancock still seemed surprised to find me at his door and kept me standing there for a moment, looking at me, until his manners kicked in. "Please come in, Mr. Rios."

"Henry," I said.

"Grant," he replied.

The room was done in shades of brown, beige, white and tan, as tasteful and antiseptic as the sitting room in a five-star hotel suite. The only personal touches were the white take-out cartons of Chinese food, the bottle of red wine on the marble coffee table and a gym bag tossed in the corner of the room.

"Can I get you something to drink?" he asked.

"Whatever you're having," I said.

He grabbed a wine glass from a china hutch filled with fine china that looked it had never been used, poured me a glass of wine from the bottle on the coffee table, handed it to me and invited me to sit down.

"I was just finishing dinner. There's plenty if you're hungry."

I shook my head. "I'm fine. I was sorry to have to be the one to tell you about Hugh."

He sat back, looked at me, and said, "I didn't believe you so I called his great-uncle. He told me it was true. An overdose?"

"That's what the medical examiner says."

He shook his head. "I just saw him. He said he was off drugs."

"You may have been the last person to have seen him alive," I said.

He absorbed this, shock slowly spreading across his handsome face. "You mean, it happened the night we had dinner? Are you sure?"

"I was with him that day. He told me he was meeting you for dinner."

A light went on in his eyes. "You're the guy he was dating."

"He told you that?"

Hancock nodded. "He said he was driving down to Linden to his boyfriend's place." He gave me a long look. "Yeah, I see the attraction. I'm sorry for your loss, Henry. I'm not sure what I can do for you."

"How was he that night?" I said.

"Hugh said you're a lawyer. Criminal defense."

"That's right," I said.

He nodded. "Okay, I understand, Henry. You want make sense of it. I would, too, in your position. What can I tell you?"

"Was he high?"

He grimaced. "That's direct." He thought for a moment. "Hugh seemed completely lucid. He didn't even have a drink."

"Can you tell me what you talked about?" He hesitated, so I continued. "When Hugh was at the drug treatment center in New York where he got clean, he started keeping this journal. He wrote down a list of people he thought he had hurt and to whom he owed an apology. Your name was at the top of the list."

I had grabbed one of the journals on my way out the door. I laid it on the table between us. He stared at it, then me.

"He apologized," he said.

"For what?"

Grant refilled our wine glasses, fingered the cover of Hugh's journal and said, "Hugh was fourteen when he showed up at my prep school. I was sixteen. My dad's a friend of his great-uncle John and he asked me to keep an eye on him. I kept an eye on him, all right," he said, picking up his glass. "I fell in love with him." He took a slug of wine. "He was a beautiful boy."

"What happened between you?"

"Drugs. There's a bad crowd at every high school, even in the backwoods of Massachusetts. Kids went down to New York or Boston for the weekend and came back with drugs or bought them from townies. Not just pot. Pills, hash, cocaine, heroin. You name it. Hugh fell in with them. He was hardcore from the start. He used drugs like he wanted to kill himself. I covered for him at first but eventually I got so worried he might hurt himself that I told him if he didn't straighten out, I'd tell his great-uncle."

"What did he do?"

He finished his wine in a single swallow. "He crawled naked into my bed one night, told me he loved me and then sucked me off like a pro. I didn't know what to think. I had just barely admitted to myself that I might be gay and here was the boy I was in love with letting me do things to him I had only dreamed about. The next day he said if I told his uncle about the drugs, he would have to leave school and we wouldn't be able to be together."

"So you kept covering for him."

"Yes. I thought now that we were, well, whatever we were, I could persuade him to give up the drugs and scumbags he was getting them from. I was in love with Hugh, but he wasn't in love with me. He loved drugs. He bribed me with sex to keep me quiet. Finally, I had enough. I told him if he didn't stop, I would tell his uncle even if it meant him leaving school."

"Did you?"

"No. He said unless I kept my mouth shut, he'd tell the headmaster I'd raped him. Talk about being sucker punched." He looked like he was still feeling it. "Then it got worse."

"How?"

"As soon as he figured out I would do anything to keep him from going to the headmaster, he started blackmailing me for money for drugs."

"No wonder you were on his list of amends."

"Yeah, that's why he called me when he got back to the city." He poured out the last of the wine. "I hadn't seen him since the day I graduated from that school and beat the crap out of him."

"You did what?"

He got up. "We need another bottle."

He disappeared into the kitchen. Hugh told me his addiction had turned him into a liar and a thief and a whore, but he'd never offered, and I'd never asked for, details. It was shocking to hear Hugh was already using sex and blackmail to maintain his habit when he was fourteen. He was twenty-six when I met him. How far down into the well of addiction had he gone in those years and how had it shaped his character? Don't trust me, he had warned me. Was I wrong about his death? Had he overdosed himself? Was I just the latest in a line of people who covered for him? I looked at the plain black and white cover of his journal. The voice in those pages was so raw and self-lacerating I wanted to believe that, whatever he had been, he had been trying to change.

Grant returned with another bottle of wine. "Help yourself," he said. "Yeah, what was I saying? Oh, so the day I got my diploma, I excused myself from my parents and went and found Hugh. He was getting high with some of his low-life friends. I told him I needed to talk to him. I took him to the woods behind the school and left him on the ground crying. I told him, 'you can tell the headmaster anything you want, asshole.' I didn't hear from him again until a month ago when he called me up and asked me to have dinner with him."

"How was that?"

"Awkward," he said with a humorless laugh. "He said he'd been in some kind of drug program and part of it was making restitution to people he had hurt when he was using. He wanted to give me money to make up for the money he had blackmailed from me. I wouldn't take it. I told him the money was the least of what he had done to me. He said he knew that." Grant's voice softened a bit. "He told me, I took advantage of the feelings you had for me. He said, I'm not asking for you to forgive me, I'm just letting you know that I know what I did and how wrong it was." Grant sighed. "As skeptical as I was about this change of heart, that got to me. I told him we were just kids. I apologized for hitting him. He said he'd deserved it. So, long answer to your question, that's what we talked about."

"He didn't say anything to you about the car accident that killed his grandmother and his uncle?"

He looked puzzled. "No."

"Nothing about his grandfather," I paused, "sexually abusing him when he was a kid?"

He stared at me. "Judge Paris?"

"Yes."

"No, and if he had I wouldn't have believed him. I clerked for Judge Paris. He's a piece of work but a pedophile? I don't think so." He sipped his wine. "Why are you asking me these questions, Henry?"

"I don't think he killed himself."

"Why would you say that?"

"He was on his way to see me," I said. "He wouldn't have shown up high. And one of the cops noticed some details when they found him that seemed suspicious to her. He also told me some disturbing things about his grandfather that make me think he would have been relieved if Hugh was out of the way."

He didn't try to conceal his skepticism. "He tell you his grandfather raped him?"

"Among other things."

"It wouldn't be the first time he made a false accusation like that," Grant observed.

"Why would he do that?"

"To get your sympathy," he said. "To keep you hooked. He talked about you at dinner. Not by name. He just said he had met someone. He told me he thought he might be falling in love with this guy but he needed to be sure. I asked him what he meant and he said he needed to be sure of his motives. He told me manipulating people was second nature to him, something he did without thinking. He said he needed to know he wasn't doing that to you."

"You're still angry at him," I said.

Grant flushed. "Yes, I am. I'm not saying it's fair and I'm sure it's not very attractive since he's gone, but when I came out to him, I let him in on my deepest secret and he fucked me over. It took me years to work up the courage to come back out."

"Did you tell him that?"

"Yeah. He said he was sorry. Sorry doesn't always cut it."

There didn't seem to be anything left to say. I stood up. "Thanks for your time, Grant."

He rose too. "Look, Henry, I'm not a jerk."

"I know that," I said. "You seem like a pretty decent guy to me and what Hugh did to you was unconscionable. You're within your rights not to forgive him."

"Yeah, well, when you put it like that I feel really small." He glanced at the journal. "Can I hang on to this?"

"Of course," I said.

"Let's trade numbers, okay," he said. "Keep in touch?"

"Sure," I said.

He gave me his card with his home number written on the back, I gave him my number. He walked me to the door.

"If it's any consolation, Hugh really sounded genuinely happy about you," he said.

"Thank you," I said.

As I rode down the elevator, I thought the more I learned about Hugh, the more elusive he became. Who was he, after all? That, more than how he had died or what his grandfather had done or not done, was the real mystery here.

The doorman acknowledged my departure with the slightest of nods. I had parked next to the park and now, as I made my way to my car, the streets were deserted. Only the racket from the distant freeway and the lumbering noise of the buses as they screeched to a halt at the nearby bus yard broke the silence. At least the night was clear, the summer fogs having finally lifted as the city approached its autumn Indian summer. I was almost at my car when I saw two men emerge from a thicket of bushes at the edge of the park. I didn't know it was a cruising park but then anywhere in the city, dark and isolated, was potentially a gay hunting ground. The men walked toward me. Something was off. Gay guys out for sex didn't usually wear stocking masks over their faces. By the time I realized I was being mugged, one of them had grabbed me and slammed me against the side of my car. Then the other one jabbed me in the neck with a syringe and that was the last thing I remembered.

I was awakened by the rat scampering across my ankles. It disappeared beneath the dumpster beside me. I was in an alley, my back against a brick wall. At the end of the alley was a streetlight. A car rolled by. Someone had puked between my outstretched legs. I tasted vomit in my mouth. Mystery solved. My head was spinning and my body felt like it was encased in cement. I raised my watch to my face. One forty-five. I had left Grant's apartment almost three hours earlier. My head settled down. I tried to remember. A needle. I felt around on my neck until I found the injection site.

So that had happened. What else? Driving around. Some guy asking questions. Someone rooting through my pockets. I felt for my wallet. Gone. Keys. Gone. I struggled to my feet and stumbled toward the streetlight.

The spire of the Transamerica pyramid loomed ahead of me in the distance. I staggered to the nearest intersection and looked at the street signs: Folsom and Tenth. There was a gay bar around here somewhere. What was it called? Febe's. Leather bar. Khakis, Topsiders and a polo shirt. Not really dressed for a leather bar. Still, any port in a storm. I saw a red light over a doorway a couple of streets down the road. Ten long minutes later I parted a leather curtain and stumbled into Febe's.

Two men were playing Pacman. One of them wore black leather pants and a harness. His nipples were pierced. The other player wore jeans that had been rubbed white at the crotch, a black T-shirt inscribed *Hardcore* and a collar studded with metal spikes. He sipped Perrier. Behind a curved bar bathed in red lights, the bartender looked at me quizzically.

"I've been mugged," I said, took a step toward the bar, and passed out.

I was awakened with a hit of amyl nitrate.

"Stop," I muttered, pushing the little brown bottle out of my face. "Enough."

Someone asked, "You all right?"

"Yeah, I'm okay," I said, sitting up.

The bartender knelt beside me. He was wearing a tight pair of Levi's and a gray and pink bowling shirt with the name Norma Jean stitched above the pocket. Most of his face was lost behind a thick beard, but there was a look of maternal concern in his coffee-colored eyes.

"That was some entrance," he said. "You said you were mugged."

I nodded. "At my car near the Embarcadero. They drugged me, took my wallet and keys and dumped me in an alley."

"I could call the cops but I got to warn you, gay bars ain't high on their priorities. You'll be lucky if they bother showing up at all."

I dug around in my pants pocket and found Grant Hancock's card. "Let me try calling a friend first."

"Sure," he said. "Come on, upsy daisy." He lifted me to my feet.

The bar was empty now and the house lights were on, revealing a homey and rather shabby tavern. The bartender sat me on a bar stool, went around the bar and put the phone in front of me.

"Call your friend. I've got to clean up."

"Thanks. I know your name's not Norma Jean."

"Dean," he said, grabbing a broom.

"Thanks, Dean. I'm Henry." He nodded acknowledgement while I dialed Grant's number.

To my surprise, Grant picked up on the second ring.

"Grant, it's Henry Rios. I'm sorry to bother you, but after I left your place I was mugged."

"What? Are you okay?"

"I think so. A couple of guys came out from the park, drugged me, drove me around, took my wallet and keys and dumped me on Folsom."

"Where are you now?"

"You know the bar called Febe's?"

There was a pause. "The leather place?"

"Yeah, I managed to crawl in here."

"Okay, sit tight. I'm on my way."

Half an hour later, there was a knock at the door. Dean shut off the vacuum cleaner and went to answer. A minute later, Grant pushed through the leather curtain in a Burberry overcoat. Behind him, Dean winked at me approvingly.

Grant came over and said, "How are you doing, Henry? You all right?"

"I think so. I'm sorry to bother you but your card was the only thing they left me with."

"Don't apologize," he said. "I'm glad you called me." He scanned the room. "I always wondered what this place looked like on the inside." He smiled. "I have to say, I'm a little disappointed. I was expecting something more dungeony."

From over the vacuum cleaner, Dean said, "That would be the back room."

Grant lifted an eyebrow. "Where can I take you? Home? Police?"

"An emergency room?"

His face filled with concern. "Are you hurt?"

"I was drugged," I said. "I want to know with what."

"Can you walk?"

"Yeah," I said.

"Okay, let's go." Then he grinned awkwardly. "Actually, you mind if I take a leak first."

"Toilet's back there," Dean said, indicating another leather curtain, this one black.

"Good luck," I said.

"If I'm not back in five minutes," he replied, "send a search party."

After he departed, Dean came up and said, "Love the shoulders on that man. I can picture him in a harness."

"I'll let him know you said so," I replied. "Listen, thanks for taking me in."

"We take care of our own here," he said.

The nearest ER was SF General, a seventy-year old pile of red brick buildings on Potrero Street that served the city's poor. It was the same place where I had picked Hugh up after his overdose. An armed guard stood at the reception desk where we checked in. The nurse directed us up to the waiting room where we sat on metal folding chairs for two hours before a harried doctor pulled us into a curtained cubicle and asked what the problem was. I explained what had happened and what I wanted.

"Are you otherwise injured?"

"I don't think so, but I would like to know what they put into my system. Could you draw some blood?"

"Yeah, fine," he said, "but you're gonna have wait for the results. That could be awhile."

I looked at Grant. "Why don't you take off? I'll be okay."

"Nothing doing," he said. He said to the doctor. "We'll wait."

"Suit yourselves," he said, and insisted on examining me for injuries. After he left, we waited some more until a nurse came and drew my blood. She sent us back into the waiting room. Two men yelled angrily at each other in Cantonese. A frightened black child clung to his mother whose bloody hand was wrapped in a kitchen towel. In a corner, an ancient woman with Kabuki-type make-up sat in a wheelchair, silently weeping. A couple of cops bustled in dragging between them a black man in handcuffs bleeding from a head wound.

Grant said quietly, "There's a lot of misery in the world."

"You don't have to stick around."

"I'm not going anywhere," he said. "You were attacked. Your wallet and your car keys were stolen. When we get the results from the blood work, you'll come back to my place, get cleaned up, and we'll see if your car's still there. Do you have a spare key?"

"In my apartment," I said. "In Linden."

"I'll drive you there and back."

"What about your job?"

He shrugged. "The firm won't go out of business if I don't make my billables today."

"You're a decent guy to go out of his way for someone he just met," I said.

He looked around the room. "It's easy to be decent when everything's been handed to you."

"Meaning?"

"Nothing," he said. "Just let me help you, okay?" He stood up. "I saw a coffee machine back there. Want a cup?"

I smiled. "If you're buying."

When he returned, we sat and drank the worst coffee I had ever tasted.

"I read about you in Martindale," I said. "We were at the university at the same time, but I was a senior when you were a freshman."

He nodded. "Yeah, I know. I looked you up in Martindale, too. Sorry we missed each other."

"You've made interesting career choices," I said, "going from Menzies to Rosenthal. Listing LIFE in your associations. Not what I would have expected from someone who looks like he captained the lacrosse team at his prep school."

"Appearances can be deceiving," he replied, sipping the coffee and making a sour face. "Like yours. When Hugh said he was involved with a criminal defense lawyer, I pictured sleazy, not movie star."

OK, so we found each other attractive. That was out in the open and, given the circumstances, awkward verging on weird. He felt it too from the way his face colored.

"Anyway," he continued. "I didn't leave Menzies, I was canned."

"What? Why?"

"I came out," he said, crumpling his empty cup. "The partners were fine with me being gay as long I kept it to myself and brought women to firm functions, but when I told them I wouldn't play the game anymore, I was fired."

"What drove you out of the closet?"

"White Night," he said. He looked at me. "Were you there?"

"I came up the next morning when the call went out for lawyers to represent the demonstrators," I said. "I drove by City Hall. It looked like a bomb had gone off."

The night the manslaughter verdict was announced for Dan White, who had murdered Harvey Milk and George Moscone, a riot broke out at Civic Center. Demonstrators set fire to police cars and smashed the doors of City Hall. Later, in retaliation, the police invaded Castro Street, pulling people out of bars and beating them bloody.

"It was a battlefield," he said grimly.

"I don't remember seeing you in lock-up the next morning."

"I managed to avoid getting arrested," he said. "But I was there. Do you remember where you were when the verdict was announced?"

"Like it was the day Kennedy was shot," I said. "I was sitting outside a courtroom in San aJose about to head in to argue a suppression motion. You?"

"I was in my office working on interrogatories," he said. "I heard some of the partners coming down the hall laughing and joking. I stuck my head out and asked what's up. One of them said, they gave Dan White a slap on the wrist. I went back into my office, closed the door and turned on the radio. I couldn't believe what I was hearing. A first-year law student could have told you that Dan White had committed premeditated murders and they convicted him of voluntary manslaughter!" His face darkened with remembered rage. "Meanwhile, it's all a big fucking joke to the other lawyers at the firm. I had to get out of there before I punched one of them. I grabbed my coat and wandered over to Castro Street. Eventually, we marched down to Civic Center, thousands of us. I didn't throw any rocks or set fire to the cop cars myself, but I didn't try to stop it either. I wouldn't have cared if they'd burned City Hall to the ground that night. I called in sick for the rest of the week and came out to everyone I knew. I told anyone who had a problem with it to fuck off. When I came back to work, I went to the senior partner, Menzies himself, and came out to him. He fired me on the spot."

"You don't do things halfway, do you?"

He gave me a sour look. "I'd done things halfway my whole life, Henry, and you know what that gave, half a life."

"You told me earlier it was the thing with Hugh that kept you in the closet."

He shrugged. "It was fear," he said. "Hugh blackmailing me didn't help. That just confirmed all the terrible things I'd heard about the 'lifestyle.' " I heard the air quotation marks in his voice. "But in the end, the only person who kept me in the closet was me." He stood up, took my empty cup and tossed it and his into the trash can. When he sat back down he said, "You know what I was doing when you called me?"

"Answering interrogatories? I hear you civil lawyers work 'round the clock."

He smiled. "No. I was in bed reading Hugh's journal."

"Tough reading," I said.

"Yeah, especially the part about his grandfather raping him." He shook his head. "When you told me he said that, I thought it was a load of crap, something he said to get your attention. But the journal was obviously private and the description of what the judge did to him, that wasn't fake. You know, I always wondered why Hugh was so sexually experienced at fourteen. He really knew his way around a man's body but when we had sex, it was like he wasn't really there. Now I understand why. It's horrible what that man did to him."

"You clerked for the judge. What's he like?"

"My dad arranged the clerkship. Thought he was doing me a favor. One of the worst years of my life. The judge was arrogant, demanding and belittling. Halfway through the year, one of my fellow clerks quit. Quitting a clerkship with a federal judge isn't something you do but she'd had enough. I don't blame her. The judge was especially hard on her. The only reason I didn't get the full treatment from him is because he and my father are friends. Well, not friends exactly but peers."

"There are lot of assholes in our line of work," I observed.

"Judge Paris is special, believe me," he said. "I can't imagine what it must have been like for Hugh."

"Did Hugh talk about his family when he was a kid?"

Grant shook his head. "No, but why would he? I knew his dad had been institutionalized and his mom was a drunk."

"How did you know that?"

"Our folks moved in the same circle and it's greased by gossip. As far as I know, though, no one said anything about what the judge did to him. If he'd told me any of this when I saw him, I might have been able to accept his apology."

"Maybe he thought if he had told you, it would sound like he was making excuses. I think he was genuinely trying to take responsibility for what he did to you."

"I didn't know him at all," he said, regretfully. "Now I never will."

A nurse appeared and called my name. We went up to her.

"You wanted to know about the drug you took," she said, flipping through a chart.

"I didn't take it, someone injected me with it."

She was not interested. "Sodium pentothal," she said. "No long-term effects. You'll be fine."

Grant said, "Sodium pentothal? What's that?"

"Truth serum," I replied.

SEVEN

"Why would a mugger inject me with truth serum?" I asked as we drove from the hospital back to Hugh's apartment.

He thought for a moment. "Do you have an ATM card?"

"A what?"

"Automated teller machine," he explained. "You see them at banks. You put in a plastic card, punch in a code and it dispenses money from your account."

"Uh, no, that technology hasn't reached the great unwashed yet. And what if I did? How would that explain the sodium pentothal?"

"They could have been trying to get your code. Where did you say your car was?"

I directed him to where I had parked my car. It was gone.

"Fuck," I said.

"You need to file a police report," he said. "For your insurance company, if nothing else. You can call from my place."

We drove into the underground garage beneath his building and took the elevator up to his condo. Outside, it was dawn and the view of the bay from his windows was spectacular. While I filed a report with the cops over the phone, Grant made scrambled eggs and bacon and a pot of coffee. We ate at a dining table that seated eight.

"You have a lot of furniture for one guy," I observed.

"My mother's an interior decorator," he said. "I get the stuff her clients decided they didn't like after all."

"The Hancocks have to work for a living?"

"She doesn't do it for the money, it's how she expresses herself." He gave me a quizzical look. "What do you have against rich people?"

"Hugh called them sharks," I said.

"Maybe his family," Grant said. "Not mine. What's your story, Henry? You from the city?"

He said "the city" with a proprietary air. "No," I said. "I was raised in the Central Valley. You're San Francisco born and bred, right?"

"Fourth generation. But I asked about you."

I told him a little bit about myself, got him to reveal a little bit more about himself, and soon we were chatting freely about this and that, as if we were on a first date that was going really well as opposed to two guys thrown together by a death. Some part of me wished it was a date. That seemed strange, but then, the whole night had been strange. And exhausting. I yawned.

"Sorry," I said, covering my mouth.

"Don't apologize," he said. "You must be wiped out. Why don't you clean up? I'll give you something to wear while I throw your clothes into the washing machine. We're about the same size." He grinned. "I didn't want to say anything before but you have a little vomit on your pants."

I glanced at the stain on my pants leg. "That's attractive," I said.

"Come on," he said. "I'll show where the bathroom is and get you some clean clothes."

I took a long, hot shower. Grant had laid out a pair of levis and a rugby shirt on his bed. He'd also left a pair of boxers—pale blue, Brooks Brothers—and it felt a little strange putting them on, intimate and undeniably kind of sexy too. I heard him on the phone and from what I gathered from his side of the conversation, it was a work call. I slipped on the boxers and sat at the edge of his bed. The dizzying weight of exhaustion laid me out on the bed. Five minutes, I thought, and closed my eyes.

The room was dark when I woke up, covered with a soft blanket. Light seeped in from beneath the closed door. I switched on a lamp. The clothes that had been laid out on the bed hung over a chair. I dragged myself out of bed, got dressed and went out into the hallway. The television was on. When I entered the living room, Grant was sitting on the couch watching the evening news.

"Hey," I said.

He looked at me with a smile. "Hey, sleepyhead."

"I am so sorry about that."

"Don't be ridiculous," he replied. "You had quite a night. You hungry? I've got a fridge full of take-out leftovers."

"Sure, if you're having anything."

He hopped up and said, "Make yourself at home. I'll rustle something up. You want a glass of wine?"

"Yeah, thanks."

When he busied himself in the kitchen, I wandered around the apartment. On a bookshelf was the same small collection of gay novels that every gay man owned: *City of Night, The City and the Pillar, A Single Man, Dancer from the Dance, Tales of the City.* He also owned *The Joy of Gay Sex* which reminded me of going through Hugh's books in the forlorn cottage where he had camped out. Grant's apartment could not have been more different, a safe, warm place that radiated stability.

"Here's your wine," Grant said from behind me. He glanced at *The Joy of Gay Sex* in my hand. "I see you've discovered my porn."

I flushed and slipped it back on the shelf. "Snooping. Bad habit."

He handed me a glass of red. "Occupational hazard of being a lawyer. By the way, won't your office be wondering what happened to you today?"

I faced him. "Actually, I'm not practicing at the moment."

"Why?"

"The short answer is burnout. The long answer is—well I'm still working out the long answer."

"I'd like to hear it when you do," he said. "Come and check out the food options."

A half dozen cuisines were represented in the collection of boxes and containers laid out on the kitchen counter. I ended up with tandoori chicken and a side of spaghetti with pesto.

"I can cook," he said, grinning as he lifted a forkful of Thai peanut noodles to his mouth. "My mother made sure all her boys could feed themselves, but take-out is easier than cooking for one person, especially with the hours I work."

"I'm not complaining," I said. "You don't have a boyfriend?"

He shook his head. "No," he said. "For most guys, the city is a candy store or like that T-shirt that says, 'so many men, so little time.' I like sex as much as the next guy, but my folks have been married for forty-two years. That's what I'm looking for." He ate some more noodles, then asked, "Were you in love with Hugh?"

"What happened between us happened very fast and it didn't last very long but while it did, I felt something for him I'd never felt for anyone."

"Which was?"

I put my fork down. "Less alone," I said. "Even when he wasn't there. Is that love?"

"Sounds like it to me," he said quietly. He sipped some wine, looked at me, and continued, "Is it really screwed up that I wish we had met under different circumstances?"

"No," I said. "I like you, too, Grant, but there's one last thing I have to do for Hugh."

"What's that, Henry?"

"Prove he didn't kill himself," I said, "and give him some dignity in death."

"You really think the judge had someone kill him?"

"Unless there's a better explanation. You still willing to give me a lift home?"

"Of course," he said. He stood up and cleared our plates. "Let me wash up and we'll go."

We talked comfortably on the drive to my place about our time at the university and about the law. When we arrived at the apartment complex, I told him to pull into my parking spot but the stall was already occupied by a gray Honda Accord.

"That's my car," I said.

He pulled in behind it. "You sure?"

"I know the license plate number."

We got out and walked around the car. It was undamaged and locked.

"They must have got my address off my driver's license," I said. "Let's check the apartment."

The door to my apartment was cracked open and there was a glimmer of light from within but I couldn't hear anyone moving around inside. I pushed the door open and called out, "We're coming in!"

Silence. The lights were on in every room, drawers and cabinets were open, clothes and papers tossed to the ground. My keys and wallet were on my desk but the documents I had taken from Hugh's apartment were gone.

Behind me, Grant said, "Someone was here looking for something."

"Yeah, and they found it."

"What's missing?"

"Documents I took from Hugh's apartment after he died," I said.

"What kind of documents?"

"They were related to the investigation of the death of his grandmother and his Uncle Jeremy in a car crash fifteen years ago."

He frowned. "You asked me about that last night. What's going on here, Henry?"

"I appreciate you coming to my rescue last night, and everything else, but I can take it from here. You don't need to get involved."

He sat down on the couch. "I'm already involved. Don't blow me off now. Or is it that you don't trust me? If you think I'm going to the judge, you're wrong. He wasn't a friend even before I knew what he did to Hugh. I think I deserve an explanation."

"Okay," I said, sitting beside him. "Hugh told me his grandfather had his grandmother and uncle killed to get control of her money because she was going to divorce him. He'd been collecting evidence and when he died, I used the key he gave me to his place and brought it here."

He absorbed this. "Was he right?" he asked. "Did the evidence support his claim?"

"I couldn't find proof that the judge was involved in the accident," I said. "Until last night, I would've said Hugh had imagined it."

"You mean the mugging?"

"It wasn't a mugging, Grant. Someone followed me to your place, waited until I came out, abducted me and shot me up with sodium pentothal, probably to find out what I knew about Hugh's allegations against the judge. I must have told them about the papers."

"So they came here and took them," he said. "But you said the papers didn't prove anything."

"They wouldn't have known that without looking at them. They were worried enough about what Hugh knew to kill him." I glanced at him. "Hugh was murdered."

"I admit this makes his death look suspicious," Grant said. "What are you going to do now?"

"Call the cop I've been working with, tell her what happened, see if she's got any new leads about Hugh's death," I said. "Talk to some other people. You know his great-uncle John. Can you get me in to see him?"

"What are you going to tell him?" Grant asked. "That Judge Paris had Hugh murdered because he was out to expose the judge for having had his wife and oldest son killed?"

"Something like that," I replied.

"Henry, this is his family you're talking about. His sister, his nephews, his brother-in-law. If he doesn't think you're crazy, he'll think you're trying to extort him."

"He was the only person in his family Hugh trusted. He should know what happened to Hugh."

"You can't walk into John Smith's office and tell him his brother-in-law is a mass murderer without proof. What would you accomplish by doing that except upset him?"

"All right," I conceded. "I see your point. I won't go to him yet. I should clean up."

"Let me give you a hand."

I was picking up files from the floor around my desk and putting them away when I found the accordion file Aaron Gold had given me with copies of the letters he said Hugh had written to his grandfather. The letters were still inside. In their haste, the burglars had either overlooked the file or missed its significance. I set it aside. Grant came over holding Professor Howard's casebook.

"I found this by the door," he said. "You use it as a door stop?"

"I took it from Hugh's house," I said. "It was with the copies of the wills."

"Whose wills?"

"His grandmother's and his Uncle Jeremy's," I said.

Grant was paging through the book. He stopped and said, "Did Hugh have a particular interest in the doctrine of simultaneous death?"

I looked over his shoulder. On page 293, a paragraph had been highlighted in yellow, typical of how law students marked up their texts.

"He must have bought the book used."

Grant closed the book and tossed it on my desk.

"I'm hungry," I said. "Buy you dinner?"

"It's getting late, I need to get home. Will you keep in touch?"

"Yes," I said. "Thanks for everything, Grant. I wish we'd met under different circumstances too."

He smiled wryly and said, "Circumstances can change."

It wasn't until after he left that I noticed the answering machine light was blinking. Terry Ormes had left a message asking me to meet her at Denny's the next morning. I ate two bowls of cereal and washed them down with a shot of Jack Daniel's. I looked at the file on my desk of Hugh's letters to his grandfather. I was exhausted, physically and emotionally. I decided that whatever was in them could wait and went to bed.

Terry was waiting for me when I arrived. As always, she wore severe attire meant to render her invisible as a woman—a black pantsuit, a white blouse. Her deliberate plainness emphasized rather than diminished her small concessions toward femininity; the thin gold chain around her neck and the gold loop earrings, her manicured fingernails, a faint floral fragrance from her soap or moisturizer. The waitress brought coffee, took my order and said to Ormes, "The usual?" Ormes smiled and nodded. When she left, we started talking at the same moment.

"You first," I said.

She took a folder out of her bag and lay it on the table. "The autopsy report," she said. "You were right about the bruises on his chest. There were also ligature marks around his wrists."

She opened the folder, flipped through it, and passed a set of photographs across the table. Close-ups of Hugh's chest and arms and hands. There were the discolorations I'd observed in his chest and faint reddish rings around his wrists. I stared at his hands which looked smaller and more delicate than I'd remembered.

"Henry?"

I passed the photographs back to her. "It looks like his hands were tied together."

"It looks that way to me too," she said.

"What caused the bruises?"

"The coroner tried to tell me it was from the paramedics' attempt to revive him, but I was there when they arrived. Hugh was already dead. I think someone pushed down on him hard. And there's something else. You said Hugh was a junkie."

"Yeah. Why?"

"There was bad bruising around the last injection site. It was a sloppy job of shooting up."

"He would've known exactly what to do," I said. "Let me see the picture of his hands again."

She gave it to me. I remembered teasing him about the scratches he'd left on my back with his long nails. Now I looked closely at his fingers and thought I saw some debris trapped beneath his nails. I pointed it out to her. She reached into her bag and pulled out a magnifier and studied the photograph.

"Could be," she said. "You think he fought his attacker and got some of the guy's skin beneath his nails?"

"The dented glove compartment, the crack in the windshield," I reminded her. "Hugh was fighting."

"You could interpret it that way," she replied. "One other thing. I went back and examined the busted tail light on his car. I saw fresh paint transfer around the bumper. That could mean the tail light was broken when someone rear ended his car."

I thought about the implications. "When two people get into a minor traffic accident, they pull over. Maybe that's how his attacker got Hugh out of his car to grab him."

"There would have been at least two of them," she said. "One to drive Hugh's car to the campus with Hugh handcuffed in the passenger seat, one to follow in the getaway car. If that's what happened."

"What else could explain this evidence?"

"The tox screen came back," she said. "Straight heroin. The coroner is sticking to accidental overdose."

"How does he explain the other evidence?" I demanded.

"Unrelated, coincidental, insignificant," she said like she was quoting him.

"That's ridiculous," I said.

"You don't have to convince me," she said. "But I don't have enough juice to get him to reconsider. It's not even my case."

"So, what next?"

"Hugh was a Linden," she said. "If someone in his family were willing to pressure the coroner into taking a closer look at his death, that might get the investigation reopened."

Our food came. Ormes dug in to her bacon, eggs and pancakes. I stared at my omelet wondering who in Hugh's family I could approach. Not his father who was in a mental institution. Not his great-uncle John who was off-limits for now.

"Let me approach his mother," I said. "She's at the university."

"Good," she said. "I told you what I know. Your turn."

I had told her Hugh said there were issues with his grandfather, but I'd kept the full story from her because I didn't think she would believe it any more than I had and that would make her less likely to investigate Hugh's death. Now I told her everything Hugh had told me, what I found out on my own, and about my abduction, the sodium pentothal and the break-in at my apartment. By the time I finished, her plate was clean.

"You realize that no one is going to believe someone like Judge Paris killed his wife and son," she said.

"Do you?"

She turned the question back on me.

"After what happened last night," I said, "I think it's worth investigating. Hugh may not have found the smoking gun that implicated the judge in the murders, but that doesn't mean there isn't one. Why else would Hugh have been murdered?"

"To keep him from exposing the judge as a child molester," she suggested.

"Maybe, but you're the one who pointed out that, legally, the judge is beyond prosecution for that. Sure, Hugh could have embarrassed him with the allegations but the judge could have fought back with a libel suit or painted them as the rantings of the family black sheep. But there is no statute of limitations on murder. That could bring him down. There's your motive."

She looked thoughtful. "It's such an incredible story, Henry."

"So was Watergate," I said.

"This isn't Watergate."

"So you don't believe it's possible that Hugh was on to something?"

"I believe the shortest distance between two points is a straight line," she said. "And I don't believe in coincidences. Hugh thought he had something on Judge Paris in the papers you took from his house, then Hugh ends up dead and the papers are stolen from you. Who would want them except the judge?" She glanced at my plate. "Your food's cold."

"I'm not really hungry."

"Eat anyway," she said.

She helped up her coffee cup and the waitress came by, filled both our cups, and cleared Terry's plate.

"I don't know if the judge killed his wife and son," she said, "and even if he did, that trail is cold. We need to focus on Hugh's murder."

"But motive—" I began.

She shook her head. "Motive isn't an element of murder. You know that."

"It's not a legal element," I replied, "but I've never tried a murder case where the prosecutor didn't feel obligated to prove motive. Otherwise, it's like a telling a story and leaving out the most important part of the plot."

"I still say let's concentrate on Hugh. Talk to his mother about getting the medical examiner to reopen the case."

"What will you do?"

"I have a friend in the DA's office and I'm going to try to get him interested." She finished her coffee. "Do you remember any details of the accident that killed the grandma and uncle?"

"I dictated some notes," I said. "The burglars missed my voice recorder. Why? I thought you said we weren't going to focus on that."

"Yeah, but you're right about motive," she said. "I'll see if I can pull the accident reports."

"Thanks," I said. I grabbed the check. "On me." I asked the waitress to box my untouched food.

I called the English Department and learned that Katherine Paris would be in her office that day. In the afternoon, on the way back from my run, I detoured to the campus bookstore. The blue-frocked sales clerk didn't bat an eye at my sweaty running clothes but directed me to the second floor where the poetry section took up several long shelves against the back wall. For a brief time in college, I wrote poetry. Like most undergrad verse, my poems were conceived in the loins rather than the mind and when I started having sex, the poems stopped. My brush with poetry, however, left me with a permanent respect for those who wrote it well. Seeing familiar names again, from Auden to Whitman, took me back to the sunny autumn afternoons when I sat alone in my dorm room searching for language to describe my latest infatuation.

Katherine Paris had published four slim volumes, including *Whirligig*, the book that Hugh had in his cottage. The collection began with a poem she called *My Body*.

> *Throat puckered like crepe*
> *right hand throbbing with arthritis*
> *right hip permanently higher than the left, right leg shorter*
> *after years of books slung from one shoulder.*

I read on, immediately taken by the humane voice, at once self-effacing and courageous.

> *sagging belly testament to fear, dieting, birth, abortion, miscarriage*
> *years of fighting booze and overeating still written in my flesh.*
> *Eyes needing bifocals now, no good for driving at night,*
> *still blue and intense, tired but my best feature—*
> *or maybe it's my hands, strong, blunt with prominent veins.*

I stopped reading, certain I was being watched. I closed the book and looked around. The boy standing at the end of the aisle quickly directed his attention to his feet.

He wore a baggy pair of khaki shorts rolled up at the bottom over a long sinewy pair of legs. He had on a white sweatshirt with a red paisley bandana tied around his neck and a small button with the lambda—the symbol of gay liberation—on it. Short, dark hair framed a round cherubic face. He looked about nineteen. When he shyly raised his eyes to mine, I realized I was being cruised, not spied on.

"Hello," I said. "I'm Henry."

"I'm Danny," he replied, bounding toward me. He saw the book in my hand. "I'm taking her poetry workshop."

"Have you met her yet?"

He nodded. "She was here last spring to give a reading and afterwards a bunch of us went to dinner with her."

"Was she like her poems?"

He tilted his head, puzzled by my question. "What do you mean?"

"Her poems are warm and compassionate. Is she like that?"

"I don't know," he said. "She gave a great reading, but she didn't say much at dinner. Just smoked and drank tea and seemed kind of tired." He took the book from me. "This is my favorite one of her poems."

> *The scent you say is not scent*
> *rises from warm ports*
> *between neck and shoulder.*
> *Scent that isn't witch hazel, vetiver, camphor, lemon*
> *but is just your skin,*
> *raises a breeze on mine . . . .*

He closed the book and gave me what I imagined he thought was a seductive smile, but which struck me as adorable and silly.

"I can see why you like it," I said. "It's very sensual."

"Sexy," he said. "Like you. Are you a grad student or something?"

"I'm a lawyer," I said.

He had edged toward me and was close enough that I felt his breath on my skin. "You're not dressed like a lawyer." He plucked the strap from my singlet. "I live close by. You want to come over?"

"Danny, I'm probably fifteen years older than you."

He grinned. "I like older men. They know what to do."

"Sorry, baby, I'm going to have to take a rain check."

He made a pretend frown. "Aww." He grabbed my hand and turned it palm up, pulled a marking pen out of his pocket and wrote his name and phone number on my skin. "In case you change your mind."

"Okay, then," I said.

"Call me, Henry," he said, with a bright smile. He waved at me from the top of the stairs and was gone.

I looked at my palm. Had I ever been as bold and innocent? No. I belonged to that generation of gay men still too deeply tainted by shame to have expressed our desire so openly. We didn't wear identifying buttons. Like Hugh and me, we recognized each other from our scars.

Billie Holiday's voice filled the room:
Love is funny or it's sad
It's quiet or it's mad
It's a good thing or it's bad
But beautiful . . .

The queen of junkies, Hugh called her. The liner notes for *Lady in Satin* said it was her last recording but one. Her voice was little more than a husky croak, but what she had lost in range she made up for in wisdom and melancholy. I played the record over and over as I sipped Jack Daniel's and read the half-dozen letters Hugh had written to his grandfather in the last months of his life. They didn't have salutations, but began as if in mid-conversation, one that I imagined Hugh had been having in his head for years before he took pen to paper.

Remember the first time? I said please stop it hurts, and that excited you, didn't it, because you wanted to hurt me. You wanted me to cry, to beg. I couldn't make you stop but I could refuse to give you that twisted pleasure you took in hurting me. I kept it all inside after that, let you fuck me without a word, without a sound, even when you made me bleed. How did no one notice my bloody underwear, the blood on the sheets? Did you pay off the maid? And my grandmother, she knew, didn't she? After a while she could barely stand to look at me. Like it was my fault. Did she look at Jeremy that way? Because you did it to him too, didn't you? Isn't that why he hated you so much? Is that why you killed him? Yes, I know about that. You killed them both. Pretty soon everyone will know what you are. Rapist, murderer, psychopath.

He was ten years old when it started. Around the same age I was when my father decided to beat the devil out of his bookish, quiet son. I remember lying in bed as Friday night turned into Saturday morning and the bars closed, unable to sleep, listening for the sound of his car pulling into the driveway, wondering if he would pull me out of bed to abuse me or pass out on the couch. I could vividly imagine Hugh's terror and hopelessness as he also lay in the dark listening for his grandfather's footsteps, knowing there was nowhere to go and no one to help him. I put the letters away, finished my drink and then another one, and went to bed listening to Billie Holiday singing she was glad to be unhappy. Two years later they would pick her up for possession of junk and handcuff her to a hospital bed where she would die of cirrhosis of the liver, age forty-four.

EIGHT

"Who did you say you were?"

The woman standing in the small office surrounded by unopened boxes and bare bookshelves bore no resemblance to the portrait she had painted of herself in verse. Katherine Paris was small, slender and elegant. Her features were a feminized version of Hugh's, once delicate, by now hardened into middle age. Her eyes were the same bright blue as Hugh's, but while his were warm, hers were arctic. The overall impression of coldness was accentuated by her silver hair. She regarded me with an expression of wariness bordering on displeasure.

"My name is Henry Rios," I replied. "I was a friend of Hugh's."

"Hugh's friends were generally bad news," she said. Her voice was throaty and warm, a performer's voice. "I will say, you don't look like an addict."

"I'm a lawyer, Mrs. Paris."

"Ah," she said. "Does he owe you money for getting him out of a jam? You can bill his estate. I'm not responsible for my son's debts."

"I wasn't his lawyer," I said. "I was his lover."

The cold eyes got colder. "His what?"

"I identified his body," I said. "I gave the police your name as next of kin. I'm not here to shake you down. I came to talk to you about the circumstances of his death."

"The police said he still had the needle in his arm when they found him," she said. "The circumstances seem pretty clear to me."

"I know for a fact that Hugh had been clean for nine months before he died. I also know he wanted to live."

"If you believed him when he told you he was clean, you're a fool," she said. "Hugh was a hopeless drug addict. It was only a matter of time before he killed himself."

"The police investigation was perfunctory," I said. "There were indications the overdose wasn't accidental."

"What are you talking about?"

"I think Hugh was killed," I said.

"I don't know what you want from me," she said, "but I want you to leave. You know nothing about my son."

"Mrs. Paris—"

Her composure broke and she screamed, "Get out, get out, get out."

I left.

I sat in my car in the parking lot at the edge of the Old Quad. Katherine Paris had given up on her son a long time ago. She would be no help. I started my car and without any idea of where I was going, I drove.

"I'd like to see Mr. Gold," I told the receptionist, a smartly dressed young woman sitting beneath a Rothko at a semi-circular desk with the most elaborate phone console I had ever seen.

She responded with an unsmiling, "Do you have an appointment?"

"Tell him it's Henry Rios," I said. "He'll see me."

She hesitated, then picked up the phone, pushed a couple of buttons and said, "There's a gentleman out here who wants to see Mr. Gold." She listened to the response, glanced at me disapprovingly and replied, "No he doesn't, but he said Mr. Gold would see him without an appointment. His name is—"

"Henry Rios," I said.

"Henry Rios," she repeated.

She waited. I waited. Then she said, "Yes, all right. I'll tell him." She hung up, plastered a smile on her face and said, "He'll be right out."

In the corner of the room was an enormous globe of the world. I drifted over to it and spun it. Behind me, the receptionist cleared her voice censoriously. So I went to the window and looked at the golden hills behind the red-tiled roofs of the campus. It was one of those bright end-of-summer days when every corner of the world seemed sunlit and all darkness banished.

"Henry."

I spun around as Gold exited a heavy door in the wood-paneled wall. He was jacketless and wearing suspenders. Under different circumstances, I would have mocked him for that yuppie affectation, but his face was grim. He was not happy to see me.

"Hello, Aaron, got a minute?"

He glanced at the receptionist. "Sure, let's go downstairs and grab a cup of coffee." He smiled insincerely at her. "Hold my calls?"

"Of course, Mr. Gold," she said.

He walked me out of the office and into the elevator. When the door closed, he said, "What are you doing here, Henry?"

I hadn't seen Gold since the day he had rescued me from the squalor of grief, self-pity and empty booze bottles. I had called him a couple of times but when he hadn't called back, I let it drop. The truth was, the more convinced I became that Judge Paris was behind Hugh's death, the more reluctant I was to have anything to do with Gold. Robert Paris was his firm's client. That drew an adversarial line between Gold and me.

"Good to see you too, Aaron," I replied. "It's been a couple of weeks."

The elevator door slid open. We stepped into a crowded foyer.

"I've been busy," he said curtly.

I followed him out of the building, down the street and around the corner to a coffeehouse I had never noticed before. Inside, it was all hanging Boston ferns and unpainted planks of wood. A chalkboard menu advertised dishes that all seemed to have tofu as their main ingredient. The smell of patchouli oil was heavy in the air.

"Welcome to 1971," I said.

"It's the last place anyone in the firm would be caught dead in," he said. "Grab the table in the corner. I'll get the coffee."

When he returned, we sat there for a moment not saying anything. I broke the silence. "I was assaulted in the city and then my apartment was broken into. You know anything about that?"

I had expected outrage and a denial but he said, "Why don't you start from the beginning?"

I told him about going to Hugh's cottage after his death, removing his files on Judge Paris, about being drugged with sodium pentothal and the theft of Hugh's files from my apartment. I didn't mention what was in them and, strangely, he didn't ask.

"You're the criminal lawyer," he said. "Is it theft when someone takes something that didn't belong to you in the first place?"

"Hugh gave me the key to his place," I said.

"He was dead," he said. "Those papers belonged to his estate. You didn't have any right to them."

"Spare me the legal nitpicking. You know something, don't you? That's why you've been avoiding me."

"I warned you to stay away from that guy," he said.

"Yes, you did, and you gave me the letters. Did you read them?"

"Of course I read them."

"Then you knew that Hugh believed his grandfather was a murderer."

"I knew that the guy was a crazy drug addict working on some kind of extortion scheme," he replied hotly. "We'd tipped off the cops. It was just a matter of time before he was arrested. Maybe I didn't want my best friend associated with that shit storm."

"There wasn't a demand for money in the letters," I said.

"It was implied," he said. "Anyway, he would have got around to it eventually. He's been begging money from the judge for years to support his habit. The judge cut him off. He wanted revenge."

"Or what he said about the judge was all true and the judge wanted to silence him."

Gold glared at me. "What are you talking about?"

"You didn't ask me what was in the documents that I took from Hugh's place. It was evidence that his grandfather was a murderer. Or maybe you already knew that."

"That's insane," he said.

"If it was so crazy, why did someone go to the trouble to steal the papers from me? Who would do that, Aaron, except your client?"

"There's nothing incrim—" he stopped himself in exasperated midsentence.

"What were you going to say?" I demanded. "There's nothing incriminating in those papers?"

He said nothing but I read the guilt in his expression.

"You've seen them, haven't you?" I continued. "Fuck, Aaron. Are you part of this? Do you know who killed Hugh?"

He gave me a cold, hard look. "What are you accusing me of?"

"I'm not accusing you of anything. I'm trying to understand what's going on here."

"You have no fucking idea the shit you've stepped into," he said. "I'm going to warn you again, Henry. For your own good, leave it alone."

"That sounds like a threat."

He stood up. "It's better that we don't see each other again."

"Aaron—" I called to his retreating back. He didn't turn around.

I sat there drawing conclusions I didn't want to believe. If the documents stolen from my house had ended up at Aaron's law firm, where he had read them, then someone at his firm had ordered them stolen. I remembered the two men who had entered Hugh's place as I was leaving. If they'd been sent by the firm to retrieve any incriminating evidence Hugh might have had on his grandfather, and hadn't found any, how would they have known to go after me? Who at Aaron's firm had known Hugh and I were lovers except my best friend? Was he behind my abduction and the burglary of my apartment? Those were crimes. Real crimes, not breaches in legal ethics. Conspiracy to commit kidnapping and burglary. And if he had been a member of the conspiracy that committed those crimes, what other crimes might he have conspired to commit? Hugh's murder? I stared at the fan slowly turning overhead. I didn't know what to do.

"Terry? It's Henry Rios, give me a call. We have to talk."
I put the phone down, picked up my glass and took a sip of Jack Daniel's. The undertow of Hugh's death had pulled me in deeper than I had ever imagined and my feet had yet to touch ground. I had no hard proof of anything, not that Hugh had been murdered or that any of his allegations against his grandfather were true; only unanswered questions and suspicious behavior. I felt like a fly trapped in a spider web, waiting for the spider to appear. It was not a pleasant feeling. As evening sifted through the windows, darkening my apartment, a chill worked its way up my spine. Paranoia? Fear? Whatever it was, I didn't feel like being alone. Under different circumstances, I would have called Gold. But circumstances had changed. Grant had said something like that. Circumstances can change. Grant. What was he doing tonight? I called him.

"Henry," he said, not masking his pleasure. "Good to hear from you. What are you up to?"

"Having a drink," I said.

"Drinking alone? Isn't that a sign of something?"

"I wouldn't be drinking alone if you were here," I said.

There was a pause. "You inviting me over?"

"If you don't have other plans."

"On my way," he said.

An hour later, he was the door carrying a pizza box from a North Beach restaurant and a six-pack of Dortmunder. He looked a little windblown, as if he had air dried his hair in the car on the drive from the city. He smiled at me, an easy, happy smile, kissed my forehead and went into the kitchen where he opened the box, releasing the fragrance of tomatoes, herbs and cheese.

"I brought dinner," he said. "Plates?"

I got plates, paper napkins, knives and forks. "Vegetarian pizza?"

"La Pantera is famous for its margherita," he said. "Thin crust, sliced tomatoes, oregano, garlic, mozzarella and basil."

"Oh," I said. "An Italian *quesadilla*. It smells great."

"We should dig in before it gets any colder."

We ate in the kitchen at the small Formica-topped breakfast table I had inherited from the last tenant. Our knees knocked beneath the table. He stretched his long legs between mine. His face was a bit flushed, his dark eyes were bright and he smelled faintly of Lifebuoy.

"You take a shower for me?" I asked.

"I was just getting home from playing tennis with my dad when you called," he said. "You play?"

"No. I run, and now and then I head over to the old gym on campus and push weights around so my arms don't atrophy."

"That all you do?" he asked, raising his eyebrows. "You must be genetically gifted."

"Looked at yourself in the mirror lately?"

He laughed. "All I see is my dad's receding hairline." He took a bite of pizza and said, "You sounded a little raw on the phone. Is everything all right with you?"

"Sometimes I spend too much time in my head. Today was one of those days."

"This about what happened to Hugh?"

"How did you guess?"

"He's our connection. What's going on?"

"I feel like I'm deep in a labyrinth," I said. "Lots of dead ends and dark corners and no obvious way out."

"You're still convinced he was murdered?"

"More than ever," I said. "I have no way to prove it. Not yet anyway. I'm not sure I ever will."

"Why pursue it if you don't think you can bring his killer to justice?" he asked, not unkindly. "I mean, it can't make any difference to Hugh."

"If you believed someone you cared for was murdered, would you walk away from it before you exhausted every lead?"

"Maybe, if all the leads were dark corners and dead ends," he said.

I shrugged. "I don't know what to do next, but I can't let go."

"How I can help you get out of your head?" he asked, his eyes meeting mine.

"I didn't call you for a hook up," I replied, weakly.

He gave me a small smile. "Yes you did. That's fine with me. I was happy to hear from you, Henry, even if it was just because you needed a warm body to keep you company for a few hours."

I looked at him. "Not any warm body, Grant. Yours."

There was no hesitation, no shyness in the way we approached each other. He threw his arm around my shoulders and pulled me in for a kiss. We made our way to the couch where, within minutes, I was lying on top of him, my tongue in his mouth, my hand stroking his hard-on through his pants. He lifted my T-shirt at the waist and ran his hand up and down my back.

I got up, pulled him to his feet, and said, "Bedroom."

I was naked on the bed. Grant was hopping 'round removing a shoe. He undid the button on his jeans, pulled the zipper down, hooked his finger on the waistband and wiggled out of them. His thighs were as big and muscled as his shoulders. He stood before me in black briefs, the tip of his hard cock poking out of his waistband.

"I need a little help with my briefs," he said.

I pushed myself to the edge of bed and removed his briefs. His cock sprang in my face. I got down on my knees and closed my mouth around it. He kneaded my shoulders and groaned. The scent of soap clung to his thick patch of dark pubic hair. His cock felt meaty but clean in my mouth. Not antiseptic but wholesome. After a couple of minutes, he gently but firmly separated us.

"You're going to make me come," he said.

"That's kind of the point," I replied.

He shook his head. "Not yet," he said. "Not this way."

"Then how?"

"Fuck me," he said.

I scooted back onto the bed. "Come on, then."

Our bodies and hair were damp with sweat and the sheet beneath us was clammy. His breath was warm against my neck, his arms around my chest, his cock, spent now, pressed against my thigh, one of his legs between my legs, the other splayed behind him. His embrace was less erotic than protective, like a big, friendly dog.

"Are you falling asleep?" I asked.

"Nope," he said sleepily. "You?"

"I'm on the wet spot," I replied.

"The whole bed's a wet spot," he observed. He rolled on his back, edged away from me. "Come over here, the sheet's drier."

After we had rearranged ourselves, he asked, "You feel weird about this, because of Hugh?"

"A little," I said. "You?"

"I'm not sorry this happened but I wish—"

"You wish what?"

"I wish he wasn't here with us, that's all."

"I'm sorry, Grant. He's a mystery I have to solve."

"You two are so different, maybe the real mystery you want to solve is why you fell for him?"

"He told me once that I was a man with a boy inside of me waiting for the kiss that would end my loneliness. Until he said that, I didn't realize it was true, much less that he was the one I had been waiting for."

"Then it was lucky you found each other," he said quietly.

"Did we? I think his loneliness was different and deeper." I hesitated, searching for the words to articulate what had been only a half-formed and painful thought. "When the cops came and told me he was dead, I was shocked but I wasn't surprised. I think I always knew I wouldn't have been enough for him. I would have failed him and eventually he would have ended up somewhere else with a different needle in his arm."

"You don't know that," Grant said. "And if he had, Henry, it wouldn't have been your fault."

"Maybe, but I still feel guilty and it still confounds me, Grant."

"What does?"

"To have been in love for the first time in my life and to have known at the same time that love wasn't enough."

"It can be," he said after a moment and pulled me into his big body so that we were chest to chest. We held each other and our eyes met but our thoughts were not the same.

I was in the shower the next morning when Grant came into the bathroom, pulled back the shower curtain and said, "There's a police officer here to see you."

Terry Ormes was in the living room chatting with Grant when I emerged from the bedroom pulling a shirt over my head. She looked at me and grinned.

"Sorry to bother you so early," she said. "I didn't know you'd have company."

"I guess you've met."

Grant said. "My turn to hit the shower. Nice meeting you, Terry."

"Same here," she said. After he left she said, "Nice guy. Definitely a keeper."

"I'll make sure to record your vote," I replied.

"I got your message," she said. "I was coming over anyway to give you what I collected about the accident. What did you want to tell me?"

"The papers that were stolen from my apartment ended up with a lawyer at the firm that represents Judge Paris. His name is Aaron Gold. I thought you might want to question him about how he got them."

She sat down on the nearest chair. "How did you find out?"

"Gold told me," I said. "Accidentally."

"You know him?"

"We went to law school together," I said. "He was my best friend."

"I think you owe me an explanation," she said.

I told her about Gold, and the letters from Hugh to his grandfather he had given me and about our last conversation.

"Why didn't you tell me about the letters earlier?" she said with quiet anger.

"They didn't seem relevant," I said lamely.

"That's bullshit and you know it," she said.

"I'm sorry," I said. "The truth is I couldn't bring myself to read them until recently and I didn't want to tell you about them until I knew what was in them."

"What if the letters proved Hugh had falsely accused his grandfather or that he was blackmailing him? You don't think I would have wanted to know that before I put my neck on the line to investigate a closed case?"

"There was nothing like that in the letters," I said emphatically. "If anything, they support what he said about his grandfather sexually abusing him."

"What about the murders?"

"He accuses him of it, but there are no details."

"I can't believe you concealed them from me," she said.

"It wasn't deliberate." I went to my desk and extracted the folder. "Here, take them."

She took the folder. "Are you keeping anything else from me?"

"No, I swear."

She pulled an accordion file from her bag and shoved it at me. "This is what I have on the accident. CHP reports, a couple of newspaper articles, inquest report."

"I appreciate this and I'm sorry."

Her expression softened a bit. "How did it go with Katherine Paris?"

"She threw me out of her office," I said.

She stood up. "That's too bad," she said. "That doesn't leave us with any leverage with the coroner."

"Will you question Gold about how he got the papers from here?"

"You have any proof he sent the guys who took them?"

"Isn't that what you'd be questioning him about?"

She gave me a sour look. "So far, everything I've done on this case has been on your say so, but I have to tell you, that's getting pretty thin. I can't walk into some lawyer's office and start asking him questions without something more solid than your word that he told you he saw the papers."

"You think I'm lying about that?"

"No," she said, "but without some solid evidence that someone somewhere committed an actual crime, this is starting to look less like an investigation than an obsession."

"You had your own suspicions about Hugh's death," I reminded her.

"Yes, and I still do, but they still don't amount to much more than suspicions. Look, Henry, I'm getting some heat for the time I'm spending on this case. If something doesn't shake loose soon—"

"I know," I said. "Let me dig just a little longer."

The tense silence between us was broken by Grant singing in the shower.

"He's a catch," she said. "Maybe you should think about dropping all this and moving on."

NINE

The documents in the accordion file Ormes gave me were copies of the papers I had taken from Hugh's house except for one, the report of the coroner's inquest. Stamped across the top of the first page were the words, "Confidential. Not to be opened except by order of the court." I remembered my conversation with Hugh about sealed records and wondered if this was the record he had been trying to obtain.

Grant came up from behind me, kissed the top of my head and asked, "What are you reading?"

"The coroner's report on Christina and Jeremy Paris's car crash," I said.

He hopped over the couch and plopped down beside me. "Anything interesting?"

"It's odd there was an inquest at all. They're only convened when there's some question about the cause of death. That wasn't the case here. It's also strange the inquest was conducted in Santa Clara County."

"The Parises live here," he said.

"But the accident was in Nevada County," I said. "If there was going to be an inquest, that's where it should have been held."

"Can I see?" he asked. I gave him a few pages of the report. After a moment, he muttered, "What an awful way to die. At least they died together."

I looked up from the paragraph I was reading describing in grim detail Christina Paris's injuries. "What did you say?"

Grant read, " 'It is the conclusion of the medical examiner that the deaths occurred simultaneously.' "

I took the paper from him and read the sentence myself. "That's not right." I dug through the CHP reports until I found the paragraph I was looking for. "According to the cops, Christina was dead when they arrived and Jeremy died a few minutes later, just as the paramedics arrived."

Grant got up and rooted around my desk.

"What are you looking for?" I asked him.

He returned with Professor Howard's textbook. He sat beside me and flipped through the table of contents, running his finger down the meticulously organized divisions and subdivisions and sub-subdivisions of the ancient law of trusts and estates.

"Found it!" he said.

"Found what?"

He quickly turned the pages to page 293 and tapped the yellow highlighted text. "Here it is, the doctrine of simultaneous death."

He scooted next to me, resting half the book on my lap and half on his so we could read it together. It didn't take long. The doctrine of simultaneous death rated less than a page and a half in Professor Howard's seven-hundred page tome. The discussion consisted of a statement of the doctrine with case citations followed by a number of hypothetical situations in which it might apply, standard law school text explication.

"So," Grant said, "the basic principle is that dead people can't inherit from living ones."

"Makes sense. Where would they spend it?" I replied.

"What's interesting," he said, "is what happens if two people die at the same time and one of them has left everything to the other one." He read, " 'In such a circumstance, the law presumes that the beneficiary predeceased the testator and the gift is void and would, therefore, revert to the testator's estate to be distributed in accordance with the rest of the testamentary scheme.' "

I skimmed the page. "The presumption is rebuttable by competent evidence. Why did the coroner rule Christina and Jeremy's deaths were simultaneous when the cops said otherwise?"

"Did the cops testify at the inquest?"

I looked at the inquest and compared it to the accident reports. The witness list at the inquest did not include the officer who had written the report and who had found the bodies. Instead, his partner and the paramedics testified.

"Not the cop who found the bodies," I said. "His partner. That's not that unusual if the first cop was unavailable for some reason."

"What did his partner testify to about times of death?" Grant asked.

"I don't know. There's no transcript of the proceedings, just a summary of the testimony and the coroner's findings."

"Henry," Grant said, grabbing my wrist. "Listen to this hypo. 'A woman of means leaves her entire estate to one of her two sons who is then killed in the same automobile accident that takes her life. The deaths are determined to have occurred simultaneously. Applying the rule of simultaneous death, who would inherit her estate?' "

"If she left everything to him," I said, "and they died simultaneously, the gift to him would be void and his portion would be distributed to her other heirs. But, if there were no other heirs named in the will—"

"Then her estate would go to her intestate heirs," Grant said.

Comprehension dawned. "Her husband and her surviving son."

"What?"

"This hypo is about Christina and Jeremy Paris," I said. "Hugh had a copy of her will. Christina left everything to Jeremy, except for a few small bequests. If they died simultaneously, the gift to him was void and since she didn't name any alternate beneficiaries, her estate would have gone to her survivors, Judge Paris and her son Nick, but Nick was already institutionalized. I wonder who his conservator is."

"Judge Paris?" Grant suggested.

"I'm willing to bet." I picked up Professor Howard's tome. "How did he know?"

"Who?"

"Professor Howard," I said. "This hypo. It can't be a coincidence." I shut the book. "I have to find him."

"You know him?"

"I took trust and estates from him."

"So he's here, at the university. Could he have known Christina?"

"That's one of the questions I plan to ask him."

"What can I do?" Grant asked.

I touched his hand. "I told you this a labyrinth. Are you sure you want in?"

"I already am," he said. "Besides, this is a lot more exciting than discovery compliance and depositions."

"I need to look at Christina's will again. Even if the simultaneous death ruling invalidated the bulk of it, there were some specific bequests. If the will was probated, you should be able to track down a copy."

"Sure," he said. "I can do that."

"Also, find out who Nick Paris's conservator is," I said.

"Check," he said. "Anything else?"

"Find out what you can about the coroner who conducted the inquest," I said. "The judge may have been forum shopping by having the inquest here and not in Nevada County."

"You think he was looking for a coroner who would give him the time of death finding he needed to invalidate Christina's will?"

"Exactly," I said. "Wouldn't it make sense that he would have more pull with the Santa Clara coroner than one up north?"

"This really is twisted," Grant observed. "But is it proof that the judge killed his wife and son?"

"If all of this pans out," I said, "it at least takes us out of conjecture and into circumstantial evidence. We may not have found the smoking gun, but we can be pretty sure that one exists."

A couple of hours later I found myself on a dead-end street in an obscure wooded pocket of the campus where retired professors lived in university-subsidized houses. While it was generally acknowledged at the law school that John Howard was still alive, he had not been seen on campus for years. Eventually, an antiquarian in the alumni office had found an address for me and, armed with his textbook, I went off in search of him.

Behind a white picket fence, across a weedy, dying lawn and in the shade of an immense oak tree stood a plain, one-story stucco house with the inevitable red-tile roof. In the summer heat, the house seemed remarkably still, like a ship in dry dock. I pushed open the gate and went up the flagstones to a red door with a brass knocker in the shape of a gavel. I lifted it and let it fall. The small noise echoed in the unmoving air.

A middle-aged Filipina in slacks and a hospital scrub top opened the door, eyed me suspiciously and greeted me with a curt, "Yes, can I help you?"

"I've come to see Professor Howard," I said.

"Is he expecting you?"

I shook my head. "No one at the law school had a phone number for him so I wasn't able to call ahead."

"Who are you?"

"My name is Henry Rios, I'm a lawyer and former student of Professor Howard," I said. I showed her the textbook. "I have a legal question for him."

"Professor Howard is very sick," she said.

"I won't take up too much of his time."

"Wait here," she said and left me at the doorway while she disappeared down the shadowy hall. On the walls of the hallway were framed photographs of professional gatherings—a banquet of the local bar association showing Professor Howard at the podium, a commencement ceremony—dusty plaques and elaborately calligraphed certificates. No family photos. I tried to remember if he'd been married but drew a blank. When I was a student, my law school professors had existed for me only from the head up. Their private lives were not a subject to which I gave any thought.

The nurse returned. "He will see you but," she warned, "only for a few minutes. I don't want you to tire him out."

"Thank you," I said. As she started down the hall, I touched her elbow to detain her. "Can you tell me what's wrong with him?"

"Everything," she said. "Come with me."

The house smelled musty and faintly sweet, a mixture of cigar smoke and lemon-scented furniture polish. I followed the nurse though an arched entryway into the living room. The furniture was too big for the room, as if purchased for a different house of grander proportions. A vacuum cleaner had been parked between two sofas upholstered in red plush. A pot of yellow chrysanthemums blazed on a coffee-table near a tidy stack of legal periodicals. On a side table in a corner of the room a cigar burned slowly into an ashtray. Enthroned in an arm chair, the same deep red as the two sofas, was a small, white-haired, wasted man wrapped in a sweater and a blanket. Professor John Henry Howard, latest edition.

"You wanted to see me?" he asked in a voice thickened with the sediment of old age.

"Yes, Professor. My name is Henry Rios. I took trusts and estates from you."

"What class year?"

"Seventy-one."

"I'd already been teaching for thirty-five years by then," he said. "I don't remember you. What was your final grade?"

"An A," I said.

He lifted his shaggy eyebrows and for a second I thought he was going to demand to see my transcript. "Well, you must have learned something." He raised a frail hand to a round table covered with bottles and glasses. "Have a drink."

"I'm fine, sir. Thank you."

He frowned. "I insist, Mr.—"

"Rios, sir. Henry."

"Henry, have a drink, if not for yourself, then for me. I'm not allowed to touch the stuff anymore. You'd think my doctors would relax that proscription since I'm dying, but evidently they intend for me to meet my Maker sober. There's a very fine, very old single malt Scotch. Balvenie. Try it."

I poked around the bottles until I found the Belvenie. I poured some into a glass and returned to him.

"Pull up a chair," he said.

I grabbed a heavy chair in gold brocade and rested it in front of him, then sat down, tipped the glass in his direction and sipped. Scotch was not my usual drink, but this hit my tongue like fiery silk and left a faint aftertaste of caramelized apples reminding me, briefly, of *tarte tatin*.

"How is it?" he asked.

"Like it was distilled in heaven."

He sputtered a laugh. "That confirms what I've suspected all along. God is a Scotch drinker. Angie said you had a legal question. You an estate lawyer?"

"No, sir," I said. "Criminal defense."

His eyebrows went up. "Are you sure you're in the right place?"

"I'm sure," I said. "My question is about a hypo in your case book discussing the principle of simultaneous death."

He went very still. "Go on, Henry."

"A wealthy woman and her oldest son are killed in an auto accident. She'd devised her entire estate to that son. The court uses the rule of simultaneous death to invalidate the will and her estate passes, through intestacy, to her husband and her surviving son, who is institutionalized. What was your source for this hypo?"

"That's not exactly the hypothetical I posed," he said. "You've added facts I omitted so you already know my source, don't you?"

"This scenario describes the deaths of Christina and Jeremy Paris."

He fixed me with a narrow, inquiring gaze. "Who sent you?"

"No one sent me, sir. Christina's grandson, Hugh, was my friend. He believed his grandfather, Judge Paris, arranged for the car accident that killed her and Jeremy. Before Hugh could expose the judge, he was killed. I believe the judge was behind that, too."

I paused, waiting for a response, but Professor Howard had arranged his features into an unrevealing mask.

"I'm right, aren't I?" I pressed him. "You knew about Christina and Jeremy Paris."

The movement of his head was more of a tremor than a shake.

"I guessed," he said, finally. "She was on her way to Reno to obtain a divorce that would have cut off his intestate rights to her estate. She'd already cut him out of her will."

"How do you know that?"

"I drafted the will," he said.

"You knew her?"

"Oh, yes," he said. "She and Bob Paris and I go back a long way."

"What else do you know, Professor Howard?"

"About the will or the marriage? They were intertwined. The marriage was hell for her but she put up with it for her sons and because she was Catholic and, not least of all, because she was Grover Linden's granddaughter and Lindens don't acknowledge failure. Oh, but she hated Bob. He used her money and position to enrich and advance himself but treated her like chattel. When she finally had had enough, she came to me. She asked me to write her a will that would cut him from any claim he had to her fortune."

"How did you do it?"

"We gave him her half of the community property. It was not an insignificant amount. That was the carrot. Everything else went to their sons. Jeremy was given his share outright and Nicholas's share was put in a trust to be administered by Jeremy and his uncle, John Smith. That was the stick."

"How was it supposed to keep him from challenging the will if she died first?"

"Bob could hardly complain he wasn't provided for since he got everything they'd accumulated together in the marriage. If he tried to set aside the will to get at her separate property, he would be challenging the rights of his own sons. For good measure, we threw in an in terrorem clause providing that if he contested the will, he would forfeit the gift of her community property. The only other way he could have inherited was through intestacy if, for any reason, the will was declared void. To prevent that, she was going to divorce him. As an ex-husband, he would been entitled to nothing if her will failed. Her estate would have gone to her boys."

"Did the judge know about the will?"

"She made the mistake of taunting him with it. When she told me, I advised her to get the divorce sooner rather than later."

"Were you worried he would retaliate?"

The old man wheezed, "Well, he did, didn't he? Let me tell you about Bob Paris. He was and is someone who takes pleasure in humiliating and degrading others. I believe sadist is the term of art for his type." He sank into his chair. "He beat her, you know."

"Christina?"

He nodded. "Beat her. Terrorized his sons. His wife and children were nothing more to him than his personal property. You can imagine his rage when she told him she was going to divorce him and cut him off."

"Why did you put the hypo in your case book?"

"Do you remember footnote four in United States v. Carolene Products?"

"Of course," I said. "It's the foundation of modern equal protection law."

"That hypo was my footnote four, the only way I had to attack the injustice of the situation. I buried it in my book and hoped that, someday, someone would find it. You have. What are you going to do with it, Henry?"

"Hugh was gathering evidence to implicate his grandfather in the murders but something was missing. Thanks to you, I've found it. I'm going to the police. There is no statute of limitations on murder."

"Well, I'm not a trial lawyer," he said, "but even I can see your case is circumstantial and it happened such a long time ago."

"Your testimony would be very persuasive, Professor," I said.

He arranged his face into a smile. "If you plan to put me on the witness stand, you'd better hurry it along, son. I'm dying."

"Won't you hang on for her? For Christina? "

He made a gruff noise of assent.

"How did you know her, Professor?"

"Many years ago," he said, "I went to a reception given by her father, Jeremiah Smith, to commemorate his twentieth year as president of the university. He was a widower by then, so Christina acted as his hostess. I was a freshly minted lawyer who had just been hired at the law school. Bob Paris was also at the reception. He was my colleague at the law school with about three months more experience than I. We dared each other to ask Miss Smith for a dance. I did, finally. I got the dance, but Bob married her. He could be charming when the need arose and he was a handsome boy. He was also ambitious enough for ten men. Courted her father as much as he did her. In the end the old man probably wanted the marriage more than she did, but in those days, girls did what their fathers told them to do. So she married Bob, but we stayed friends. We were always friends." He pointed at the Scotch. "Give me that glass."

I held it out to him. He took it with trembling fingers and drank it down in a long, slow swallow.

When I got back to my apartment, there was a long message from Grant. He had obtained a copy of Christina's will and had also discovered that, after her death, Judge Paris had become sole conservator of his surviving son, Nicholas.

"And listen to this, Henry," he said. "The coroner who conducted the inquest was later elected to the Superior Court. Guess who was his biggest single contributor? Robert Paris. Talk to you later."

I went through the accident reports again and began a list of possible witnesses to testify that Christina and Jeremy had been murdered: Warren Hansen, the man who claimed to have seen a second car drive the Paris's car off the road. The CHP officer who found the Parises and wrote in his report that Christina had died first. Professor Howard. Would it be enough to persuade a DA somewhere to pursue murder charges in their deaths? Maybe not. The case was cold, the witnesses, if they were still alive, could hardly be expected to remember the accident. Even if the evidence wasn't enough to convict the judge for the murders of his wife and son, it could be introduced in a trial charging him with Hugh's death to show motive. One way or the other, we would get the story out.

I was interrupted by a knock. I shoved the papers into my desk, went to the door and opened it.

"Mrs. Paris," I said, unable to conceal my surprise.

She managed a faint smile. "Mr. Rios. May I come in?"

"Please," I said, and stepped aside.

She took a couple of steps into the room and paused. Standing there in her elegant clothes, dark blue silk shirt over white linen slacks, red leather bag, I could only imagine what she made of the bachelor squalor I lived in, empty pizza box on the coffee table, stench of beer in the air, lumpy sofa covered with a cheap India print, orange crate book and record shelves, framed UFW *Huelga* poster next to a Picasso print of the man with the blue guitar.

"I promise you the furniture's safe to sit on," I said.

She looked amused. "No, it's not that. It reminds of my freshman dorm room. Well, except there aren't ashtrays overflowing with cigarettes and a bong."

"It *is* my freshman dorm room," I said. "Transported to every place I've lived in since."

"Are you quite sure you're gay?" she asked.

"I'm sure," I said. "Have a seat. May I get you something to drink?"

"No, thank you, but may I smoke?"

"Of course," I said. "I've got an ashtray in the kitchen somewhere."

I searched through the cupboards for an ashtray, couldn't find one, and returned with the saucer to a cup that had disappeared a long time ago. She was perched at the edge of the armchair with *Leaves of Grass* opened on her lap, a cigarette burning between her fingers. I set the saucer down.

"The book was open to the *Calamus* poems," she said.

"I was going to read them to Hugh."

She gazed at me steadily, then at the book, and began to read in a richly expressive voice:

> *Or, if you will, thrusting me beneath your clothing,*
> *Where I may feel the throbs of your heart, or rest upon your hip,*
> *Carry me when you go forth over land or sea;*
> *For thus, merely touching you, is enough—is best,*
> *And thus, touching you,*
> *would I silently sleep and be carried eternally.*

"Were you going to read him that one?"

"Yes," I said. "He inspired poetry. But you know that. You wrote a poem for him, *The Lost Child*."

"I wrote many poems for him," she said. "Maybe all of them." She closed the book and put it on the coffee table. She tipped her cigarette into the saucer and reached into her bag.

"I know you're surprised to see me here after yesterday," she said, pulling out a thick envelope. "This is from Hugh. It was forwarded from Boston. I got it just after you left. He writes about you quite a bit." She took the letter out of the envelope, unfolded it, scanned it and read, "*I know I can't stay clean for anyone but myself, but he makes me want to be a better person, if that's possible, if I'm not so broken that I can't love, that love can't heal me. When you meet him, you'll see why I love him.*"

I looked away from her, unable to speak.

"You and his father are the only people Hugh ever told me he loved. After I read his letter, I felt terrible about how I treated you. So here I am, Mr. Rios. What do you want to tell me about my son's death?"

I found my voice. "Before I do," I said, "can you tell me about Hugh and his father and you? There's so much I don't know."

She picked up her cigarette and drew on it, exhaled a jet of smoke. "The thing you need to know about our family is that Nick, Hugh's father, is schizophrenic."

"Hugh told me that."

She crushed the cigarette into the saucer. "Nick and I were kindred spirits, Mr. Rios. We both came from wealthy, proper families. His was wealthier, mine was more proper. Money and propriety—they were straitjackets we couldn't wait to escape. We met in college."

"At the university?"

"Oh, God no," she said. "Nick wanted to get as far away from his family as he could. Harvard for him, Radcliffe for me. I went to a mixer and there he was, handsome and wild. He took me into the garden and we shared his silver flask and talked about art and love and poetry. After that, we carried on like we were the second coming of Scott and Zelda Fitzgerald. Eventually dropped out of school, eloped and moved back here, to North Beach, just as the beatniks were leaving and the hippies were arriving. It was a fantastic time to be young." Her eyes clouded. "Then he got sick. When the illness first struck Nick, it was like watching a gorgeous bird suddenly drop from the sky and crawl around on the ground. You know something must be broken but the wings are intact, the plumage is still dazzling, the song is the same. For a while, anyway. And for a while, the bird manages to fly again, maybe shorter distances and not so high, but it's still flight."

"And then, he falls to the earth and can't fly at all?"

"It was some time before I understood how sick he was. You have to understand, our friends were artists and they were all passionate and eccentric. Crazy was a compliment in our circle. So, when Nick started behaving oddly, I just thought it was temperament. But then he began to experience delusions he couldn't shake and after that, the hallucinations started. I finally got him to a psychiatrist who diagnosed him. I thought it was the worst day of my life. I was wrong."

As she spoke about her husband, her glacial, patrician façade cracked and another woman emerged, a young woman, sensitive, unguarded and terrified. The poet.

"Nick refused traditional treatment," she said. "He believe he could cure himself by expanding his consciousness because he thought his illness was simply a figment of his ego. We went to ashrams in India where he fasted and meditated for days on end, to *curanderos* in Mexico who drove the evil spirits out of him with drums and rattles, to a psychiatric commune in England where patients smeared their shit on the walls and the psychiatrists administered LSD. The delusions, the hallucinations only got worse."

"Hugh told me his father thought the family was under a curse."

"Ah, yes," she said, lighting another cigarette. "The Chinese curse. That's what eventually led to his institutionalization."

"Why the Chinese curse?"

"Nick was always deeply conflicted about his family's wealth. He felt undeserving of it but he couldn't bring himself to renounce it either. He said he felt like an animal in a trap whose only escape was to gnaw off its limb. What made it worse for him was how sensitive he was to the suffering of the poor people we encountered in places like India. He would draw out huge amounts of money at the bank and walk around the slums of Delhi and Mexico City giving it all away."

"That sounds dangerous," I said.

"Of course it was," she said. "He was robbed more than once and after the Getty boy was kidnapped in Rome, I was terrified that Nick would be abducted too. I think he courted that danger. He wanted to be punished for being rich. Thus the curse."

"The Chinese curse."

She nodded. "As he got sicker, Nick became obsessed with his great-grandfather and read everything he could about him. Somewhere in his research he learned that hundreds of the Chinese workers Grover Linden imported to build his railroad were killed in accidents. The story stuck with him. He began to believe the angry spirits of these workers led by what he called a warlock were pursuing Linden's descendants seeking vengeance. Nick became terrified of anyone Chinese. He believed the warlock was going to send people to abduct Hugh and sacrifice him to atone for Grover Linden's crimes against their ancestors."

"The peach tattoo on Hugh's chest was to protect him."

"Yes. It's an ancient Chinese symbol to ward off evil spirts," she replied. "Nick had Hugh tattooed without telling me. I was furious. It was one thing for me to deal with Nick's delusions but I didn't want him scaring Hugh with them."

"Hugh seemed to adore his father."

"It was mutual," she said. "After Hugh was born, Nick got better for a while as if the love he felt for Hugh left no room for the disease. Hugh was too young to understand Nick was ill. All he experienced was Nick's devotion. And then Nick tried to kill him."

"What? Hugh never said anything about that."

"I doubt if he remembered it," she said. "Nick's delusions about the Chinese warlock got tangled up with the story of Abraham and Isaac. You know it?"

I nodded. "God commanded Abraham to sacrifice his only son as a test of his piety and then, at the last moment, stopped him and sent a ram in Isaac's place. What did that have to do with the curse? I thought you said Nick was trying to save Hugh from being sacrificed."

"Schizophrenic delusions grow and change in the schizophrenic's mind," she said. "Nick got it into his head that if he showed he was willing to sacrifice Hugh himself, the warlock would intervene at the last moment, save Hugh, and lift the curse. I came home late one night and found Hugh asleep on a kind of altar that Nick had made out of leaves and flowers and surrounded by candles and incense burners. Nick was kneeling at the altar, holding a knife above his head, chanting in some made up language. I screamed at him and he dropped the knife. I grabbed Hugh and ran to the neighbors and called the police. They took Nick to a psychiatric ward. Hugh never knew what happened. Nick had apparently drugged him."

"How old was Hugh?"

"Six," she said. "When he woke up, he didn't remember anything."

"What happened to Nick?"

"The doctors put him on Haldol. It stopped the delusions but left him feeling like a ghost. So he would stop taking it and the delusions would return. One afternoon, he walked into a restaurant in Chinatown where he thought he had tracked down the warlock. He was carrying a semi-automatic pistol. Fortunately, a couple of police officers happened to be having lunch there and they overpowered him before he hurt anyone."

"Was he prosecuted?"

She raised an eyebrow. "The great-grandson of Grover Linden prosecuted? No. Calls were made, checks were written and Nick was committed to the asylum in Napa where he was been for the last fifteen years." She looked frail and sad. "Where he will die."

"I'm sorry," I said. "I can't imagine what it must have been like to lose your husband that way."

She stubbed out the cigarette. "The marriage was over long before that happened. I dealt with Nick's illness by drinking. By the time Nick was committed, I was a hopeless drunk. I became as much a danger to Hugh as Nick. Bob Paris threatened to have me declared unfit unless I let them have Hugh until I straightened myself out. I agreed. Bob gave me some papers to sign that he said were necessary for him to make decisions about Hugh's care without having to track me down and get my consent. I signed them without reading them. Only later, after I got sober, did I realize I had signed away my parental rights. I tried hiring a lawyer to regain custody but no one would touch the case, not against Bob and not with what he had against me."

"What was that?"

"Adultery, alcoholism, drug use," she drew impatiently on her cigarette. "More than one suicide attempt. Even after I got sober, no judge would have given me custody of Hugh. I begged him to at least allow me visitation rights. He refused." She looked at me. "After that, the fight went out of me, Mr. Rios. So, yes, you could say at that point I abandoned Hugh to his grandfather."

"Did you explain all this to Hugh?"

She made a derisive noise. "Mr. Rios, when a child asks 'Why did you leave me?' it's not a question, it's a shriek. No answer is ever enough. Over the years, he would show up at my place in Boston when he needed money or a break from killing himself with heroin. We'd have a good day or two and then he'd start up with the accusations and we'd get dragged back into a circle of guilt and rage that never resolved anything." She stared at the letter. "He blamed me for his addiction. I told him that belonged to him."

"Do you believe that?" I asked.

"I'm a drunk," she said. "A sober drunk, but still a drunk, and there's one thing I am very clear about. You don't get to blame your using or drinking on someone else. No one else puts the needle or the glass in your hand. That's a choice each addict makes. No one else can put them down for you. That's your choice too."

"Addiction is a loss of control," I said.

"No," she said, firmly. "It's not like Nick's schizophrenia. Using, drinking, they're compulsions, that's true, but as long as you're alive there is always the option of stopping. I'm not saying it's easy or that most people can stop on their own. I was fortunate enough to stumble into AA at a moment when I would have done anything to stop drinking. I prayed that moment would someday arrive for Hugh." She touched the edge of the letter. "It seems like it did. He says he was clean. Is that true?"

"He had one relapse," I said. "When he went to visit his father. Other than that, he was clean for the nine months before he died."

"He went to see Nick?"

I nodded. "It was too much for him."

"God," she said. "He shouldn't have gone by himself. Nick is—" She put out her cigarette and lit another. "Nick is as good as dead. Mr. Rios. What do you think happened to my son the night he died if it wasn't an overdose?"

"I'd seen him earlier. We'd spent the day together. He had dinner with a man he'd known in prep school, Grant Hancock. Then he drove down here. On his way, he was rear ended by someone who I believe was following him. When they pulled over to exchange information, the other driver or someone else in the car with him grabbed Nick, restrained him and drove him to the campus where they injected him with a lethal overdose and left him to die."

"Oh, God," she said, and I could see her picturing the scene in her mind's eye. "Who did this?"

"Mrs. Paris, I think it was your ex-father-in-law."

"Bob? Why? Is this about the sexual abuse?"

"You knew about that?"

"It was one of the things Hugh blamed me for."

"You believed him?"

She hesitated. "I don't know," she said, "but I do know if he planned to accuse Bob publicly, Bob would have fought back, not killed him. He would have enjoyed the chance to humiliate Hugh as a homosexual drug addict and extortionist."

"Hugh thought he had something else on his grandfather," I said.

"What was that?"

I told her about the accident and the wills and the simultaneous death finding that had secured the Linden fortune for Judge Paris.

"That's incredible," she said. "Can you prove any of it?"

"I'm think I'm getting close."

"And you say Hugh knew about this?"

"Yes,"

"And he told Bob?"

"In a letter," I replied.

She sat quietly for a moment, smoking. "I don't know if any of this is true," she said. "But I hate Robert Paris and I'm grateful to you. What do you need from me?"

"Have you buried Hugh yet?"

"His body is in a mortuary in San Francisco," she said. "I'm flying him home next weekend to bury him with my family. I can't stand the idea of him being anywhere near the Lindens. Why?"

"The country coroner ruled his death accidental overdose but both I and the police detective I'm working with saw indications on his body that were inconsistent with that ruling. I'd like an independent forensic pathologist to examine his body for signs that he was murdered. A second, independent autopsy."

A look of horror briefly crossed her face, but then she nodded, slowly. "Yes, all right. What do I need to do?"

"There's a pathologist in the city I've used before in some of my cases. Will you authorize the mortuary to release Hugh's body to Doctor O'Hara?"

She nodded again. "I'll call them this afternoon." She stood up. "I don't know if I should thank you."

"I understand," I said.

"Goodbye, Mr. Rios." She paused at the door. "You know, Nick was right. We are cursed."

TEN

Some of the Chinese laborers who built Grover Linden's railroad were lowered in wicker baskets over mountainsides to set dynamite charges, and died in the explosions when the baskets could not be reeled up fast enough. Others were entombed in tunnels that collapsed on them or in avalanches. The number of the dead is not known but when their bodies were exhumed and returned to China for burial after the railroad was completed, one newspaper estimated that twenty thousand pounds of bones made the journey.

These details of the construction of the transcontinental railroad were not in my fourth grade California history text. I'd had to dig through some pretty obscure sources at the university library to find them. Among the stories were photographs of the Chinese railroad workers. I studied the faces beneath the broad-brimmed straw hats and derbies, surprised at how young most of them had been. On further thought, it made sense that Linden would have recruited the youngest and strongest men for his railroad. He had been mocked when he had first recruited Chinese workers who were considered physically weak and effeminate because of their small stature. "Linden's monkeys," the newspapers called them. But they proved to be tireless and disciplined and brave. That didn't prevent Linden from paying them half the wage of white workers and cutting off their food when they struck for equal pay.

Behind every great fortune lies a great crime. Balzac's phrase came to me as I sat in the university library's Special Collections room, shuffling through the photographs with gloved hands. The room was so quiet I could hear the scratching of a grad student's pencil on paper behind me. The lights were filtered to prevent the old documents preserved in the collection from fading and the room was antiseptically clean and odorless. A morgue where history came to be dissected, autopsied. A place of forgotten achievements and forgotten suffering. But for Nick Paris, the sins of the father had not been forgotten or forgiven and the suffering would not end without a sacrifice; blood for blood.

"The special collection room closes in fifteen minutes," the librarian said in a hushed voice. "Please return your materials."

I slipped the photographs into their folder, as haunted by the eyes of the young men as Nick Paris must have been when he conceived his anguished idea to sacrifice his son. Blood for blood. Perhaps the sacrifice had been completed when the cops found Hugh with a needle jammed into his arm.

The framed diploma from John Marshall Law School had been issued to Wendell Ronald Patterson but the nameplate on the desk identified the occupant of the office as Sonny Patterson, Deputy District Attorney. He glanced up from the autopsy report he was reading, noticed me looking at his diploma and said, "What?"

"Wendell," I said.

He took a drag from his cigarette, scattering ashes on his pale green shirt and bright orange tie. "I been Sonny since I was two years old." He returned to his reading.

Hick was written all over his puffy potato face, but Ormes, sitting beside me, assured me that it was an act, like his loud mismatched clothes. He had told her he got jurors to like him by letting them think they were smarter than he was. "Don't be fooled," she said. "He's sharp."

She had persuaded me to come to him with everything we had collected on Hugh's death. I'd agreed on the condition that she not mention that Hugh was a Linden descendant or anything about Judge Paris. I didn't want Patterson's view of the evidence colored by the Linden family association. Patterson reached the end of Jack O'Hara's independent autopsy report, squashed his cigarette in a frog-shaped ashtray and leaned back in his swivel chair, pulling apart the shirt buttons over his belly to reveal a white T-shirt.

"Why are you bringing me this shit, Terry?" he asked.

"Wanted your opinion," she said. "Was it an accidental overdose?"

"If it wasn't," he replied, "someone went to a lot a trouble to make it look that way."

"Exactly," I said. "Someone did."

He threw me a dismissive look. "Still not sure why you're here."

"I represent the interests of the victim's mother," I said, which wasn't precisely untrue. "She wants to know what happened to her son."

"So she hires a criminal defense lawyer," he said, clearly disbelieving me.

"Come on, Sonny," Terry said. "What do you think?"

"I think this ship has sailed, but if you'd brought this to me when the kid died, I'd have made Torres work it a hell of a lot harder than he did before writing it off as accidental."

"You don't think it was accidental," I pressed.

"I didn't say that," he replied. "Even if you'd brought it fresh, we'd be miles away from a prosecution. What I have here is suggestive, that's all. First thing we'd have to establish is that it was a homicide. Of course, we might be having a different conversation if you'd been straight with me. Did you think I wouldn't recognize the victim's name? He's a Linden."

"How did you know that?" I asked.

"The university is the only reason this town exists," he said. "Biggest landowner, biggest employer, biggest taxpayer and the source of most crime. I make it my business to know everything I can about Linden University and the Linden family. What else are you holding back?"

"I think Hugh was killed on his grandfather's orders because he was threatening to expose Judge Paris's involvement in the deaths of his wife and son Jeremy."

Patterson looked at Ormes. "Is he serious?"

"Hear him out," she said.

He went through three cigarettes while we told him the rest of the story. His cramped office reeked of smoke. He crushed the third cigarette into the ashtray, then dumped the butts in a paper-stuffed trash can. I half-expected it to burst into flames.

"That's the damndest story I ever heard," he said.

"That doesn't mean it isn't true," I replied.

He grinned. "We're lawyers, Henry. We don't deal in what's true, we deal in what's provable. Applying that standard, you got nothing."

"Circumstantial evidence of motive," I said.

"Straw in the wind. Even if this witness, Hansen, testified the other car ran the Paris car off the road, you've got nothing to connect the driver to the judge."

"*Cui bono*," I said.

Patterson smirked. "We spoke English at my law school."

"Drop the yokel act. You know damn well what it means," I said. "Who profits? Who gained the most by the deaths of Christina and Jeremy Paris? Robert Paris."

"Entirely coincidental unless you have something that directly ties him to the accident. Do you?"

I shifted in my seat. "Hugh's murder, the theft of the papers at my apartment. The judge obviously believed Hugh had gathered evidence to prove he was involved in the accident, so he had Hugh killed and ordered the burglary. That connects him to the accident."

"Lawyers don't say obviously unless they're desperate," Patterson remarked, lighting yet another Marlboro. "You're bootstrapping, Henry, plus where's the evidence that connects the judge to Hugh's murder or the burglary, and don't throw some fancy Latinism at me."

"Who else has any motive?" I snapped. "You know, Sonny, there is a point when a chain of coincidences becomes too fucking unbelievable to be coincidental."

"Cussing doesn't make your case any more obvious," he said, clearly enjoying my discomfort. "But because I like conspiracy theories as much as the next guy, I gotta tell you, you missed something."

"What's that, Sonny?" Ormes replied.

"Why was he dumped at the university?"

"Okay," I said. "I'll bite. Why?"

"The university runs by its own rules," he said "and it has its own interests. We poor fools out here want to solve crimes and punish the guilty. The university wants to protect its image. What do you think the university would do if one of the Lindens was murdered on campus?"

"Cover up," I said. "But how would anyone know Hugh was a Linden? He didn't have any ID on him."

"Who was first on the scene, Terry?" Patterson asked.

"The campus police," she replied.

"Do you know how long it took them to call you after they got to the scene?"

She shook her head. "I assume they called in right away."

He dug through the papers on his desk and pulled out an incident report on university police stationery that had a lot of black lines across the text.

"Fifty-five minutes," he said. "That's how much time passed before they notified the department. Plenty of time to do a lot of things, including removing the kid's wallet."

She skimmed the report. "I haven't seen this before," she said. "Why is it all blacked out?"

Patterson stubbed his cigarette out. "Redacted to protect the privacy of the victim. That's what the university lawyer told me. Which is bullshit, of course. I'm willing to bet my pension that the first cops on the scene saw the same things you did, Terry, the signs of a struggle, the drag marks, the clumsy way he was injected, and they came to the same conclusion, that something didn't add up. For all we know, there might have been even more evidence pointing to homicide."

"Are you saying the university cops tampered with evidence?" I asked.

"I'm saying that once someone figured out who this kid was, death by accidental overdose had to look a lot more manageable PR-wise than a Linden heir murdered on the university campus. But you're missing the point, Henry."

"Which is what?"

"Whoever dumped him on campus knew that his identity would be discovered and that the university would cover up any evidence of homicide."

I nodded. "So whoever abducted and killed Hugh and dumped his body on campus knew who he was."

"That's right," Patterson said.

"That points back to Judge Paris," Terry said.

"Or is that another straw in the wind too?" I asked.

"Well, it's not obvious," Patterson replied with heavy sarcasm, "but as far as I'm concerned, it's one coincidence too many."

"Why did you ask the university for this report?" I asked.

"I told you," he said, "I make it my job to keep tabs on what goes on at the university. When Terry told me what she wanted to talk about, I did my own little investigation. I noticed right away how long it took the university cops to call the department but it didn't mean anything until I heard your story."

"Do you believe me now?"

"I believe the university knows more than what it's saying about the kid's death."

I indicated the blacked-out police report. "The university doesn't seem eager to share the information."

"That's why I'm going after them," he chortled.

"With what?"

"I'll tell the university's lawyers if they give us what they have on Hugh's death, I'll drop my investigation into the deaths of Christina and Jeremy Paris."

"That case is even more circumstantial than Hugh's murder," I said. "Why wouldn't they just tell you to fuck yourself?"

"Because, like I said, the university is all about image and in the court of popular opinion the standard of proof is a lot lower than guilt beyond a reasonable doubt. I'll have them shaking in their shoes if I spin them your story about how the accidental deaths of the granddaughter and grandson of the university's founder maybe weren't so accidental. That's just not the kind of publicity the university wants. They'll cave."

"But if there's evidence Hugh was killed, it leads back to the judge," I said. "You can't separate the two cases."

Terry spoke up. "Henry, you told me what you wanted out of this was to prove Hugh didn't die a junkie's death. You wanted to give him back his dignity. Won't it be enough if we can change the cause of death from accidental overdose to homicide even if we can't prove who did it?"

"That's all we may be able to accomplish," Patterson said. "Because even if the judge killed all those people, we're never going to get him on it. Rich people have their own law. You know that, Rios."

"Yeah, I do," I said. "Okay, fine. Sometimes all you have to fight injustice is to bury the truth in a footnote and hope that someone, someday will discover it."

"What are you talking about?" Patterson asked.

"Nothing," I said. "What do you need from me, Sonny?"

"Everything you've got on Christina and Jeremy Paris. I'll go through it and then we'll have another meeting and make the strongest case we can before I call the university lawyers for a meeting. Rattle their cages, see what I can shake loose."

"You really have it in for the school, don't you?" I said.

He lit another cigarette. "Last year I had to dismiss a brutal gang rape case that happened in one of the dorms because the girl recanted after the university's lawyers got to her. A few months later, she killed herself. Like I said, the university operates by its own rules. I don't think it should."

I returned Grant's call when I got home and it led to a dinner invitation in the city that I accepted. Driving up, I was forced to admit to myself that this was a date and it felt awkward, as if I were cheating on Hugh. The awkwardness disappeared when Grant opened the door to his apartment with a big smile and the phone pressed to his ear. He covered the mouthpiece and said, "Make us drinks. I'm almost done."

As I fiddled with ice, glass and bottle in the kitchen I heard the words "gay cancer." When he hung up, I brought the drinks into the living room, handed him his, and asked, "What was that all about?"

"Apparently there's a new STD going around New York that people are calling the gay cancer. One more plot to drive us back into the closets."

"How would that work?"

He frowned. "Gay sex equals disease. I mean, if we're not shoving gerbils up our asses, we're giving each other cancer. As if most of us don't already have enough shame and guilt to work through." He gulped his Scotch. "Sorry, stuff like that gets me on my soapbox. How was your day?"

As I told him about my meeting with Terry Ormes and Sonny Patterson, the awkwardness returned. Not that Grant was anything other than sympathetic and interested, but on the subject of Hugh he listened from a distance of time and feeling while for me Hugh was still present and my feelings for him still raw. Yet, I was also undeniably attracted to Grant and I knew he liked me. A lot.

"It sounds complicated," he said when I finished.

"Translate that into Latin and you've got the Linden family motto," I said. We were sitting on the couch. He began to massage my neck with his big, strong fingers. "Do you know about the Chinese railroad workers?"

"I don't think so," he said.

"Grover Linden and his pals brought twelve thousand of them to build the transnational railroad. Recruited them from villages all over China, shipped them across the ocean to a place that must have seemed as distant and strange to them as the moon. They died by the hundreds. Their friends buried them in temporary graves and after the railroad was built, they dug up the bones and sent them back to China, to be buried with their ancestors. Ten tons of bones, Grant. That's what Grover Linden built his railroad on."

He stopped squeezing my neck. "Would it have been better if it hadn't been built, Henry?"

"He could have done it with a little less suffering," I said.

"You would think that," he said. "That's one reason I admire you."

"Not following," I said.

"I've never suffered, Henry. Dealing with being gay is the closest I've come and that was a cakewalk compared to a lot of stories I've heard. But you know suffering first hand, don't you?"

"Suffering is not a virtue, Grant. It tends to maim people, like Hugh."

"Or deepen their compassion," he said. "Like you."

"Don't make me out to be a saint or anything like that," I said. "I'm as screwed up as the next guy. I'd just like a world where people don't treat each other as the means to an end."

He rested his hand on my neck and asked. "What did you want to do about dinner?"

"This," I said, and kissed him.

Later in his bed, after sex. He'd switched off the lamp, casting us into darkness like a raft adrift on a slow-moving stream. We were turned toward each other. Grant's breath grazed my chin. The coarse hairs on his legs abraded my thigh when he dragged his leg between mine. I gripped his bicep, hard and round and warm and kissed him, softly, because we had gone at each other hard.

"I have this little game," he said, his voice husky from sex.

"Uh-oh," I said. "Where is this going?"

"No, listen. The first time I meet someone, the way I know whether I'm going to like them is that I try to imagine them as a child."

"Explain."

He pulled me closer, our chests touching. "Don't you remember when you were a little boy and you saw another kid for the first time. You didn't know who he was or where he lived or what his dad did for work. You start playing with him and if you liked the way he played, he became your friend. Simple as that. It's the same principle. Before I know anything else about you, I have to know, do I want to play with you?"

"Did you want to play with me?"

He ran his tongue lightly along my cheek and up to my earlobe and whispered, "From the moment I saw you."

"I like playing with you too," I said.

He pulled away a bit at that but grinned to hide his disappointment.

Ormes and I provided Sonny Patterson with everything we had gathered on the deaths of Christina and Jeremy Paris. I called Katherine Paris and explained where we had left the matter with Patterson, thanking her again for consenting to the second autopsy. She told me she had returned to Boston with Hugh's body and buried him. I carried that image with me on my runs through campus, now alive with students returning for the new school year. They made me feel old and I had to wonder what I was still doing in Linden ten years after graduating from law school. Admittedly, Linden was the first home I had chosen for myself after throwing off the fetters of my family and it had provided me with stability and peace. But maybe it was time to leave the nest. And go where? And do what?

I spent time with Grant and it was easy time. Unlike Hugh, Grant seemed free of shadows. But then, I had enough shadows for both of us. He coaxed them out of me, gently but persistently. I found myself telling him things I'd never told anyone. I even told him about the death penalty case that had driven me from the law.

My client, Eloy Garza, was charged with the grotesque rape, mutilation and murder of a middle-aged nurse in her suburban home in a quiet neighborhood. He was a Chicano handyman, she was an ER nurse. He had a long record of prior offenses, including a prior rape conviction that the judge allowed into evidence to demonstrate a pattern of conduct. Over my objection, the court allowed the prosecutor to dismiss the only two Chicano prospective jurors with peremptory challenges. Again and again, at gratuitous length, the prosecutor emphasized the brutality of the murder, the vulnerability of the victim and Eloy's prior rape conviction. My objections were consistently overruled by a judge who had himself been a prosecutor. Helplessly, I watched the prosecutor instill into the jurors a primal fear and anger.

"This could have happened in your neighborhood," he argued. "Miss McDonnell could have been your neighbor. Your friend. Your sister, or aunt or mother."

"Objection, Your Honor."

"Overruled. Continue, counsel."

When I stood up to give my closing argument, I knew by the crossed arms and hostile stares that I had already lost them.

One morning I picked up the local paper and read on the front page that Eloy Garza had been given the death penalty. I called Mike Burton, my ex-boss, to tell him I would sign a declaration saying my representation had been incompetent if that would help on appeal.

"Well, sure, Henry, we're going to have to argue ineffective assistance. You called the jury a lynch mob. I think we can assume that prejudiced them against the defense in the penalty phase. But listen, I read the reporter's transcript of the guilt phase. Between the judge and the prosecutor there was no fucking way our guy had any chance at acquittal. They double-teamed you from day one. Don't worry about the appeal, we have plenty of ammunition."

"I should have—"

"Should have what, Henry? You did a good job but you were pissing against the wind. I wish you hadn't lost it there at the end, though. I also wish you hadn't quit. If you want to come back, we can talk about that."

"Thanks, Mike."

"Listen to me, Henry," he said. "Racism is part of the social climate and so is fear of crime, especially violent crimes committed by strangers, stuff people believe they can't protect themselves against. Add to that a biased judge and a gung-ho DA, and you walked into the perfect storm on this case."

"Eloy was innocent, I should have got him off."

Mike said, "The case isn't over yet. We have years of appeals ahead of us, and if we lose, then, yeah, maybe the state will end up executing an innocent man. That's on the state. The thing you have to ask yourself is this. If you're in the business of saving people, are you going to let the next one die because you weren't able to save the last one?"

Even with Valenzuela pitching, the Dodgers were losing to the Giants at Chavez Ravine. I watched Valenzuela leave the game with mixed emotions. I wanted the Giants to win and keep their post-season hopes alive but, like every other Chicano baseball fan, I'd been caught up in Fernandomania. In a perfect world, he'd be playing for the Giants. The Dodgers fans were giving him a round of applause—he'd kept the game close—and there were cries of "Toro, Toro." I thought he was built less like a bull than a *luchador*, big-bellied and massively strong. My father loved the *luchadores* and for a while, before he decided to disown me, he would take me to the Mexican movie theater in our farm town to watch *luchador* movies where *Mil Máscaras* and *Tinieblas* and *El Santo* would battle mummies and space aliens. We shared popcorn and I drank orange soda while he sipped the beer he had told me to hide in my coat. My dad. The hardest part of having a father who had come to hate you was the memory that he had once loved you. I picked up the beer bottle on the coffee table. Budweiser. His brand. I emptied the bottle in a swallow and turned my attention back to the game. The Dodgers had called up a new, young leftie from the bullpen. His name was stitched on the back of his jersey, DeLeon. I watched him give up back to back home runs.

The phone rang. I grabbed it.

"Henry," a voice slurred. "'s Aaron."

"Aaron. You drunk?"

"Never mind that. Need to see you. You got it all wrong."

"What are you talking about?"

"Not over the phone. Come over. Need to tell you."

The urgency in his voice cut through the alcohol and alarmed me. "You calling from home?"

"Mmm, home," he said. "Need to talk to you." The phone seemed to fall from his hand and then the line went dead.

Aaron lived in a small house set back from the street by a big yard shaded by two massive oak trees. His black BMW was crookedly parked in the driveway. Lights were on behind the drawn curtains and I could hear the last inning of the Dodgers-Giants game on his television. I stood at the front door, about to knock, when I heard an explosion inside the house. I pulled at the door but it was locked. Then I pounded on it and called his name. The back door slammed shut as someone ran past me. I glanced over my shoulder and saw a dark figure scaling the fence that separated Gold's yard from his neighbor. I ran toward him and grabbed his left foot, trying to pull him down. He gave me a startled, angry look, then lifted a gloved hand and began flailing it at me. Something heavy, hard and metal smashed into my skull. I let go of his leg and collapsed on the ground. I heard an object drop with a thud beside me as he scrambled over the fence. I sat up and saw the gun he had hit me with. Black, .22 caliber. Still dazed, I picked it up, pulled myself to my feet and went around the back of Gold's house. I let myself in through the unlocked kitchen door.

"Aaron!"

Nothing.

I followed the sound of the television to the living room where Aaron was slumped back in his armchair with a bullet hole just above his right eye. On the table beside him was an empty Jameson bottle and a half-filled glass. Outside a siren, the sound of a car jerking to a stop and then someone at the front yelling, "Police. Open up."

Numbly I went to the door and pulled it open. Three cops crowded the porch. One of them shouted, "He's got a gun," and in an instant, three revolvers were aimed at my head.

"Drop it," the first cop said.

I dropped the gun. "My friend's been shot," I said.

I no sooner got the words out than I was slammed against the doorpost, handcuffed and dragged to one of the two patrol cars parked in front of Aaron's house. A moment later, the paramedics arrived.

By then, I'd been pushed into the back seat of the patrol car and was having my rights read to me. The whole thing was surreal.

"Do you understand these rights as I have read them to you?" The cop's harsh tone cut through my confusion.

"Yes," I said.

"Do you want to speak to a lawyer?"

"I want to talk to Sonny Patterson in the DA's office."

The cop gave me a surprised look. "You know Patterson."

"Yes, I'll talk, but only to him."

ELEVEN

I stood in the sally port until the steel door rolled back with a clang and then stepped into the jail. My hands were cuffed and my head throbbed. The deputy in the control room stared as I passed through to booking. It was my old friend Novack.

"What the hell?" he said, storming out of the room.

The officers who had brought me in stopped. One of them—Jackson? No, Johnson—said, "What?"

"Do you who this is? He's a lawyer. A PD." He looked at me. "What's going on here, Henry?"

"He's under arrest for a one eighty seven," Johnson said, using the penal code section number for murder. "Caught him with the gun in his hand and the vic sitting in a La-Z-Boy with a hole in his head."

Before he could respond, Novack was distracted by the phone ringing in the control room. He went to answer it, closing the glass door behind him. Johnson and his partner jostled me toward booking. Novack held up his hand, gesturing them to stop. We watched him listen, nod, and briefly speak. He came out again.

"That was the sheriff," he said. "The DA is on his way. In the meantime, he goes into a holding cell."

"After we book him," Johnson said.

"You'll book him when I say you book him," Novack said. "You two start your paperwork. I'll take him from here."

Johnson shrugged. "He's all yours."

"Cuffs," Novack reminded them. Johnson uncuffed me. Novack took me by the elbow and guided me through the familiar rooms to the holding cells. They were empty. "Looks like you got your choice, Henry. What's it going be? The presidential suite or the honeymoon special?"

"Hey, anywhere I lay my hat is home."

He opened the cell door. "I don't know what shit you got yourself into, but it's deep if I have the sheriff calling me and Sonny Patterson on his way."

"It's not what it looks like," I said.

He locked the door and laughed. "You know how many times I've heard that before? Do I need to take your belt and shoelaces?"

"Give me a break," I said. "Thanks for the hospitality."

He smirked. "I pride myself on it."

There were two bunks in the cell. I sat down on one of them and looked around. Cells looked different when you were on the wrong side of the bars. Smaller, much smaller. The strong antiseptic the trusties poured down the metal toilet did not completely conceal the smell of piss. The concrete floor shone dully in the dim light and I imagined I could make out a faint groove where thousands of inmates before me had paced the room waiting for a lawyer or a meal or to make bail. Hugh might have been in one of these cells. That night seemed so long ago, but it had only been four months since the deputies had brought him into the interview room and my life had changed. My head hurt. I touched the spot where I'd been hit with the gun. It was tender and a little damp. I examined my finger. Blood. I considered calling Novack, but if I told him I was injured, they'd have to take me to a hospital and I'd miss Patterson. Better to tough it out. Blood. Aaron's blood. Aaron was dead. I lay down on the bunk and closed my eyes for a minute.

A voice called me out of a dark dream. When I opened my eyes, Sonny Patterson was standing on the other side of the bars. "Henry, you all right?"

"I fell asleep," I said.

"You look bad, pal."

"I've had better days." I went over to him. "I didn't kill Aaron."

"I know," he said. "The neighbor who called 911 saw the whole thing. Why did you pick up the gun?"

"I don't know," I said. "He hit me pretty hard in the head and I wasn't thinking straight. Maybe I was afraid he would come back for the gun. I honestly couldn't tell you what I was thinking." I touched my scalp. The bleeding had stopped.

"They should have taken you to the hospital. There could be a concussion."

"I didn't tell them what happened. I said I would only talk to you."

"Did you get a good look at the guy who hit you?"

I shook my head. "About my height, athletic build, white. Wearing gloves and a stocking cap. I only saw his face for a few seconds."

"The department's treating it like a home invasion robbery," he said. "Interrupted by you. Why were you there?"

"Aaron worked at the law firm that represented Judge Paris," I said. "He called me, drunk, told me he had to see me. Said I'd got it all wrong."

"Got what all wrong?"

"I don't know," I replied. "Someone shot him before I could ask."

"You think this had something to do with the Paris murders?"

"Aaron warned me off the case. Said it was dangerous."

"He was feeding you privileged client information?" he asked incredulously.

"He was trying to protect me," I said. "Now he's dead. It's not a coincidence. The judge was behind this."

"Yeah, about Judge Paris," Patterson said. "He's dead."

I grabbed the bars. "What?"

"Massive stroke this morning. Died two hours ago. About the same time someone was shooting your friend." His forehead furrowed. "Maybe you should sit down. You look like you're about to pass out."

I was. My head was spinning and my legs were crumpling. I staggered back to the bunk and collapsed.

"He's really dead?"

"I'm afraid so, Henry. And your friend, Aaron? That was a robbery. It was just his bad luck that he was home. You relax for a minute while I get you out of here."

I nodded dumbly.

"I don't believe it," I told Terry Ormes. "I don't believe Aaron was killed in a robbery. It has to be related to the Paris murders."

We were back at her booth in the Denny's across from the station. The same waitress, the same pile of pancakes on Terry's plate, the same omelet on mine.

"The judge was dying in a hospital room in the city when your friend was killed," she reminded me.

"Who said he gave the order that day?" I replied. "He could have done it before the stroke. I'm pretty sure he didn't plan on dying that evening."

"Okay," she said, "But why? Why kill your friend?"

"Maybe Aaron found the memo in the judge's client file where he admits to killing his wife and son," I said irritably. "I don't know why, Aaron didn't get a chance to tell me. But he must have something pretty incriminating."

"Except you said he told you that you got it all wrong. What do you think he meant by that?"

"I don't know," I admitted. "But don't tell me it was a coincidence that a lawyer with access to Judge Paris's client file calls me to say he has important information about the judge and is shot dead before he can tell me what it is. He just happened to be robbed that night? I bet you didn't find anything missing from his house."

"All that proves is that you interrupted the robbery before the robber could get away with anything," she said.

"You don't really believe that," I said.

"No," she allowed. "I don't think it was a coincidence either, but it's moot because the judge is dead."

"The judge is dead, but not the man who killed Aaron," I reminded her. "Or the men who killed Hugh. They're still out there."

"The investigation into your friend's murder is ongoing," she said. "But Sonny's dropping Hugh's case. He lost any leverage he might have had with the university when the judge died. Look, if you're right, and the man who killed Aaron Gold was acting on orders from the judge, and we catch him, he may implicate the judge in Hugh's death. He may even have been Hugh's killer."

"You'll never catch him," I said. "Not with what you've got. A vague description and a street gun."

"Like I said, it's an open investigation."

"Don't bullshit me. You know as well as I do that unless you get incredibly lucky the investigation into Aaron's murder will end up in the unsolved pile, gathering dust in a file cabinet somewhere."

"I promise you I will personally do everything I can to close the case."

I knew she would and I knew she wouldn't, but now was not the time to be a jerk about it.

"Thanks," I said. "I appreciate that."

I sprinted down University Drive toward the Old Quad at the end of a ten-mile run that had taken me around the perimeter of the university and into the foothills. The road in front of the quad was clogged with limousines and in their midst, a hearse. I ran up the steps, came to a slow stop, stripped off my shirt and used it to mop the sweat on my face and chest. Undergrads darted in and out of classrooms or lolled on benches in the warm September sun. The massive doors of the church had been thrown open on their great, iron hinges and the grave voices of a requiem choir floated through them into the still air. I picked up a pamphlet abandoned on the ground. On the cover was the photograph of a wizened old man. *In memoriam, the Honorable Robert Prescott Paris, A Life Well-Lived.* I glanced at the church. That's what was going inside: the judge's funeral. There were other photographs in the pamphlet. The judge in his robes, a family portrait where, for the first time, I laid eyes on Christina, Jeremy and Nicholas Paris. It was an old photograph. Two little blond boys, an elongated woman with a worried face and the judge smiling blandly for the camera. Nick Paris must have been ten or eleven but I could still see traces of Hugh's features in his face. Jeremy Paris was a little older. His father's hand rested on his shoulder. Maybe it was my imagination but Jeremy seemed to be flinching.

I skimmed the program. The eulogy was being delivered by a former Governor. The music I had heard was *In paradisum* from Fauré's *Requiem*. In paradise? Really? Is that where the murdering son-of-a-bitch had gone? I crumpled the pamphlet. At that moment, there was a burst of organ music. A moment later expensively-dressed men and women tumbled out of the church and into the quad where, immediately, cigarettes were lit and the chatter assumed cocktail party levels of raucousness. There was a brief pause in the noise as eight elderly men carried a bronze-colored casket out of the church and shuffled across the quad toward the waiting hearse. My first and last glimpse of Judge Robert Paris. His mourners were middle-aged and elderly, the ladies fanning themselves with their programs, the men cackling at each other's remarks. No one seemed particularly broken up by the occasion.

I couldn't help but contrast the scene to the funeral in Los Angeles I had attended three days earlier to bury Aaron Gold. A half-dozen people, all family, except me. His parents frozen in postures of grief as his coffin was lowered into the ground.

"A father shouldn't have to bury his son," Mr. Gold keened.

I thought, too, of that other son whom a parent had to bury. What had gone through Katherine Paris's mind when Hugh went into the grave?

Young men dying—it was unnatural. This old man being carried out of the church in a metallic casket through the throng of important people was, I was certain, responsible for both those earlier deaths. Where was the justice in that?

The funeral party had begun to notice me, standing shirtless and sweaty in their midst. Hostility from a few of the old men, more than casual interest from a couple of others. I turned to go but someone clasped my arm and a deep, familiar voice said, "Henry?"

Grant was impeccably turned out in a perfectly cut black suit that emphasized his broad shoulders, narrow waist and long legs. He was stunningly handsome, all the more so because he radiated the careless confidence that comes from belonging. These rich, oblivious people were his tribe. I choked off the wave of resentment before it reached my mouth and I said something stupid.

"Henry," he repeated. "Are you all right?"

"Yeah, I was finishing my run when I saw the commotion. I didn't know it was the old bastard's funeral. You come to pay your respects?" I said, more acidly than I had intended.

He flinched a bit at that. "My dad asked me to come. He reminded me that I clerked for the judge and said it was the proper thing to do."

I bit back a sarcastic response. "I've got to go."

He gently but firmly took my arm and steered me to an archway at the edge of the crowd. "I haven't talked to you since you got back from L.A. How was Aaron's funeral?"

"It was hard," I said, surprised and embarrassed to hear my voice breaking.

He enfolded me in his arms and pressed me against his big male body and said, "You should have let me go with you like I suggested."

"I'm going to ruin your suit," I mumbled.

"Don't worry about my suit," he said. I rested my head against his shoulder and breathed in the smell of his cologne. After a moment, he said quietly, "My dad just saw us. He's heading over." I began to pull away but he held me more tightly. "It's okay, Henry. May I introduce you?"

"It would be weird if you didn't," I replied.

He released me. I turned and saw an older, grayer and slightly thicker around the trunk version of Grant approach, in an equally well-cut suit. I hurriedly put on my sweaty shirt.

"Dad," Grant said, when his father reached us. "This is my friend, Henry Rios."

Mr. Hancock, seemingly oblivious of my running garb, grabbed my hand and smiled warmly at me. "Henry, how nice to meet you. Grant has told us so much about you."

That was a surprise. "It's a pleasure to meet you, too, sir." I said.

"I gather you weren't here for the funeral," he said.

"No, I was out running and I more or less stumbled across it."

"Grant tells me you're a lawyer too. Did you ever meet Judge Paris?"

"No, I knew his grandson, Hugh."

Mr. Hancock shook his head. "That was a tragedy. Hugh had a difficult life, but I always thought he was basically a good boy."

"A good man," I said.

"Of course," Mr. Hancock said. "You must forgive me. The last time I saw Hugh he was a child and," he continued, wrapping his arm around Grant's shoulders, "at my age everyone under thirty looks like a kid."

"I'll be thirty in two months, Dad."

"I'm thirty-three," I said.

"Oh God, now I really feel old. Henry, I know you want to be on your way but would you be kind enough to wait here just for a moment while I find my wife? She'd never forgive me if I didn't introduce you."

When he stepped away, I said, "You've talked to them about me?"

Grant flushed a bit. "Yes, I talk about you a lot. Does that bother you?"

"No. It just caught me off-guard."

He looked at me, a little anxious and a little exasperated. "I really like you, Henry, so yeah, I talk about you."

Before I could respond, Mr. Hancock returned with a small blonde woman. Her shellacked hair framed an expensively made-up, sharp-chinned face that I imagined her friends described as "pixieish." In a pink-and-black wool suit she looked like all the other rich matrons milling around the entrance of the church except that her eyes danced with life.

"Elizabeth," Mr. Hancock said. "This is Henry Rios, the young man Grant has been telling us about. Henry, my wife Elizabeth."

She appraised me with her lively eyes on me and said, "Oh my, Henry, you're even better looking than Grant said you were."

Beside me, Grant groaned.

She waved a small hand at him, gold bracelets jangling on her wrist. "Oh, Grant, don't be such a fuddy-duddy. He's adorable. Come to dinner so we can get to know each other. It will be so much more fun than standing around in this heat and pretending to be sad about Bob Paris when nobody could stand him."

Grant groaned a little louder. "Mom, people can hear you."

She looked around. "I don't hear anyone disagreeing." She took her husband's arm. "Come on, dear, I'm sure the boys would like to be alone. Henry, I'll expect you at dinner before the end of the month."

Mr. Hancock gave me another firm handshake, another warm smile. "That was an ultimatum," he said. "A word of advice from a guy who's been married to her for forty years? Give her what she wants. Seriously, Henry, we'd love to see you under happier circumstances."

"I'd like that, too."

"Good. You and Grant pick a day. Goodbye, Henry. Such a pleasure to meet you."

"Ta, boys," his mother said. "See you soon."

After they left, I said, "Your dad seems like a mensch."

He smiled. "Is that Spanish?" Before I could explain, he said, "I'm teasing you. I know what it means. And that's exactly what he is. A mensch."

"Your mom is—"

"The phrase you're looking for is 'a hoot'," he said. "Would you really come to dinner or were you just being polite?"

"I'd love to come to dinner," I said. "I like you too, Grant."

"Great," he said happily. "I have to go to the post-burial reception or whatever they call it. Can I come over afterwards?"

"Yeah, that would be nice." I smirked. "Should I shower?"

His eyes got wide. "Oh," he said. "Don't go to any trouble for me."

He kissed me quickly but not furtively and headed toward his parents who were making their way to their car.

I got up in the middle of the night to piss and when I slipped back into bed I was wide awake. Grant was on his side, his long back turned to me, breathing softly. His leg twitched and he rolled onto his back. Half-awake, his hand groped for my hand and when he found it, he folded our fingers together and sank back into sleep. In the drizzle of a streetlight outside the window, I watched him. His face, untouched by thought or feeling, revealed the abiding kindness that was his was essence, his soul.

It was only his kindness, and not fear of rejection, that prevented him from telling me he was in love with me. He was waiting for me to give a sign I was ready to consider his feelings for me, whether I could reciprocate them or not. I gently released his hand and got out of bed. I pulled on a pair of boxers and picked his suit up from the floor where he had shed it and hung it over the back of a chair.

"You look like a prince in that suit," I had told him when he arrived at my place.

"Me, no? You're the one who looks like he stepped out of an El Greco painting."

"What are you talking about?"

He grabbed a beer from the refrigerator and plopped down on the couch beside me. "There's a famous El Greco painting in a little church in Toledo called *The Burial of the Count of Orgaz*. Have you ever seen a picture of it?"

"No, never."

"The central figure is a Spanish count who is being laid to rest in the arms of two men in gold vestments who are supposed to be saints, I forget which ones. The count wears black and gold armor but his face is uncovered. I was eighteen when I saw that face. Long and dark and elegant. I was stunned. I actually had to stop myself from touching him and getting my mom and me thrown out of the church. Looking at him, something moved inside of me the way it does for all of us when we begin to realize we're different from other boys. When we realize we feel about other boys the way they feel about girls." He took a deep swallow of beer. "You look a little like him."

"The dead count?"

He nodded. "Sometimes when I look at you, I feel the way I did standing in that little church with butterflies in my belly." He laughed. "Tell me I haven't made a complete fool of myself with that story."

I touched his arm. "No. I'm incredibly flattered."

I could see in his eyes he had hoped for a different response. "Anyway," he said, "the point is, if there's a prince in this room, it's you, not me."

"I'm the son of a construction worker," I said, "from a long line of *campesinos*. Pretty sure there are no counts in the family tree." I straightened the collar of his shirt. "As good as you look in that suit, you'd look even better out of it," I told him as we headed into the bedroom.

Now, I slipped out of the bedroom. I poured myself a nightcap in the kitchen and wandered into the living room where I sat at my desk. There, beneath a pile of junk mail was the copy of *The Little Prince* I had taken from Hugh's house. I opened it to a random page and read: *It took me a long time to learn where he came from. The little prince, who asked me so many questions, never seemed to hear the ones I asked him. It was from words dropped by chance that, little by little, everything was revealed to me.*

Hugh. As opaque as Grant was transparent. As complicated as Grant was straightforward. When Hugh slept, his face was a question mark and that's what he had left me with, a question mark. *The little prince, who asked so many questions, never seemed to hear the ones I asked him.* And now he never would.

I heard Grant shuffle into the room and felt his hands on my shoulders.

"Bedtime story?" he asked about the book.

I closed it. "I woke up and couldn't get back to sleep."

He took the book from me. "I've never read this." He flipped through the pages. The photograph of Hugh and him slipped from its pages and fluttered to the desk. He picked it up. "Where did you get this?"

"Hugh gave it to me," I said. "This was his book."

He sighed. "Hard to compete with a beautiful guy who died a tragic death."

"It isn't a competition," I said.

"You were in love with him," Grant said.

"Yes," I said. "But I'm not going to spend the rest of life pining after him if that's what you think. I'm not sentimental. I just need time and—"

"Closure?"

"If you want to be clinical about it. I would say I need to know what happened to him and why."

"You know I would do anything to help you find out."

"Then get me in to see his great-uncle John."

This sigh was exasperated. "Why, Henry? What good will it do? Bob Paris is dead."

"The people who killed Hugh and Aaron are still alive and free. I need someone with clout to keep the cops from shoving their deaths into the cold case files."

"From what you've told me," he said, "the police have no real leads."

"All the more reason to keep them at it," I said.

"When will enough be enough, Henry?" he asked softly.

"Do this one thing for me, Grant. Get me into see Smith and whatever he says, that will be the end of it."

"I can't get to Smith directly but I know the guy who runs security for him. If you can convince him it's worth the old man's time, he can get you in."

"Thank you," I said.

"I'm going back to bed. Are you going to stay out here?"

I downed the bourbon. "No. This should knock me out."

I followed him back to bed and as soon as I closed my eyes, I felt myself drifting off to sleep but, as I did, I was dimly aware that now it was Grant who was awake.

Grant hadn't told me how he knew Peter Barron, but I could make an educated guess from looking at the man. Barron had short-cropped hair, a carefully-trimmed moustache and, beneath the conservative gray suit, an athletic body. He was blandly handsome. His dark eyes seemed friendly at first glance but beneath the friendliness was the hard glimmer of someone used to getting what or who he wanted. A Castro clone. One of the gay men for whom San Francisco was a gay Utopia playground as long as you looked like one of them. That Grant knew him was not surprising but it still disturbed me because I didn't think of Grant as belonging to that world. Considered objectively, though, Grant fit right in.

"So," Barron said in a smooth baritone. "Grant said you wanted to talk to me about Mr. Smith's grand-nephew, Hugh Paris."

"I had hoped to talk to Mr. Smith himself," I said.

The hardness surfaced in his eyes and his voice. "Mr. Smith is a busy man but if you have information I think he needs to know, I'll pass it on."

Unaccountably, now that he had dropped his friendly manner, he seemed familiar to me. Somewhere, I was sure, we had encountered each other and the meeting had not been pleasant. Still, he was my link to Smith so I needed him on my side.

"Of course. I appreciate that, Peter. The police and the DA have been looking into Hugh's death because there is some evidence it wasn't an accidental overdose."

"Why would they think that?"

"There was some physical evidence at the scene that indicated one, maybe two other people were present when he died. A private autopsy revealed some marks on his body inconsistent with accidental overdose."

He had leaned forward against his desk and was listening with rapt attention. "A private autopsy? Who authorized that?"

"His mother," I said. "Katherine Paris."

He frowned. "What marks?"

"There were bruises on his chest where someone might have held him down. Ligature marks around his wrists where he might have been bound. The injection site was clumsy, as if he'd been shot up quickly or by someone who didn't know what he was doing."

"You say the police know about this?"

"Yes, and the district attorney."

"Do they have any suspects?"

"No," I said. "In fact, they've closed the case."

He relaxed into his chair. "So, why are you here?"

"Because whoever killed Hugh is still out there," I said. "The cops and the DA should still be looking. Mr. Smith is an influential man. If he leaned on them, they'd reopen the case."

Barron looked at me for a moment and again, I felt the quiver of recognition.

"This is the first I've heard that anyone thinks Hugh's death was anything other than an accidental overdose," he said. "If Mr. Smith thought differently, he would have told me, so we can assume he doesn't."

"I'm telling you now," I said.

"But who are you? Not a cop, not a DA. Just some random guy. How did you even know Hugh Paris?"

"He was a friend," I said.

Barron smirked. "Right, a friend. Okay, well, thanks for the information. I will pass it on to Mr. Smith."

"That's it?"

"I'm afraid so, Mr.—what was your name again?"

"Rios," I said. "Henry Rios."

"Yeah, Mr. Rios. Thanks for coming in."

I stood up. "Have we met?"

That startled him. "Uh, I don't think so, bud."

"You're sure? You look and sound familiar."

He shrugged. "It's a small town, Henry. Maybe we've run into each other, but I don't remember you, sorry. You'll have to excuse me. I've got work to do."

"Sure," I said. "Thanks for your time, Peter."

I stalked from Barron's office through the Financial District to the restaurant where I was meeting Grant for lunch. I had been prepared for a polite hearing and a noncommittal response but with Barron the rejection had felt personal. He was lying when he said he didn't remember if we had met before. We had met and whatever the occasion had been, it had not ended well. That's why he had hustled me out of his office as soon as he could, worried maybe that I would remember. Because it felt from the moment I had stepped into his office that something had happened between us. The air was bad from the start. I tried to think where I had met him, but fury clouded my mind.

Grant was already in the restaurant when I arrived. It was one of those pre-1906 landmarks that locals called an institution but was really a fossil representing San Francisco at its most affected and self-congratulatory. Housed in the same narrow room since 1860, the walls and floor were oak and the tables covered with stiff white tablecloths. The waiters moved through the room in white jackets and black ties and pegged the quality of their service to the quality of their customer's suits and shoes. Grant occupied a booth at the end of the restaurant, a prime spot that reminded me, again, that he and Peter Barron had more in common with each other than I did with either of them.

I waved away the waiter who attempted to pull out my seat for me and sat down.

"How did it go with Peter?" Grant asked.

"He's a dick," I said. "How do you know him?"

He shifted back slightly in his chair as if to escape the force of my hostility.

"We dated," he said, quietly. "I don't know what happened between you, but I don't think you're being fair. Peter's a good guy."

"Only if you're a member of the same club," I said.

"Which club would that be?"

I indicated the room. "This one."

He frowned. The waiter returned to the table with oversized menus he laid before us and asked us for our drink order. Peter asked for iced tea. I ordered a double Jack Daniel's on the rocks.

"What's got into you, Henry?" Grant asked, after the waiter left.

"Barron. He could barely be bothered to hear me out before he dismissed me."

"I'm sorry it didn't go well," Grant said. "Would you like me to call him?"

"Will he be friendlier to you because you fucked him?"

"Okay," Grant said, evenly. "Now you're just being a jerk."

The waiter brought our drinks.

"I am tired of running up against the Peter Barrons in this town," I said. "Smug, white gay guys with their gym bodies, little moustaches and condescending attitudes."

"Is that really what you think of us?"

"I wasn't talking about you."

"Hey, Henry," he said. "I'm gay, I'm white. I work out at a gym. I even had a moustache for a while."

"Are you smug and condescending?"

"You tell me," he said. He sipped his tea. "I admire so much about you, Henry, but I don't understand these chips on shoulders."

"You don't? Look around this room, Grant. Here we are in the heart of the Financial District. Lawyers, bankers, financial advisors. The only people who look like me are clearing off plates and glasses. You're not aware of it because, why would you be? I am never not aware of it. And by the way, a chip on my shoulder? That's condescending."

"I'm aware that life is a lot easier for me than it is for most people," he said, quietly. "Have I thought about why? Believe it or not, I have, though clearly not as much or as deeply as you. Are you going to write me off because of that, Henry? What about Hugh? Did you have this talk with him? Because he was a member of my club, too."

"Hugh's father was insane, his mother was an alcoholic, his grandfather raped him and he ended up hooked on heroin. What's lucky about any of that?"

"You don't want a boyfriend," he said. "You want a cause."

The waiter returned and asked if we were ready to order.

"I was just leaving," I said. I pulled a twenty out of my wallet. "This should cover my drink."

I heard Grant say, "Henry, I'm sorry," but I left without looking back.

I woke up in the middle of the night, still half-drunk from all the booze I'd consumed to relieve my guilt from unloading on Grant, when it came to me with perfect clarity where I had met Peter Barron before. Met him twice. His voice was the voice of one of the men who had abducted me. And his face? I'd glimpsed it as he was scaling the fence in Aaron's yard, just before he coldcocked me with his gun.

TWELVE

"Are you sure?" Sonny Patterson asked for the third time.

I tried to keep the exasperation out of my voice. "Yes, I'm sure, Sonny. Peter Barron was the guy I saw at Aaron's that night. I'd swear to it in court."

Patterson rubbed his temples. "You told me you only saw the guy for a few seconds before he coldcocked you with his pistol."

"I'm telling you, it was Peter Barron."

"Not enough for an arrest," he said.

"An eyewitness identification is not enough?" I said, incredulously.

"Not if it's all I've got," he said. "Any half-decent defense lawyer could take your identification apart. Plus, this guy's a war hero."

Patterson, Ormes and I were in his office with its overflowing ashtray and cigarette stench. On his desk was a file Terry had compiled about Peter Barron. Patterson was referring to the bronze star Barron had earned on one of his three tours of duty in Vietnam. He was also an ex-cop, five years in the San Francisco Police Department where he quickly climbed the ladder before going into the private security business. Needless to say, he had no criminal record. He'd worked for John Smith for the past six years.

"What about the fact that he kidnapped me?"

Patterson said, "Come on, Henry, your voice I.D. is even weaker than your visual I.D. Anyway, unless we can draw some connection, the mugging is irrelevant to Gold's murder. Plus, it didn't even happen in my jurisdiction."

"My apartment was tossed by whoever kidnapped me," I reminded him. "That did happen in your jurisdiction."

"You're going to blame that on Barron, too?" Patterson said. "Look, your whole theory of the case is that Judge Paris was behind these murders. Barron works for John Smith. Explain that."

"I can't," I snapped. "Ask him."

Terry said mildly, "You have to admit, Henry, it muddies the water."

"I know that," I said. "But all I can tell you is what I saw. What it means is up to you guys to figure out. Even if it's not enough to arrest him, it's still a lead, right? Don't you guys follow leads? Or are you afraid to because on paper he looks like a Boy Scout?"

"I didn't say I was going to let him off the hook," Patterson said. "I plan to invite him down here for a talk."

"Keep me in the loop," I said.

"No way," he said. "You're a witness now."

Ormes walked me out of the DA's office. Before we parted, she said, "Be careful, Henry. If you're right about Barron, he's already killed two people. Once we call him in for questioning, it won't be hard for him to figure out who implicated him. Watch your back."

A couple of days later, Patterson called me.

"Barron's in Japan for work," he said. "He's expected back Friday. Smith's people assured me he'd cooperate."

Friday came and went, then the weekend, then half the next week. On Wednesday Patterson called again.

"Barron's in the wind," he said.

"What?"

"He left Japan the day I called you. No one knows where he is."

"What does that mean?" I asked.

"It means I've got a search warrant for his apartment and his office," Patterson said. "I'll be in touch."

A week later, another call from Patterson.

"Hey, John Smith has asked for a meeting with the District Attorney and the Chief of Police. Ormes and I are also invited. I'm inviting you."

"What does he want?"

"His lawyer says he wants to make a statement about Barron. Ormes will pick you up tomorrow morning at eight-thirty."

I put on my best suit, my nicest tie and buffed my shoes. Ormes arrived in her dress blues.

"Look at us," I said. "You'd think we were meeting God."

We drove into the city where Smith lived in his grandfather's house at the top of Nob Hill. The residence had once been surrounded by the mansions of other nineteenth century robber barons, but the demands of a growing city, the dispersal of the old families and the earthquake had led to their demolition or conversion to hotels, schools or other uses. Only the Linden House remained a private residence, a nineteen thousand square foot, forty-four room, Renaissance Revival structure in gray granite on a quarter acre of the most expensive real estate in the city. The gates swung open for Ormes's car. We drove up a circular driveway to the sweeping entrance staircase that led to a door carved out of California oak where Sonny Patterson was waiting for us.

"Remember, you're here as a courtesy," he told me. "So keep your mouth shut."

"Scout's honor," I said.

Patterson rang the bell. A maid opened the door and we stepped into a long hall illuminated by gilded wall sconces decorated with oak leaves and sheaves of wheat. The walls themselves were covered with medieval tapestries and lined with ornate chairs, tables and cabinets that seemed to serve no other purpose than to take up space. I remembered Hugh's comment that his uncle collected antiques. That was an understatement. We were led down the hall on a thick Oriental carpet to a two-story oak-paneled library—oak seemed to be a theme here—the shelves of which were filled with leather-bound books apparently chosen more for their size and color than their content. Above the fireplace was a framed Bear Republic Flag, not the one that served as the state's flag but one of the original flags that had flown over Sonoma in 1846 when California briefly became an independent country. I knew this because the small brass plaque on the bottom of the frame identified it as such. The Santa Clara DA, and Linden's Chief of Police, sitting uncomfortably on a settee upholstered in pink silk, gave me the stink eye as I wandered around the room. Ormes tugged my coat sleeve like an impatient mother with an errant child and quietly told me to sit down. Before I did, I saw that a couple of tall bookcases were filled with mystery novels; I caught sight of books by Agatha Christie, Raymond Chandler, Dashiell Hammett, Rex Stout, Ross Macdonald and John D. MacDonald and even, interestingly, the gay mystery writer Joseph Hansen. These weren't the beat-up paperbacks I bought at used bookstores when I wanted to kill a couple of hours, but pristine first editions.

"Henry," Ormes whispered again. "Sit down." I sank into a leather armchair and looked up. The ceiling was so high I expected to see clouds passing overhead. There was, instead, a crystal chandelier. The windows, separated by pilasters, were heavily draped, apparently to block out the view of the twentieth century. The carpet and furnishings were Victorian era. I doubted they were reproductions.

The maid wheeled in a trolley with a coffee service and for a few minutes we all busied ourselves with that. We talked in whispers, as if we were in a museum or a church. The DA and the police chief continued to eye me suspiciously, but before either of them could question my presence, two old men shuffled into the room.

One of them, short, stout, white hair curling over his shirt collar, was garbed in the uniform of the legal profession—gray chalk-stripe suit, rep tie, gold cufflinks. The other man, the elder of the two, tall, thin, stooped, his pate covered by wisps of white hair, wore khakis, a red-and-white striped button-down shirt, a shapeless navy blazer and red carpet slippers. His blue eyes—the Linden blue—were glazed with age. He glanced at me appraisingly and allowed himself a tiny smile. What had Hugh told me? The old bachelor who collected antiques. I smiled back at him.

The two men sat down and introductions were made. Patterson glossed over my presence by introducing me simply as "my associate, Mr. Rios." I thought Smith's eyebrows climbed a bit when he heard my name, but I could have imagined it. After we all got chummy, Smith's lawyer, Mr. Caldwell, cleared his throat and began.

"Thank you for coming, gentlemen and Miss Ormes. Mr. Smith wanted to make a statement about one of his former employees, Peter Barron."

Former?

"As soon as we learned the police wanted to talk to Mr. Barron about the shooting in Linden, we called him in Tokyo and asked him to return to San Francisco immediately. We told him we expected him to cooperate fully with the police. As we informed you earlier, however, Mr. Barron did not return. At the moment, his whereabouts are unknown."

"You have no idea where he might be?" the DA asked.

"I'm afraid not," Caldwell replied coolly. "Mr. Barron served as an intelligence officer during the Vietnam War. We assume he retained some useful contacts in Southeast Asia. It wouldn't be hard for him to disappear."

"I thought he was Army," Patterson said.

"That was a cover," Caldwell replied. "He was CIA. In any event, after he failed to return, we launched our own internal investigation." He turned to the DA. "Mr. Bradbury, thank you for holding off on the execution of your search warrants to allow us to complete our investigation."

I glanced questioningly at Patterson. He shrugged.

"I can tell you now what we've learned," Caldwell continued. "We have evidence that Barron and another man abducted and killed Hugh Paris. That other man was Aaron Gold. We believe that Barron and Gold had a falling out that ended with Barron killing Gold."

Only Terry's hand squeezing my arm kept me from jumping up and demanding proof that Aaron had anything to do with Hugh's murder.

"Why?" she asked. "Why did these men kill Mr. Paris?"

"That requires some background." Caldwell said. "I expect everything I am about to tell you remains private. Yes?"

Bradbury, apparently speaking for all of us, said, "Of course."

"Thank you," Caldwell said. "A few month ago, Hugh Paris came to Mister Smith with some rather incendiary charges against his grandfather." Caldwell paused, looked at Smith, who nodded slightly. "Hugh alleged that his grandfather had sexually abused him when he was a child. He wanted compensation from the judge and he asked Mister Smith for his help. Mister Smith assigned Peter Barron to look into the allegation. This involved questioning some of Judge Paris's associates. When Judge Paris learned of the investigation, he had one of his lawyers, Mr. Gold, approach Barron and, basically, suborn him. The judge offered Barron two million dollars to terminate the investigation."

"Terminate meaning kill him," I said, unable to hold my peace.

Caldwell did not deign to look in my direction. "What the judge intended can't be established for obvious reasons but what followed is that Barron and Gold killed Hugh Paris. You can draw your own inferences."

"Why did Barron kill Gold?" Patterson asked.

"Again, without Barron here, we can't say definitively. They have may quarreled over money or perhaps Mr. Gold's conscience troubled him and he wanted to turn himself in. Whatever the exact reason, Barron was worried enough that he decided to eliminate his accomplice."

The DA asked, "You have proof of all this, Mister Caldwell?"

"Much of our evidence is circumstantial. Logs of phone calls and so forth. Some of it is necessarily inferential, perhaps even conjectural. But we are certain of the basic facts. Barron and Gold killed Hugh, and then Barron turned on Gold. We'll give you everything we have so that in the event Barron is ever apprehended you can prosecute him. I think that's all Mister Smith has to say at this time."

"Thank you, Mister Caldwell, Mister Smith," the DA said.

Now everyone was on their feet. There was much portentous shaking of hands and solemn "Thank you's" and "You're welcome's" and then we were all firmly moved toward the door. Was I the only one who had noticed that Smith had given a statement without ever having said a word? But then he spoke. He laid a hand softly on my arm and subtly pulled me away from the others.

"You were Hugh's friend," he said quietly.

"I was," I replied.

"He spoke about you. If there is anything I can ever do for you, Mr. Rios, you must let me know. You can reach me through Caldwell."

"Thank you, sir. May I ask you one question? Are you sure that Aaron Gold was involved in Hugh's death?"

"Oh, absolutely," he said. "Did you know him?"

"He was a friend," I said.

"Ah," he said. "Then you have a double loss. My condolences."

"Henry," Terry said. "Come on."

"Goodbye, Mr. Rios," Smith said. "Don't forget what I told you."

"What was all that about with Smith?" Terry asked me on our way back to Linden. We were on Interstate 280 passing through the thickly-wooded hills where private roads and locked gates marked the enclaves of the rich. It was a perfect autumn day. In the woods, knots of trees were beginning to change color, red and orange and yellow. Thin, vaporous clouds unfurled themselves across the sky. I thought about John Smith and his 44-room mansion. How many of those rooms did he actually occupy? What did he do with the others? Fill them with priceless gewgaws and leave them to gather dust? Except, of course, they wouldn't gather dust. That's what the maids were for.

"He said Hugh had spoken to him about me, and that if I ever needed anything to let him know."

"That's a big chip," she said.

"I don't plan to cash it in," I said. "He doesn't have anything I want. It's strange Caldwell didn't mention Hugh's other allegation against the judge."

"The murders?" she said. "Maybe Hugh didn't tell him."

"He told me he did," I said. "He told me Smith didn't believe him."

"Then that's why Caldwell didn't say anything about them."

"Did I understand correctly that the DA really called off the search warrants on Barron to let Smith's people do a private investigation?"

"Yeah," she said curtly.

"That's okay with you?"

"No one asked my opinion."

"When Caldwell turns over the evidence implicating Aaron in Hugh's murder I want to see it."

She glanced at me. "You know that's not going to happen, Henry. You're a witness in this case. We're not going to have some defense attorney claiming collusion."

"I don't believe Aaron had anything to do with it."

"We've always thought two people were involved," she reminded me. "The killer and the driver of the getaway car. My money is on Barron as the killer."

"The driver would have the same liability as an aider and abettor," I said. "Both of them would go down for murder. That's not Aaron Gold."

"He would only be an aider and abettor in murder if he knew that's what Barron had in mind."

I grunted. It was a slender reed, but I hung on to it.

She exited the freeway and drove me home. When I got out, she said, "I'll let you know what I can. I'm sorry about your friend."

Here was my quandary: if, as I believed, Aaron Gold was incapable of helping Peter Barron kill Hugh, then why had Barron killed Gold? What motive would he have had other than to keep Gold quiet about Hugh's murder? I went 'round and 'round in my head trying out scenarios that exonerated my best friend, but in even the most generous ones, I came to the inescapable conclusion that Gold knew Barron had murdered Hugh and kept quiet. Whether he was an aider and abettor, a conspirator or an accessory after the fact, Aaron was implicated in Hugh's murder. I thought back to our first year seminar in theories of justice. Aaron claimed to live by the principle that nothing is inherently right or wrong, but that everything is a means to an end. He liked to say there is no justice, only power. I never took him seriously. But maybe he really believed that and I refused to see it because if I had, we couldn't have stayed friends. Ironically, the strongest evidence of Aaron's involvement in Hugh's murder wasn't the possibility he was a moral opportunist; it was how he had consistently and adamantly warned me away from Hugh. Whatever else he may or not have believed in, Aaron believed in our friendship. He had tried to protect me. I was left to wonder what exactly he had tried to protect me from, and whether that included his participation in murder.

In the midst of my ruminations, Aaron's sister Leah called me. I had given her my number at his funeral and told her to let me know if there was anything I could do for the family.

"The police said now that they know who killed Aaron, we can collect his things," she said, after our awkward hellos.

"Ah," I said. It made sense that since the cops thought Aaron's murder was solved, they'd release the crime scene. "I'd be happy to help you pack up his house."

"No, we can manage that," she said. "but it's just that, no one's been in the place since he was . . . killed. To clean up, you know? I'm worried about my parents walking into the room where . . . he died and seeing . . ."

"I understand," I said. "I have a key. I'll take care of it before your parents arrive."

"I would be so grateful," she said. There was a pause and then she said, "The police say Aaron helped commit a murder and that's why he was killed, to keep him quiet. I don't believe it."

"I know, it is hard to believe."

"Do you believe it?"

"Of course not," I said.

"Thank you," she whispered.

After Leah's call, I went out for a run to clear my head. When I returned, Grant was standing at my door with a paper bag in his hand. His smile was tentative. He held the bag out to me and said, "I brought you peaches."

I opened the bag. Inside were two large, beautiful, fragrant peaches. "Why?" I asked him.

"Because flowers seemed too corny but I didn't know what else to bring to apologize. I'm an idiot, Henry. I was wrong about Peter Barron."

"Oh, you heard."

"That he killed Hugh? Yeah, I heard. The other man he killed, he was a friend of yours?"

"Yes," I said.

"And I sent you to him," he said.

"I don't think I was in any danger from Peter Barron, if that's what you think. If he'd wanted to hurt me, he could've done it the night he abducted me."

"He was behind that too?" Grant asked, eyebrows lifted in disbelief.

"I recognized his voice."

"This just gets worse and worse. Do you hate me?"

"Now you are being an idiot."

"I dated the guy and he was a murderer."

"You didn't know that," I said. I took the bag. "Come inside, Grant. I've missed you."

He smiled shyly. "I've missed you, too."

Later, in bed, he said, "I'm crazy about you."

"I need to tell you something."

"What's that?" he asked warily.

"Remember you said I didn't want a boyfriend, that I wanted a cause."

"That was stupid, I'm so sorry."

"No, listen to me. My dad knew I was gay before I did, and he hated me for it. Even when I understood why he hated me, I never felt I had done anything to deserve it, but I knew better than to admit who I was. So I lied until I could escape him. When I got to the university I thought I could finally be myself. I was right, about the gay part. I didn't have to hide that anymore. I realized, though, that most of the kids I met assumed that everyone there was like them. I wasn't. Just being around them and in their world made me feel like I was still lying. All that lying was hard for me because I'm not a liar. Lying violates my nature."

"I know that about you," he said.

"Then maybe you understand when I say I've never felt like I belonged anywhere because there's never been anywhere I didn't feel forced into one lie or another. My life feels like it's been a struggle to tell the truth. Like I've been swimming up from deep water, my lungs about to burst, trying to reach the surface and breathe. Hugh understood that. He didn't fit into the family he was born into and he didn't fit into the streets where his addiction took him. He was trying to make his way to the surface too. He wasn't my cause. He was my mirror."

Grant reached for my hand and squeezed it. "I'd like to think you'll never feel forced into a lie with me," he said.

"I'm through telling lies about myself or letting people make false assumptions about me. That may not always be comfortable for you."

"I said goodbye to comfortable when I told old man Menzies I was a queer," Grant said. "I know it's not exactly the same as what you're saying, but we've both stepped off the path, Henry. You know what I mean? Marriage and kids and a gold watch at sixty-five. Whatever our lives are going to be, they won't be like that. We'll have to make our own way. I hope," he continued, taking a big breath, "that maybe we could do that together."

In the silence that followed, I felt, for the first time we'd been together in my bed, it was just the two of us. Hugh was gone.

"I want to try," I said.

Grant insisted on coming with me to clean up Aaron's place. It was a bright, fragrant autumn morning but inside the house the air was dead and creased with shadows. The surfaces of the living room were covered with a fine, black film. Grant ran a finger along a bookcase, examined it and said, "What is this?"

"Fingerprint powder," I said.

He wiped it on his jeans. "It's like a morgue in here."

I only half-heard him. I was staring at the armchair where Aaron had been shot. The headrest was stained black with dried blood. Grant came up beside me.

"Is this where . . . ?"

"Yes," I said. "We have to get rid of it before his folks arrive. This isn't going to fit into my car."

"We passed a U-Haul on El Camino," he said. "Why don't I go back there and get a truck while you start cleaning up?"

"Thanks," I said.

He slipped his arm around my waist. "I'm sorry, Henry."

"Go on and get the truck," I said. "The sooner we get this thing out of here, the easier it will be to deal with the rest of the place."

"Sure thing," he said. He kissed my cheek and left.

I cleared a space around the chair so we could get it out the door when he returned. I picked up the ottoman in front of the chair. To my surprise, the top came off. Inside was a large envelope. My name was written on it. I picked up the envelope, removed the thick bundle of legal-sized paper within and unfolded the pages. It was the copy of a document captioned "Amendment." I flipped through the pages, uncertain of what I was looking at, until I came to the signature page at the end where there were two signatures: John Smith and Robert Paris. Below their signatures was a date fifteen years earlier and a notary public stamp. I turned back to the first page and began reading.

THIRTEEN

This time I had called ahead and Professor Howard's nurse let me into the house without an interrogation. I found him where I had left him, sitting in his overstuffed chair, another cigar in an ashtray sending up plumes of smoke like incense in the church of the past.

"You're back," he said, smiling. "Are you looking for more free legal advice?"

"Something like that," I said, pulling a chair up to him. "I have a document I'd like you to read and explain to me."

"Okay, you've got my attention," he said. "Let's see it."

I gave him the document I had found hidden at Aaron's house.

Professor Howard took the papers, leafed through them and gave me a hard look. "Where did you get this?"

"From an attorney at the firm that represents Robert Paris," I said.

He lifted a disapproving eyebrow at the violation of client confidentiality and then returned to the document, raising one page at a time to his face with unsteady hands and dropping the pages to the floor as he finished them. The last page slipped from his fingers and he said, "Extraordinary. Unbelievable." He looked at me. "What do you want to know, Henry?"

"All I know about trusts is what I remember from your class so I'm not sure that my interpretation of the document is correct."

"How do you interpret it?"

"It seems to amend a provision in the Linden Trust that gives the two trustees equal authority in the management of the trust and makes one trustee, Judge Paris, completely subordinate to the other trustee, John Smith. Is that right?"

Howard's wheezy laughter ended in a coughing fit. When he recovered, he said, "Subordinate? It made Bob into Smith's lapdog. No authority to direct investments or distribute income without Smith's approval. It reduced Bob to a figurehead."

"So I did read it correctly. What does it mean in the larger scheme of the trust?"

"How much do you know about the Linden Trust?"

"Mostly that it paid for my tuition and room and board when I was an undergrad."

"Ah," he said. "You were a Linden Scholar. You must have been one very bright boy, Henry."

"And a very poor one," I said.

"Yes, that too," he agreed.

The Linden Scholar program had been set up by the trust to give a full ride to the university to a couple of dozen students from families below the poverty line. I remembered my astonished joy when I got the letter informing me of the scholarship. It had been nothing less than a lifeline.

Professor Howard poured himself a glass of water from a decanter on the table beside him. He took a sip and said, "I suspect Grover Linden would have approved of you. He was a very interesting magnate. Have you ever read any of his writings?"

"I didn't know he was a writer."

With enormous effort, Howard got up from his chair and shuffled to the bookcase that lined one wall of the room. Mumbling to himself, he searched the shelves until he found what he was looking for, a musty volume in a brown leather cover with gilt lettering on the spine. He carried it across the room, sank back into his armchair and opened the book, flipping through the pages.

"Linden's memoir," he said, and began to read. " 'Immense power is acquired by assuring yourself in your secret reveries that you were born to control affairs.' That's not the passage I'm looking for though it does open a window into the man's character, does it not? Oh, here it is. 'Surplus wealth is a sacred trust which its possessor is bound to administer for the good of the community.' "

"That sounds remarkably charitable for a robber baron."

Professor Howard closed the book. "He was no ordinary robber baron. When he died, he left the bulk of his fortune to the Linden Trust. The income from the trust was to support the university for the next one hundred years. He specified that there would be only two trustees and that they must be his lineal descendant or descendants by marriage to a lineal descendant. The trustees were obligated to meet annually with the president of the university to discuss the school's funding needs but they were given unfettered discretion in deciding which of those needs, if any, they would fund. The only restraint Linden imposed on their discretion was his command that the income be spent to elevate the university to the first rank of educational institutions in the world."

"All to the greater glory of its founder," I observed.

"I'm sure that occurred to him," Howard said, "but he was a genuine philanthropist, and for his time and station in life, rather progressive. From the start, he specified the university would accept male and female students at a time when women were not encouraged to obtain a university degree. As a young man, he was an abolitionist and after the Civil War he set aside money to fund a scholarship for colored students, as they were called then. Not to Linden University, of course. To black schools. And, of course, he created the Linden Scholarship for boys and girls like you."

"How did he reconcile his abolitionist beliefs with his company's treatment of the Chinese workers who built his railroad? When they went on strike to get the same wage as white workers, he cut off their food and starved them into submission."

"I said he was progressive for his time. Like most of his peers, he was violently anti-labor. He thought the unionists were no better than thieves trying to steal his profits."

"They were trying to provide a decent life for his workers," I said. "He sent his goons to break their strikes and hired scabs to take their places. Linden Scholar or not, I know blood money when I see it."

Professor Howard shrugged. "Most fortunes are built on someone's back, Henry, but not all rich people worry as much as Linden did about the fate of his soul. You remember from the gospel Jesus's colloquy with the rich young man? Jesus says it's easier for a camel to pass through the eye of a needle than for a rich man to enter heaven." He touched the book in his lap. "Linden was obsessed with that passage. He devotes several pages in his memoir to explaining why it did not apply to him."

"Didn't Jesus tell the rich man all he had to do was give his money away to the poor? Why didn't Linden do that? Why found a university?"

"He was a social Darwinist: if the poor were poor, it was because they were mentally and morally inferior to the rich." He opened Linden's memoirs and consulted it for a moment. "Here's what he says about charity. 'It were better for mankind that the millions of the rich were thrown into the sea than spent so as to encourage the slothful, the drunken, the unworthy. Of every thousand dollars spent in so-called charity today, it is probable that nine hundred and fifty so spent produce the very evils which it hopes to mitigate or cure.' "

"Darwinist, abolitionist, union-buster, Christian. This guy was all over the map."

"Decidedly a complicated man," Professor Howard said. 'Though remember, Henry, Christianity is very much like the law. It's not about the text, but the exegesis. Linden believed that educating an enlightened ruling class at his university would be more beneficial to the poor than simply handing out money and in that sense more Christian."

"I don't think the poor would have agreed," I said.

"The poor never get a vote in these matters," he said. "The first trustees were Linden's daughter Alice and her husband Jeremy Smith who was also, not by coincidence, the first president of the university."

"So President Smith only had to consult with trustee Smith and Mrs. Smith on how to spend the money."

"Exactly," Howard said. "Smith decided the school needed graduate programs to achieve greatness so he founded the law school, the medical school and the engineering school. Mrs. Smith was a devout Christian, so she insisted on the divinity school. They spent liberally to steal away some of the most distinguished teachers from the Ivy League by offering them unheard of remuneration. Grover Linden founded the school, but the Smiths turned it into a great institution. They inculcated this responsibility into their children, John and Christina, who in the fullness of time, succeeded their parents as trustees."

"Judge Paris was shut out even though he was a lineal descendant by marriage to Christina?"

Howard nodded. "Remember, there can only be two trustees at any given time and direct lineal descendants are given priority over descendants by marriage. So, yes, Bob was shut out." His eyes twinkled. "He didn't like that. In fact, he worked very hard to persuade his wife and brother-in-law to amend the trust to add a third trustee. John refused even to consider it. That was the beginning of the bad blood between them."

"Why did the judge push so hard to become a trustee?"

Howard raised his shaggy eyebrows in disbelief. "Are you serious, Henry?"

"Yes, what was in it for him that so important?"

"Power, Henry! The power to shape one of the world's great universities in your own image. To found graduate schools, hire famous architects to construct iconic buildings, start great archival and artistic collections, fund groundbreaking medical research at a state of the art hospital, provide seed money for a presidential library, endow chairs and prizes and a press. All of those activities at the university have been funded by the income of the Linden Trust. Building a railroad across the continent is all fine and well but creating a great university that you have named after yourself, that's legacy, my boy. That's immortality. Grover Linden understood this. So did Bob. The man was a megalomaniac and it killed him to stand aside while his wife and brother played king and queen."

"What's the value of the trust?"

"The last time I looked, it was just north of five hundred million dollars."

And then in a stroke, it all fell into place for me. "Wait," I said. "That's why the judge killed Christina and Jeremy. It wasn't for her money. It was to replace her as trustee and to eliminate Jeremy as a rival."

"I knew you were a smart boy," Professor Howard said. "Go on, explain it."

"It wasn't enough to kill Christina because Jeremy would have succeeded her as Linden's direct lineal descendant. He was the only one who could have. Nick Paris was insane, Hugh was a minor, which made either of one of them incompetent to succeed Christina as trustee."

"Precisely," he said.

"Why didn't you tell me this the first time I came to see you?"

"You didn't ask about the trust, Henry. You only asked about Christina's will."

"But this information provides a much stronger motive for him to have killed her and Jeremy."

"I would agree," Professor Howard replied, "but for this document." He indicated the papers on the floor beside his chair. "This amendment to the trust stripped Bob of any effective authority as trustee and transferred it to John Smith."

"If Judge Paris was a megalomaniac like you said, he would never have voluntarily agreed to this amendment."

"Yes, so, a carrot or a stick?" Professor Howard said. "Think, Henry. What could have induced him to sign this document?"

Aaron's words in that last phone call came back to me. *You've got it all wrong.*

"Smith knew," I said. "Smith knew the judge killed Christina and Jeremy and he used that knowledge to blackmail the judge into signing away his power as a trustee."

"I can't think of any other reason why Bob would have agreed to this humiliating agreement with a man who sickened him."

"Sickened him? Why?"

Professor Howard closed his rheumy eyes and whispered, as if fearful that his voice might carry into the next room where his nurse was knitting. "John Smith is a homosexual."

"Yeah, I know. Hugh told me as much."

He opened his eyes. "Hugh knew this about his great-uncle?"

"Hugh was also gay, professor."

He stared at me. I could almost hear the gears turning in my head. "Are you a homosexual as well?"

"Yes," I said.

"And Hugh was your—" he stopped, searching for a polite description. "Your special friend?"

"Yes, professor."

"My word," he said. "The times really have changed. I would never have guessed looking at you, Henry."

"No, we don't generally have horns and a tail."

He laughed. "Or cloven hoofs? Don't worry, Henry, I'm an old man who has seen enough of life to have discarded most of my biases."

"We were talking about why the judge accepted this amendment."

"Yes," he said, somewhat reluctantly returning his attention to the previous subject. "Yes, well, I believe you are correct to assume John Smith blackmailed him."

"Why didn't he go to the police?"

"The police?" he said incredulously. "Can you imagine the sensation that would have created? Grandson of Grover Linden accuses federal judge brother-in-law of double murder of wife and son? How do you think Bob would have responded? He would have gone directly for Smith's jugular and exposed him as a homosexual." He permitted himself a little smile. "Which, evidently, carries more opprobrium for men of Smith's generation and mine than it does for yours. No, rich people don't air out their dirty linen in public. By blackmailing Bob, Smith avoided a public battle and got to exercise power over the man who had killed his sister and nephew."

"If the judge despised Smith so much, then Smith's evidence must have been compelling to force the judge to sign the amendment."

Professor Howard nodded. "He must have found the proverbial smoking gun."

"The one that Hugh was looking for when he was murdered," I said. "Smith had it all the time. Whatever it was."

We sat in silence for a few minutes. Finally, I stood up, gathered the papers that the professor had scattered at his feet and said, "Thank you, Professor Howard."

"No, my boy, thank you. I haven't had this much mental exercise in years. It's invigorating!" He took Linden's book off his lap and handed it to me. "Here. Grover Linden's memoirs. Bedtime reading."

"Thank you, sir."

"You realize," he said, "that if what we have hypothesized is correct, then the motive you ascribed to Bob Paris for killing your friend Hugh is no longer a valid one."

I nodded.

"So either," he continued, finishing the thought, "Bob had another motive for killing Hugh Paris, or someone else killed Hugh." His trembling fingers touched my hand in valediction. "And the killer may still be out there. Take care of yourself, son."

Grover Linden's account of receiving his first wages, age twelve, from working in a textile factory: *I cannot tell you how proud I was when I received my first week's earnings. One dollar and twenty cents made by myself and given to me because I had been of some use to the world! Many millions of dollars have since passed through my hands. But the genuine satisfaction I had from that one dollar and twenty cents outweighs any subsequent pleasure in money-getting. It was the direct reward of honest, manual labor; so hard that, but for the aim and end which sanctified it, slavery might not have been too strong a term to describe it.*

In light of his later business practices, the passage was profoundly ironic. He worked a six-day week, twelve-hour day with a single thirty-minute break at noon, conditions he recognized as approximating slavery. Yet he would impose upon his Chinese railroad workers conditions that were more arduous and dangerous without a second thought and starve them when they struck for the same wage as white workers. How did he justify it? Money. His little wage of one dollar and twenty cents "sanctified" the brutal work demanded of him. The tiny wage his Chinese workers earned should have, in his mind, sanctified theirs.

This was his epiphany, his road to Damascus moment— money gave meaning and purpose to life's struggles; money was sacred.

Therefore, a life spent in pursuit of wealth was a worthy, even a holy vocation. And if, in that pursuit, lesser mortals fell behind, that was a necessary consequence of what he called "the law of competition." "*Whether the law be benign or not, we must say of it: It is here; we cannot evade it; no substitutes have been found; and while the law may be sometimes hard for the individual, it is best for the race because it ensures the survival of the fittest."*

Illuminating every page of his memoirs was the simplest of truths: Grover Linden worshiped money. Money was his God and the acquisition of wealth was his religion. A cold God, a brutal religion. The memoirs, written toward the end of his life, hinted at his internal struggle between the god of money he worshipped in life and the Christian God to whom he would have to account for himself in the afterlife; the same god who had driven the money changers from his temple. In that light, his decision to give away his money felt less like philanthropy than panic as he looked for a loophole into heaven a lot wider than the eye of a needle. And then he found it: all he had to do was to arrange to give away his money posthumously. After pages and pages celebrating his business acumen and the amassing of his fortune, in the final chapters of his memoir he recast himself as *"the trustee and agent for his poorer brethren,"* whose duty was to distribute his wealth *"in the manner which, in his judgment, is best calculated to produce the most beneficial results for the community."* The year after his memoirs were published, he founded the university.

I thought about my scholarship to his school. Did my acceptance of it and the education it provided to me implicate me in his crimes or in his salvation? Because surely I was connected to the man by the long tendrils of his money, that fortune he amassed and celebrated and then which, as he faced his mortality, terrified him. I was connected to Linden in another, more personal way too, through his descendant Hugh Paris. Hugh's murder, his killer, and the motive for his murder was evidence that Linden's money still dripped with blood.

I drove to the mansion at the top of Nob Hill in the rain. A maid met me at my car with an umbrella and walked me into the great hall where John Smith was waiting. He was dressed much as he had been the last time—blazer, khakis, carpet slippers. The maid took my coat. I walked down the silent hall to where Smith stood. He extended a trembling hand.

"Henry, I didn't expect to have the pleasure of seeing you again so soon after our last meeting."

His tone was polite but the blue eyes were calculating and wary and I read in them the unasked questions: *What do you want? What will this cost me?*

"Thank you for agreeing to see me," I said.

"Come in," he said, gesturing toward a room off the hallway. "We'll talk."

It was a different room than on my last visit but no less ornately decorated and furnished. The predominant color was yellow in all its shades, from lemon to gold, from carpet to drapes to upholstery, and it was filled with the same ponderous and uncomfortable Victorian furniture. A silver coffee service was set out on a marble-topped table.

"Please," he said, indicating it. "Help yourself."

"May I pour you a cup?"

"No, thank you. Caffeine no longer agrees with me."

I poured coffee into a bone-china tea cup decorated with blue hibiscus flowers and a gold rim. Smith had seated himself on a cane-backed settee and patted the seat beside him.

"This is a beautiful room," I said, stalling.

"You think so?" he replied. "My grandfather's will specified that nothing in the house was to be changed. Other than necessary replacements and maintenance, it looks exactly the same as when he was alive. Sometimes I feel as if I'm living in a museum."

"Surely you could live anywhere."

"Why would I?" he said. "It's my family's home. Caldwell said you had something you wanted to talk to me about."

I had worked out my speech in my head on the drive up from Linden but now, confronted with Smith in the flesh and surrounded by Grover Linden's artifacts, I wavered. Accusing a man of murder was considerably more anxiety-producing in life than in the crime novels that Smith collected. I steeled myself with thoughts of Hugh and Aaron.

"After my last visit here," I said, "I went to clean up the house where my friend Aaron Gold was murdered. I discovered a document he had left for me that I think his killer might have been after. It was an amendment to the trust instrument creating the Linden Trust."

"Ah, yes, Mr. Gold was your friend, you said."

"We were classmates at the law school. He worked for the firm that represented Judge Paris."

"And this is where he found this document? Isn't it impermissible for a lawyer to share his client's confidential records?"

"It is," I said. "But he wanted me to see this document because he thought it explained who killed Hugh."

"We know who killed Hugh," Smith said. "Peter Barron and Mr. Gold himself. That being the case, I would think you would be skeptical of any attempts by Mr. Gold to exonerate himself."

He spoke with such conviction that I faltered for a moment, before saying, "Aaron was like a brother to me, sir. Whatever you and Caldwell may have cooked up to implicate him, I can't believe he had anything to do with Hugh's death."

Smith leaned back slightly and I thought I saw a glint of amused interest flash across his eyes. "Cooked up, you say? Please, go on."

"I believe Aaron was killed because he discovered who actually commissioned Barron to murder Hugh. It wasn't Judge Paris."

"I'm sorry but you're not making any sense," he said lightly. "If it wasn't Bob, then who?"

"The man Barron worked for," I said. "You."

I expected his next words to be a threat or a directive to get out of his house. Instead, he laughed.

"How extraordinary! I was the only one in our family who cared for Hugh. I supported him all those years he seemed intent on destroying himself. And you think, after all that, I had him killed?"

"Yes," I said.

"What motive could I have possibly had to injure the boy?"

"Control of the Linden Trust," I said. "Hugh wasn't going to expose his grandfather as a pedophile, he was going to expose him as a murderer. He was gathering evidence that Judge Paris killed his wife and son, your sister and nephew. He tried to convince you to help him, but you'd known the truth about their deaths for years. You used your knowledge to force Judge Paris to sign the amendment to the trust that gave you complete control over it. If Hugh had brought these allegations against the judge, he would have been forced to resign as trustee and Hugh would have replaced him. But Hugh wouldn't have been bound by the amendment you forced the judge to sign. Hugh would have had authority over the trust equal to yours. You needed to stop him. The only thing I don't understand is why that possibility was so threatening to you."

I had spoken in a great, clumsy gust, getting the words out before my nerve deserted me entirely. When I finished, I was perched at the edge of the settee, my hands in a fist, breathing hard, as if I'd just finished a sprint.

"What an astonishing story," Smith said, smiling charmingly.

I was incredulous; he appeared to be enjoying this. My anger overcame my nerves. "Is this a game to you, sir?" I demanded.

The amusement went out of his eyes. "Young man," he said, "if you haven't already, you will soon discover that life is a game, but we are not the players. We are the pieces, moved around a board of which we see only the smallest part, a square or two, and which is beyond our comprehension." The smile reappeared. "Do you read mysteries, Henry?"

The abrupt change of topic disconcerted me. "Uh, sometimes."

"They're my favorite reading," he continued, "because mystery writers know about the game and about our pathetic attempts to control it. They understand the law of unintended consequences and the good intentions that pave the road to hell. This scenario of yours has all the elements of a really top drawer mystery."

"Mr. Smith, do you deny that you had Hugh killed?"

"Of course, I do," he said. "I loved Hugh. I understood Hugh. I knew what he was. What you are."

"What you are," I said.

"What I was perhaps, once, back when my heart still pumped warm blood. A long time ago, I assure you. I am not that thing, now. Not a protagonist like you, Henry, filled with youthful ardor and an unshakeable conviction in his own rightness. No, I'm an antagonist. An old spider in the middle of a dusty web."

"Are we back to mystery novels?" I asked.

"If this were," he said, "I'm afraid the reader would find some holes in your plot."

"What do you mean?"

"Let's assume the antagonist in your story really did have his beloved nephew killed. Your reader will ask the same question you do. Why? Why would the antagonist have been so worried about sharing authority over this trust with his nephew that he had him killed?"

"How would you answer that?"

"Let's say that this trust will, by its own terms, dissolve one hundred years after the death of the man who created it at which point the principal will be distributed to the institution it supports. Let's say further that this will occur in three years. Let's say, finally, that our antagonist, the sole trustee, has been diagnosed with a fatal, incurable but slow-moving disease like Parkinson's." He held out his hand and the tremor I had observed when I shook his hand took on a different meaning. "Our antagonist has devoted his entire life to his grandfather's legacy and now he finds himself in a race with time and his own decaying body to carry out his grandfather's last bequest. He has sacrificed everything to do this, even going so far as to accept the murder of his sister by a man he loathes and the murder of a nephew who held such great promise by the same man. And now, as the moment approaches when his life's work is coming to an end, his grand-nephew threatens to create a scandal that will not only expose the murderer, but also expose our antagonist's complicity in those murders. Do you think our antagonist could survive the scandal? Or would he be forced to resign his position as trustee and turn the trust over to an unstable, drug-addicted boy?"

"If the trust provides for its own dissolution in three years, what would it matter who was the last trustee?"

"Because trusts can be amended or broken or redirected," he said. "And this boy, filled with resentment against his family, and who would suddenly have enormous resources at his command, might well have decided to rewrite the terms of the trust out of sheer spite and frustrate the purpose for which it was created."

"Or not," I said. "Maybe our antagonist didn't give his grand-nephew enough credit."

"No? Well, that couldn't be chanced," he said. "Our antagonist couldn't risk his grandfather's legacy on the possibility that the boy had finally grown up."

"And that's why you had him killed?"

"Me? I had no one killed," he said. "But in your story, yes. Of course, you will have to make the reader understand that from the antagonist's point of view the boy's death served a greater good."

"Be that as it may, ordinarily in mysteries, the killer is punished."

Smith said, "Oh, the killer was. He fell from the balcony of his room on the fifteenth floor of a hotel in Jakarta."

"Barron," I said. "What about you? What's your punishment?"

"Punishment takes many forms. One of them is to awaken in terror in the middle of the night, night after night, and to know the cause of the terror is not a dream or an illusion but a real thing and it is coming for you."

"You deserve whatever happens to you," I said.

"Perhaps so," he said. With a hard smile, he added, "A word of advice, Henry. You shouldn't be so trusting of your bedmates."

"Hugh never gave me any reason not to trust him," I replied.

"I'm not talking about Hugh," he said. "I meant Grant Hancock."

I went home, poured myself a drink and considered my options. I could go to Ormes and Patterson with my story but even if they believed me, I doubted their bosses would. The law likes simple problems and easy answers. Smith had given the District Attorney and the police chief a killer and a motive in the murders of Hugh and Aaron. I was certain that whatever evidence his people had fabricated to support his story would look more plausible than what I had. A legal document stolen from a client's file by one of the men Smith said had killed Hugh. A single document and a convoluted story that had its beginning a hundred years earlier in the directive of the man who had founded one of the world's great universities because, like John Smith, he was terrified of what might be coming for him.

The case was over, the story was ended.

Except for one final detail.

EPILOGUE

Summer arrives in San Francisco in early September after the tourists leave and the fog disperses when, for a few weeks, the days are warm and the sky is achingly clear and blue. We were in October at the tail end of Indian summer. The days were a little shorter and a foreshadowing chill had crept into the night.

We'd had lunch with Grant's parents at their house in Sea Cliff at a table set with Talavera plates and blue goblets, from Puebla, his mother told me. I appreciated that she had intended the table settings as a welcoming gesture, so how could I tell her my family ate off cheap plates from Woolworth and drank out of plastic tumblers? When their maid brought the food to the table, I felt Grant's gaze on me, watching for my reaction. Not wanting to be impolite, I caught his eye and smiled. The conversation was light and witty, his parents bantering affectionately when they weren't beaming at us, and then his father mentioned having seen John Smith and how ill he had looked and my mind drifted back to his poisonous parting comment. I had tried to dismiss it as the old man's vitriol, a curse on me for having exposed him for what he was but I couldn't stop thinking about it and now, today, I would have to confront Grant with what I thought it meant. I hoped I was wrong.

After lunch, we went for a walk along Ocean Beach. A flock of pelicans dipped and soared above the slowly churning surface of the sea.

"There used to be an amusement park called Playland on the other side of the Great Highway," Grant said. "My dad would bring me sometimes. It was kind of broken down but I loved it. My dad said we could see Japan from the top of the Ferris wheel."

"And did you?"

"It was always too foggy," he said. "But I did see a whale spouting out there in the ocean once. That was very exciting." He pressed my hand. "My folks really like you, Henry."

"I like them, too," I said.

"My dad finally has someone he can talk to about baseball and my mom, well, my mom likes beautiful things. She wasn't too gushing, was she?"

"A bit," I said.

"Is something wrong, Henry? You seem a bit checked out."

We passed circles of rocks that held the ashes of fires. At night, the beach was bright with these autumn fires, a tradition the city tolerated. A smooth log had been rolled down to the beach and left in front of a fire pit.

"Let's sit for a minute," I said.

We sat facing the ocean. Gulls shrieked above us, dogs ran off the leash into the water, splashed around and ran back to their owners. A line of sea foam hissed on the sand when the tide came in.

"I have some questions for you, Grant," I said. "And I need for you to answer truthfully."

"That sounds ominous," he said lightly. When I didn't respond, he said, "Of course I'll answer truthfully. Ask away."

"How did Peter Barron know that I'd left your apartment the night he grabbed me?"

He had pressed himself against me and now I felt him go absolutely still.

"I'm not sure I understand the question," he said after a moment.

"Did you tell him I was coming to your place?"

His retreat was subtle, just a small movement that made a little space between our bodies. "How did you figure it out?" he asked.

"Originally, I thought Barron had followed me from Linden to your place, but he wouldn't have had any reason to follow me unless he knew I was snooping around Hugh's death. Someone had to have told him. Then I remembered when I asked you to talk to Smith for me, you said you couldn't get to Smith directly, but you could get to Barron. That's who you talked to the day I called you and told you Hugh had been killed. Not Smith. Barron. You told him about me. Didn't you?"

"Yes," he said quietly. "I talked to Peter that day."

"Did he tell you to invite me to your place to talk?"

"Peter said Smith was really upset by Hugh's death and the last thing he needed was someone making trouble. He wanted me to talk to you and see what you were all about. I swear, I wasn't trying to set you up."

"But you did," I said. "You knew it was Barron who grabbed me, didn't you?"

"Not at first," he said. "But yes, after we went to your place and I saw it had been ransacked, I called Peter and asked him. He admitted it."

Now I looked at him or, rather, at his profile because he kept his eyes trained on the ocean. Slowly, he turned his face to mine. He was so handsome, so hapless, his eyes so shamed that for a moment I wanted to throw my arms around him and tell him I understood, that it was nothing. But those would have been lies and there had been enough lies between us.

"What else did you tell him?"

"I told him what you had told me, that there was nothing in the stuff Hugh had collected that proved the judge had anything to do with the car accident. I told him he should leave you out of it."

"And none of this seemed important enough for you to mention it to me?"

The fog had begun to roll in from the ocean. The air was colder, grayer.

"You have to understand, Peter was an old friend and Smith and my dad go way back. I wanted to believe that whatever they were doing was to protect the family."

"But you were wrong," I said. "They did what they did to cover up Hugh's murder."

"I had no way of knowing that," he said.

"Even after you knew Barron had grabbed me and broken into my apartment, you sent me to see him," I continued, pressing him.

"I had to. You insisted on talking to Smith," he said.

"What did you tell Barron before I went to see him?"

"That you still believed Hugh had been murdered, that you weren't going to drop it."

"You told the man who killed Hugh that I was after his killer. Did it occur to you that Barron might make me his next victim?"

"I didn't know he had killed Hugh," Grant protested.

"Are you sure?"

Now he stared at me, his face coloring. "What are you talking about, Henry?"

"Barron had an accomplice when he murdered Hugh. Smith claimed it was Aaron Gold but we know now that that was a lie. The second man, Grant. Was that you?"

"You can't seriously believe I helped Peter kill Hugh," he said.

"You never forgave Hugh for what he did to you when you were in prep school."

"So I helped kill him twenty years later? What kind of a person do you think I am, Henry?"

"I honestly don't know, Grant."

He looked back toward the ocean, scanning the horizon as the fog continued to drift in, looking for what? Japan? A way out?

"I lied to you about Barron," he said in a flat voice. "But I had nothing to do with Hugh's death or covering it up. I didn't know you from Adam when you called me and told me Hugh was dead. Of course I called Peter. Of course I agreed to help him find out who you were and what you wanted. I don't apologize for that, but yes, I should have told you."

"Why didn't you?"

"Your world is black and white, Henry," he said. "Good guys and bad guys. Us versus Them. I didn't want you to think I was one of Them." He stopped and exhaled a long breath. "Not after I started to fall in love with you." He looked at me. "Can't you forgive me?"

"If I hadn't figured it out for myself about you and Barron, would you have ever told me?"

A quick, almost involuntary shrug. "What would have been the point?" he asked softly. "It was over."

I said, without looking at him, "Goodbye, Grant."

I heard him get up and listened to his footsteps padding softly in the sand as he walked away. I sat there alone until the fog obliterated all traces of the sun. Then I got up and went off in search of the nearest bar.

AFTERWORD:

The Making of Henry Rios

Photograph of 25 year old Michael
Nava in 1980, a recent Stanford Law
School graduate. While studying for
the bar, Nava worked nights at the
Palo Alto jail and there he began to
write what became the first Henry
Rios novel. Published 30 years ago as
The Little Death, the first in the Henry
Rios series has been completely
revised and retitled into the book you
hold in your hand today–*Lay Your
Sleeping Head*.

I.

I became a mystery writer, if not precisely by accident, then not by design. I began writing this book in the summer of 1980. I had just graduated from Stanford Law School, and was cramming for the California bar exam during the day. At night, I worked at the Palo Alto jail where I interviewed arrestees to determine whether they were eligible for release on their own recognizance. There weren't that many arrests in our sleepy university town. In the down time, there was only so much studying I could endure and so, late one night, I began to scribble a scene in my notebook about a lawyer interviewing a prospective client in a jailhouse room much like the one where I was sitting. The lawyer was as yet nameless but I already had a title for the book—*The Little Death*.

But let me back up.

2.

My childhood, briefly. I was born out of wedlock and never knew my father, who was a Cajun from Lafayette, Louisiana. I was raised entirely by my mother's Mexican-American family in a Sacramento *barrio* called Gardenland. When I was four, my mother married a Mexican man who was a violent drunk, a sometime drug dealer and, if I understand the diagnosis correctly, a sociopath. By the time she was thirty, my mother had six children under the age of ten. We were very poor. Had it not been for my mother's parents and Aid to Families with Dependent Children, we would have gone hungry and homeless. Like all children, I had no choice but to accept my family's reality without any ability to improve it. From an early age, I set out making a better life for myself. I had two advantages: my maternal grandparents and my intelligence. My Mexican immigrant grandmother loved me above all her grandchildren and my Yaqui grandfather, although forbidding, provided me with an alternative model of manhood to my demented stepfather. Their house became my refuge from his sociopathy. From the start, my intelligence was verbal and literary; I have always loved words. One of my earliest memories is walking home from school repeating the word "eternal" for the beauty of its sound. For my teachers I was a dream child—the poor boy with promise—and they doted on me, providing me with the love and attention I did not receive at home.

One morning, when I was twelve, walking to school by myself, I heard a voice say, "You're a queer." I looked around to see who had called me that name and realized it was me. From that moment forward, I knew who I was, and while I also knew I had to keep it secret, there was never any question in my mind that I could change. Around that time, I began to write, looking for a language to express the torrent of feelings I could share with no one. I found that language in poetry. Elliptical, sentient and sensuous, poetry gave me a way of speaking without saying. I also discovered among the poets a fraternity of queers who wrote more or less openly about the themes that were all-consuming in my hormonal teens and early twenties—homosexual desire and alienation. Poets as different in style and temperament as Cavafy and Whitman, Auden and Ginsberg, Hart Crane and Frank O'Hara and Lorca wrote out of the same consciousness of difference that set me apart. I read them on many levels and for many reasons, but above all I read them because in a loneliness that often bordered on despair, they represented for me what Auden called "an affirming flame." There were, by contrast, no comparable voices that spoke to me in fiction. So, until I was in my early 20s, I read, studied and wrote only poetry.

3.

An irritated aside: Some readers assume the Rios books are literally autobiographical; that all I have done is apply a thin veneer of fiction to events and people taken from my own life. This is not true. Beyond the obvious similarities—Rios are I are both gay, Mexican-American and Stanford-educated lawyers—the parallels between events in my life and the novels are general, not specific. By that I mean, for example, that because I lived through the AIDS epidemic as it decimated the gay male community from the late 1980s to the mid-1990s, so did Rios. While his observations of the impact of the plague were drawn from my own, our actual experiences were quite different. There was, for instance, no equivalent in my life of Josh Mandel, Henry's HIV-positive lover, first introduced in *Goldenboy*.

I deliberately selected parallels between my personal experience and Rios's to serve a narrative or thematic purpose or to illuminate character, not to expose my private life. For example, Rios's father, like my stepfather, was cruel and violent but for a different reason. As Rios explains in *The Hidden Law*, his father's violence toward him was occasioned by his father's perception that Rios was homosexual; he was punished for a quality inherent in his nature that was morally neutral. The injustice of this punishment meted out by an authority figure helps explain why Rios chose to become a criminal defense lawyer, the archetypal defender of the despised, challenger of authority and seeker of justice.

This is not my story. My relationship with my stepfather was not the same as Rios's relationship with his father and I have a different understanding of my stepfather's violence—he was mentally ill—than Rios drew about his father's.

My point is that the Rios novels are fictions, not autobiography, and they should be read that way.

4.

At Colorado College, I was befriended by Ruth Barton, an adjunct professor in the English department who taught creative writing. Ruth was the first person to give me the permission I needed to think of myself as a writer by taking seriously the work I presented to her.

Forty years after I met Ruth, I delivered one of the eulogies at her memorial service. This is how I remembered our first meeting: "Ruth Barton was my first teacher at Colorado College; I took a course from her called Creative Writing. In typical Ruth fashion, we met, not in one of the sterile English department classrooms at Armstrong Hall, but in a lounge at Montgomery Hall, a residential hall with windows that framed Pikes Peak. On that morning in September 1972, the ten or so of us young writers arranged ourselves on chintz-covered chairs and couches and waited for Professor Barton—who was late."

"Time passed and still no Professor Barton. We glanced at our watches, sneaked looks at each other, but no one spoke. Finally, the door opened and shambling into the room was a small woman in cat eye glasses who, in my memory, was clutching a sheaf of books and papers and a cup of coffee with a big black purse slung over her shoulder. She arranged herself in an armchair, brushed dog hair off her blouse, pushed her own thick, black hair back from her sharply pointed face, smiled warmly at us, and lit a cigarette."

"Good morning!' she exclaimed cheerfully. "I'm Ruth Barton."

That voice! Slightly gravelly, rather low, a little breathless. Ruth's voice was her signature: you could hear the Sweetwater, Texas childhood; you could hear the flat Midwestern and Western intonations from her years at the University of Wisconsin and in Colorado; but, most of all, you could hear in her voice the lively, inquisitive, humorous, and skeptical intelligence that made her such a compelling presence, notwithstanding her unassuming appearance."

"Ruth did not look like a college professor to my seventeen-year-old eyes. She looked like one of the nice lady librarians who worked at the reference desk at my hometown library. But Ruth was to a small town librarian what an astrophysicist is to a high school science teacher; same genus, very different species."

Among the many gifts she gave me, Ruth introduced me to mysteries. She was an avid fan of Rex Stout and I consumed all the Nero Wolfe novels he had written to that point. Having exhausted his work, I began to read other American and English mystery writers. I was aware, of course, that these were "entertainments," but because Ruth had recommended them, I was unaware they were considered unliterary. She was a brilliant Yeats scholar and, while unpretentious, supremely cultured. She would never give me junk to read. (And anyway, hadn't so magisterial a figure as T.S. Eliot proclaimed that poetry, my undergraduate end-all and be-all, was "only a superior form of entertainment"?) As a reader of fiction, I did not distinguish between "literary" and "genre" fiction. I read novels that gave me pleasure and that spoke to me. Those are still my criteria for fiction.

After college, I continued to read mysteries appreciatively if randomly, hopping from Ross Macdonald to John D. MacDonald, from Josephine Tey to P.D. James. Just before I started law school in 1978, I discovered the novels of Joseph Hansen. At that point, he had published three of his twelve mysteries: *Fadeout* (1971), *Death Claims* (1973), and *Troublemaker* (1975). Although Hansen's protagonist, David Brandstetter, was an insurance investigator rather than a private detective, the tone was classic American noir as was the setting, Los Angeles and environs.

Rereading *Fadeout* after thirty-five years, I am still struck by Joe's distinctive style, brisk, spare and poetic. Joe, too, began his literary life as a poet. (Aside: as I explain below, Joseph Hansen and I became friends and I cannot think of him as other than Joe.) *Fadeout* begins with Brandstetter standing on a wooden bridge in the rain looking down at the swirling waters where, a couple of weeks earlier, a car belonging to a man named Fox Olson, insured by Brandstetter's company, crashed through the railing. The mystery: Olson's body has not been recovered. Without proof Olson is dead, Brandstetter's company will not pay the claim.

"Fog shrouded the canyon, a box canyon above a California ranch town called Pima. It rained. Not hard but steady and gray and dismal. Shaggy pines loomed through the mists like threats ... Down in the arroyo water pounded, ugly, angry and deep." The mood set, we are introduced to Brandstetter who is carrying a near-suicidal burden of grief. He describes driving across the bridge *"with sweating hands. Why so careful? Wasn't death all he'd wanted for the past six weeks? His mouth tightened. That was finished. He'd made up his mind to live now. Hadn't he?"* And then, a few pages later, we learn the source of his grief: *"Bright and fierce, he pictured again Rod's face, clay-white, fear in the eyes, as he'd seen it when he found him in the glaring bathroom*

that first night of the horrible months that had ended in his death from intestinal cancer."

My pulse quickened: *Rod?*

Brandstetter is grieving the loss of his lover, a man named Rod Fleming. In chapter six, we get the whole story. In a flashback, Brandstetter, recently discharged from the army at the end of World War II, enters a furniture shop on Western Avenue in Los Angeles to buy a bed. He sees, across the crowded room, as it were, a young salesman, short and dark, with a dazzling smile. "*'I want you,' Dave thought and wondered if he'd said it aloud because the boy looked at him then, over the heads of a lot of other people. Straight at him. And there was recognition in the eyes, curious opaque eyes, like bright stones in a stream bed.*" The young salesman, Rod Fleming, sells Brandstetter a ridiculous white wicker bed which he ends up sharing with Brandstetter for the next twenty-three years until his cruel, painful death six weeks before *Fadeout* begins.

How can I explain to younger people the impact of Joe's work on a gay reader like me? Maybe some context helps. I read *Fadeout* in 1976 or 1977. At that time, there was not a single city, county or state in the United States where an employer could not legally have fired me for being gay or a landlord not refused to rent an apartment to me. Indeed, in almost every state, I could have been imprisoned for having sex with another man. The American Psychiatric Association decreed homosexuality was no longer a mental illness in 1973, and California had only repealed its sodomy law in 1974. Even so, almost universally, gay men and lesbian women were still outlaws, widely regarded as sick, sinful or criminal.

Whether our individual lives were actually touched by these oppressive laws and social attitudes, all of us were embattled by their very existence. It is terribly hard to be hated for a characteristic over which one has no choice and no possibility of changing. To be hated for this reason is morally, psychologically and emotionally exhausting; no human being should have to endure it. Even those of us who fought the hatred sometimes surrendered to feelings of hopelessness when it seemed like things would never get better. In these moods we wondered whether *they* were right about us; that we were, in some fundamental way, diseased and condemned.

Most of the gay fiction I read at the time seemed to be by writers who accepted this morose formulation of homosexuality. The so-called post-Stonewall fiction emanating from New York in the mid-1970s was anything but liberating. These celebrated novels were about doomed, self-hating queens who took drugs, went to dance clubs, had emotionless sex and no visible community. As a high school student, I had buried myself in the stacks of the Sacramento public library surreptitiously reading anything I could find about homosexuality. For the most part, these were abnormal psychology texts in which homosexuals were presented as skinny, flamboyant, white men who lived in big cities, wore women's clothes and trolled public toilets for sex. The gay fiction I encountered in the mid-1970s was scarcely more advanced in its depiction of gay men. Nothing could have been more alien to my life, my experience of myself or my aspirations.

I was a bookish, upwardly mobile Mexican-American boy from the hinterlands. I experienced myself as a fundamentally decent human being. I declined to view myself as doomed or depraved because I was homosexual and I refused to live a life characterized by self-hatred or secrecy. If there was no space for the kind of gay man I wanted to be, then I, along with what turned out to be millions of other gay men and lesbian women, would create it. Joe's books legitimized my hopes and aspirations. Brandstetter was the kind of grown-up I could imagine myself becoming: a competent professional who was also unapologetically gay and who demanded to be respected on both counts. For me, Joe's novels were the fiction of gay liberation.

5.

About Joseph Hansen. After the publication of *The Little Death*, for which he provided a generous blurb, I met Joe and for several years he and I had a standing monthly lunch date. There was a thirty-plus year difference in our ages and while over the course of those lunches I learned a great deal about Joe and his life, I cannot say we became intimate friends. We had two topics of conversation. The first was novels and novelists. Joe never went to college but he was a lifelong autodidact who had a vast knowledge of European and American literature. He sometimes chided me on all the gaps in my reading of fiction—I had mostly read only poetry, remember—and once loaned me a volume of Chekhov's stories which were, he assured me, the greatest short stories ever written. "Tsk, tsk," he said, when I returned them with an uncomprehending shrug.

The other subject of our conversations was Joe himself. On that topic he was a charming, polished raconteur, although not necessarily the most trustworthy narrator. In his deep, melodious voice, he told stories about his life in which he edited out all the squalor of emotion. Nonetheless, it was impossible not to listen to his stories without sensing the hardship and discouragement he had endured for most of his life as he struggled to make his mark on the literary world. Joe was a writer who, more than most of us, needed the validation of a devoted readership but it was decades before he found his audience. He published his first poem in 1942 in *The Atlantic*, age nineteen. *Fadeout*, his first novel from a New York press appeared in 1971 when he was forty-eight. In the twenty-nine years between those events his only published works were pulp novels, some gay, some not, that he wrote under assumed names. His publishers were often just one cut above pornographers.

During those years, Joe was also active in in the homophile movement—the precursor to gay liberation. He founded the pioneering gay journal *Tangents* in 1965 and hosted a radio program called *Homosexuality Today*. As important and courageous as these activities were, however, he never considered gay activism to be his primary vocation. Indeed, he disliked the word "gay" and preferred "homosexual." He was first and last a literary man and the years of obscurity and rejection weighed heavily on him.

In *Fadeout*, Fox Olson, the subject of Brandstetter's investigation is a frustrated novelist who achieves success late in life as a kind of folksy, Garrison Keillor-style radio personality. It was not the success he wanted; he had aspired to be a great writer. Olson's wife shows Brandstetter a file cabinet filled with his unpublished manuscripts. She says, " *'He wrote this one in 1953, 1954. How fine I thought it was.' With a small, sad laugh, she closed the covers, bent and pushed the manuscript back into its slot. 'It wasn't, I guess. Nobody would publish it.' She stood and watched her foot as she rolled the drawer shut. 'There are twelve novels in this cabinet. Three plays. Fifty short stories. Hundreds of poems.' She looked at Dave and her voice was dry with remembered resentment. 'Out of it all, only a handful of poems ever saw print.'"*

As I reread that passage, I realized Joe was writing about himself. The long years in the desert left him with a thirst for recognition that even the success of the Brandstetter novels could not slake and perhaps he thought writing mysteries was a step down from the kind of novels for which he had hoped to be celebrated. Despite the great reviews and literary honors the Brandstetter books brought him, Joe could be arrogant, touchy and resentful (though never toward me, to whom he was always kind), all the more so because his late-life success was relative. Joe was critically acclaimed but his courage in creating a heroically ordinary gay protagonist limited the commercial appeal of his mysteries. Even at the height of his career, he made only a modest living and he died poor.

At one of our lunches he said a psychic had told him he would achieve his greatest fame posthumously. I hope she was right. He deserves it.

6.

Law school, I quickly discovered, was not the study of justice but an immersion in the minutiae of the law that was both complex and tedious. When I wasn't floundering, I was bored senseless.[1] By the end of my first semester, I was ready to drop out. Fortunately, I met a young lawyer named Matt Coles. Matt, then twenty-eight, shared office space on Castro Street, and sometimes collaborated with the first gay legal organization in the country, Gay Rights Advocates. He came to Stanford to give a talk about the legal rights of gays and lesbians which were, in 1979, basically nonexistent. Even so, he was indefatigably optimistic and energetic and adorable in a fast-talking, wise-cracking East Coast way. He persuaded me to stay in law school and we dated for a while.

---

1   A few quirky bits stuck with me from my law school education, things that appealed to the writer in me, like the doctrine of simultaneous death, which became central to *The Little Death.* Happily, the practice of law was infinitely more engaging that the study of it and although I was, at best, a mediocre law student, I developed into a very good appellate lawyer.

On weekends I took the train up from Palo Alto to San Francisco where we would hang out in his basement apartment or drive around the city in his land yacht of a convertible or go drinking at a dive bar on Bush Street that had a great jukebox and was run by a female bartender who looked like Elizabeth Taylor in the actress's later, zaftig incarnation.[2] One of our shared passions was for mysteries. As we lay in bed or ate breakfast at Coming Home restaurant on Castro Street, we concocted the plot of a mystery novel we would write together about a young gay lawyer. Although we never got around to giving our protagonist a full name (we called him Nick), we did come up with a title for the book: *The Little Death*, a double-entendre that alludes to both murder and ejaculation. We thought it was a clever gay twist on a classic noir title. Matt reminded me recently that the plot of our novel involved a massive insurance scam but all I remember is that at one point our hero stumbled into a notorious leather bar on Folsom Street called Febe's.[3]

Gradually but definitely, in law school I stopped writing poetry. The impulse to write, however, did not go away. Entering my third year, I began to think about writing a novel, but I didn't want to write the autobiographical, self-disclosing and self-indulgent novel that most first-time, young, would-be novelists produce. I wanted to write something that would force me to construct a plot and create characters that were not simply <u>repurposed versions of myself. I</u> remembered *The Little Death* but

2 The Bushfly wasn't our only hangout. We liked to drink. Late one night, as we were walking to or from another dive bar through the Mission (San Francisco's Latino neighborhood), we saw three tough looking *hombres* approaching from the opposite direction. They passed us with a sneer and then we heard their footsteps stop. Matt whispered, "I think we're in trouble." I replied, "What do you mean 'we' white boy?" They resumed walking and so, perhaps, a little more briskly did we.

3 Matt went on to have a heroic career at the ACLU where, as director of its LGBT project, he was counsel in Romer v. Evans, the U.S. Supreme Court decision striking down Colorado's ban on laws protecting LGBT people from discrimination, and counsel for amici in Lawrence v. Texas, in which the U.S. Supreme Court declared sodomy laws unconstitutional. He argued cases challenging the ban on LGBT people in the military and bans on adoption by gay people and he has tried discrimination cases. He was the primary drafter of California's law banning sexual orientation discrimination and he wrote the nation's first domestic partnership law. We remain friends.

school, job-hunting and my first serious boyfriend kept me from immediately returning to it.

Midway through my third year I was hired at the Palo Alto jail to be the "O.R." or own recognizance officer. This, as I said, involved interviewing men—it was an all-male facility—after they had been hauled in and booked by the cops to determine whether they should be released on their written promise to appear in court or if they would have to sit in jail until morning when a judge would set bail. I had less discretion than the job description suggests. Basically, I asked questions from a form and wrote down the answers to determine the strength of the prisoner's community ties, whether he had any prior criminal record and, if so, the nature of those offenses. After I questioned them, I looked at their rap sheets to see who was lying about his prior record. I added or subtracted points depending on their answers. You got lots of points if you owned a house in Palo Alto and were married with children and had no criminal record. Minus points if you lived in a motel, were single and had prior misdemeanors. Any felony conviction automatically disqualified you from your own recognizance release.

Predictably, white, middle-class guys picked up for drunk driving or some other booze-driven offense (disturbing the peace because of a bar fight or indecent exposure because they'd pissed into someone's rose bushes) had no trouble qualifying for O.R. release. Young black guys from East Palo Alto (the poor black neighborhood on the wrong side of the 101 freeway) picked up for stealing a six-pack, dealing pot or breaking and entering did not fare as well. However, I tended to fudge the numbers of the black and Latino guys to let them out if I could. Also, in close cases, I could call a judge and get him to sign off on their release. There were two judges, old white men (I say old but they were probably both younger than I am now), who I could call. One of them was a hard-liner who never let anyone out, the other was either squishy or kind-hearted, depending on your point of view, and I could usually talk him into an O.R. release.

The sheriff's deputies figured me for squishy right away, yet another civilian undermining their hard work of keeping the streets safe, and treated me with benign contempt. (Most of them never bothered to learn my name and just called me "O.R.")

When I told one of them I had been hired by the Los Angeles City Attorney's office as a prosecutor, he snorted and said, "You're too soft to be a DA. You should be a Public Defender."

Still, I loved the job. After three years of sitting in the back tiers of Stanford's amphitheater classrooms and trying to care about the Rule Against Perpetuities and the Administrative Procedures Act, here was the law operating at its crudest and most compelling level. Palo Alto's jail was a windowless collection of cells and rooms in the basement of City Hall. I sat at a beat-up wooden desk in a big room between the reception area where prisoners were brought in through a sally door and the cell where they were strip searched. After being dressed in jumpsuits, they were either brought to me to be interviewed or I was called back to the holding cells to talk to them. In addition to the holding cells, there were also rows of cells for inmates serving misdemeanor sentences (sentences of a year or less; any sentence longer than a year required a transfer from county jail to a state prison.) One set of cells was reserved for homosexuals and transsexuals dubbed by the jailers the "queens tank." I was a good-looking boy and any time I happened to be in that area, I drew whistles and catcalls, much to my mortification and the amusement of the jailers.

The atmosphere of the jail was relentlessly male and, from my point of view, unmistakably homoerotic. The jail was permeated with the raw stink of men, what I would describe in *The Little Death* as "a distinct genital smell." I had encountered that stink in only one other place—the gay bathhouses in San Francisco. Also evocative of the bathhouses was the scene in the strip search cell—a group of men watching another man strip and display his body in postures that included bending over and spreading his cheeks. I tried, as the nuns had admonished us in catechism class, to keep "custody of my eyes," but I couldn't help but peek from time to time. To a horny twenty-three year old gay boy, the jail could be a bizarrely sexy place which was undoubtedly one reason I liked hanging out there. But I also liked the realness of the place, the cynical and casually profane jailers, the corn-rowed trustie who sullenly mopped the floors in the middle of the night, the vile decaffeinated coffee that was all the inmates were allowed to drink, the inmates themselves, some touchingly young and innocent appearing, and others who looked like they had been there cheering on the snake when it talked Eve into biting into the forbidden apple.[4] After years of reading noir novels, I felt as if I had stepped into the pages of one.

And so, one June night in 1980, I began to write what became the first pages of *The Little Death*. They were my homage to those opening scenes in classic noir fiction where the beautiful, seductive dame shows up at the private eye's shabby office with an implausible story and troubles no sane man would want to touch. But in my scene, the private eye is a burned-out, gay public defender and the dame is a handsome gay boy brought in on drug charges who claims to have no memory of the events that led to his arrest. The lawyer is skeptical but also, in classic noir style, immediately smitten. And that, for the next three years, was as far as I got.

7.

In September of 1980 I went to work for the Los Angeles City Attorney's Office. The City Attorney was responsible for all of the city's civil law work, from conducting contract negotiations with public employee unions to defending police officers sued in federal court for excessive force to representing the city in tort suits arising from slip and fall accidents at bus stops. Unusually for a city attorney's office, the L.A. City Attorney also prosecuted criminal cases, though these were limited to misdemeanor violations occurring within the city limits (the District Attorney prosecuted all felonies.)

Although misdemeanor connotes a relatively minor offense, in California a section of the Penal Code allows more serious crimes—domestic violence and assaults with a deadly weapon for example—to be charged either as felonies or misdemeanors at the discretion of the District Attorney. My caseload as a Deputy City Attorney often included crimes that the District Attorney had kicked down to misdemeanor status because there were problems of proof or the victims and witnesses were as unsavory as the defendant or because, as in the case of domestic violence against women, the crimes were not taken seriously.

---

4 I have since been in other jails and prisons, including Death Row at San Quentin. They are warehouses of human misery.

Following a six-week training program, I was escorted by my supervisor into a courtroom at the Criminal Courts Building on Temple Street in downtown Los Angeles, shown where to sit, handled a couple of dozen case files, given her phone number which was to be used only in the case of extreme emergencies, and left to sink or swim. It was terrifying! It was exhilarating! This was what I had imagined it meant to be a lawyer and after the bloodless tedium of law school I threw myself into it.

Over the course of the next four years, I tried 60 or so cases to a jury, another dozen or so to the court sitting without a jury and argued innumerable motions. In addition to staffing a trial court, I worked the arraignment court, a job that included the responsibility of reading arrest reports and deciding which crimes to charge. I also worked the master calendar court which is where all cases came after arraignment to be, in theory, sent out for trial. With over two hundred cases a day, and limited trial courts, most of those cases were either continued, resolved by pleas or, for one reason or another, dismissed. Nonetheless, our witness coordinators had to call the witnesses in every case to make sure they had been properly subpoenaed and were available should a case go to trial. (Our most effective witness coordinator was a thin, middle-aged African-American guy named John Freeman, a fount of weary wisdom. Years later, when I needed an investigator for Rios, I remembered John and patterned Freeman Vidor after him.)

My job was all-consuming. Writing receded into the distance. Yet, there was that part of me that was apparently taking mental notes of my encounters with defense lawyers, cops, judges, defendants, jurors, victims and witnesses. These impressions bubbled just beneath my consciousness and were, unbeknownst to me, forming themselves into characters and stories that would eventually rise to the surface and demand to be told.

And what characters and stories they were. L.A. cops, I observed, seemed to think of themselves not so much as public servants but an occupying military force, particularly in the city's poor black and Latino neighborhoods, regarding the inhabitants of these areas not as citizens but potential enemies. Defense lawyers seemed to fall into three categories: the zealots for whom prosecutors like me were tools of an oppressive system; marginally competent lawyers who made their living taking court appointments and who could be counted on to plead out their clients at the earliest opportunity; and the occasional first-rate, big-time, privately-retained defense lawyers, slumming in misdemeanor land, who were polished, prepared and dispassionate, a joy to watch in trial even when they beat me.

The municipal court judges were also a quirky lot. Municipal court was the first stop in a judicial career and the up-and-comers rarely stayed for more than a few years. At the time, in the 1980s, however, many of them were appointees of a liberal Democratic governor who had been succeeded by a reactionary Republican. They found themselves stalled trying drunk driving cases when what they really wanted was a seat on the Superior Court or the appellate bench. These frustrated judges tended to be a little cranky which, combined with their liberal tendencies, made for a rough ride if you were the prosecutor. There was nothing like being dressed down in front of jury for having interposed a perfectly legitimate hearsay objection by an enraged judge known behind her back as Cocaine Annie. Then there were the lifers on the bench who had, upon their elevation, reached (or even exceeded) the limits of their competence. One of my favorites was a red-faced, white-haired, jowly ex-police detective turned lawyer turned appointed judge whose post-lunch, bourbon-scented breath wafted across the well of the court to where I was standing arguing against a suppression motion. He regarded me with bloodshot eyes and interrupted me with a muttered, "Motion denied," before departing the bench for a pick-me-up in his chambers. There were also some quite excellent judges, some demanding, some gracious, all of them briskly intelligent and thoughtful.

After every trial, win or lose, I would talk to some of the jurors about the case and what had persuaded or failed to persuade them to convict the defendant. These were rarely edifying conversations. The things that moved jurors in one direction or another often had little to do with my meticulously prepared case. They based their decisions on which of the witnesses or lawyers they liked best, as if a trial were a high school popularity contest. When I figured this out, I used it by trying to stack the jury with jurors with whom I registered high on the likeability quotient. I did particularly well among older women (I was in my mid-twenties at the time and looked several years younger) in whom I evidently triggered a maternal instinct; they wanted me to succeed and would vote to convict for that reason alone. Once, after a trial, one of these women said, affectionately, "You're too young to be a lawyer," and actually pinched my cheek!

The victims were the people who ultimately drove me out of the prosecutor's office because their suffering reminded me that trials were not, after all, a sporting event. There was rarely any justice for the victims of crime in the criminal justice system, even when the defendant was convicted, because his crime had rent the fabric of their reality in ways the law could not repair. Contrary to TV lawyer shows, most crimes are committed by poor people against poor people who are usually black or brown. It is difficult and inconvenient enough to be poor in this society without the added stress of being beaten or robbed or sexually assaulted. This was brought home to me in a car theft case. The woman whose car had been stolen appeared faithfully for trial every time the case came up and every time the case was continued by the defense. She grew increasingly frustrated by the delays and I finally negotiated a plea bargain to settle the case so she wouldn't have to come back to court. When I told her, I expected thanks, I guess. Instead, she burst into angry tears. Didn't I understand that the loss of her car meant she had no way to work and had lost her job? What was I going to do about that? Nothing, I could do nothing, except send the thief to jail for six months for joyriding. I held her while she sobbed. I have never forgotten the futility and pointlessness I felt at that moment in my efforts to achieve "justice" for her.

8.

At the end of my second year at Stanford one of my classmates and I became boyfriends. After graduation, Bill had a clerkship with a federal judge in his hometown of Cleveland. When that ended, we reunited in Los Angeles and he went to work for a big law firm. We found friends among other young gay and lesbian professionals. One of them was a surgeon who wrote science fiction. I told him about *The Little Death*. As it happened, John was taking a private writing class from a man named Paul Gillette. John suggested that I come to the class and show Paul what I had written. Hastily, I typed up the few pages of *The Little Death* and went with John to his class to present them to Paul.

Paul's 1996 Los Angeles Times obituary is captioned *"Paul Gillette; Novelist, Wine Expert and Scriptwriter."* This captures the scope of his professional activities but doesn't begin to hint at his larger-than-life personality. Like many people in L.A. who had rubbed up against the movie industry, Paul was a performer and the class was his stage.

Paul was a journeyman writer who enjoyed his greatest success in the 70s when he produced a series of novels including *Play Misty for Me*, which Clint Eastwood made into a movie. *Play Misty for Me* is about a playboy radio DJ who starts a casual affair with a woman who turns out to be psychotic and stalks and attempts to murder him. The themes of the novel say a lot about Paul. He was shaped by the "Sexual Revolution" of the 60s which promised (with the help of the birth control pill) to liberate men and women from the restraints of conventional sexual morality but which for many straight men seemed to end up being a weird mishmash of licentiousness and misogyny. Guys might feel free to go bed hopping with no commitments but they couldn't shake their underlying fear of women as personified in Paul's novel as a knife-wielding maniac. Paul combined a *Playboy* magazine ideal of male worldliness with the social and sexual anxieties of a small town boy (he hailed from Carbondale, Pennsylvania, current population 8,891).

Paul was, physically, a florid man. He was overweight but he carried his bulk like an athlete and seemed powerful rather than fat. A photograph of himself in military uniform standing beside John F. Kennedy showed he had been a handsome young man, but twenty-plus years later his face had a balloon-like quality as if it had been inflated by the passage of time, too much rich food and many, many bottles of wine.

Paul's class met on Thursday nights from 7 to 10 in his third-floor offices in a boxy, run-down building on Sunset Boulevard a little east of Highland from which he conducted his publishing business, producing what the *Times* obit described as "beverage industry trade newsletters." There was a small reception area that led into a large office fronting Sunset. He sat at his desk while we students—at any given time there were ten to fifteen of us—arranged ourselves in a semi-circle around him on folding chairs. Behind us was a good-sized storage room filled with cases of wine and stacks of his novels. (Rios's office on Sunset Boulevard is modeled on Paul's.) There were always a half dozen open bottles of wine on Paul's big desk from which we were free to imbibe. He himself kept his glass filled, using it as a prop while he passed judgment on our weekly literary offerings.

The first time I walked into his office and surveyed the landscape—big man in a blue blazer, white shirt and rep tie sonorously holding forth to a middle-aged group of acolytes with a half-filled wine glass he deployed like a conductor's baton—I nearly turned around and walked out. This was not the sedate literary gathering I had expected. But I stayed and listened. The set-up was that students signed up the week before to present their pages which were critiqued in 30-minute sessions, first by their fellow students and then by Paul. Paul listened intently to the student comments, mostly patrolling them for civility, and then, clearing his throat, would announce, "And now it's my turn." He delivered a detailed and always acute analysis of a scene's strengths and weaknesses, plausibility and implausibility, graceful or clumsy style before seizing upon a particular point—a plot turn, a bit of dialogue, description or characterization—and using it to launch into a mini-lecture on that subject before summing up with his invariable, "Excellent work."

He was a magnificent teacher, shrewd, knowledgeable about craft, generous and patient. Moreover, Paul approached writing in the same way that his blue-collar forebears in Carbondale had approached mining or plumbing or selling dry goods—writing is a job and to do it well you worked hard to master the fundamental elements of which literature is constructed. Paul's class was all nuts and bolts; there was no drifting into the ether. His working-class approach to writing resonated deeply with me because it assured me that writing a novel was not a grace bestowed upon the fortunate few but an achievement within the grasp of a born striver like me. At the end of that class, I shyly handed Paul the opening pages of *The Little Death* and told him I wasn't sure if I had anything but would he call me during the week to let me know if he thought this was something worth pursuing? A couple of days later he called and announced, "This is a book that must be published and I will help you do it."

Over the course of the next year—this was 1982-83—I presented a chapter a month in Paul's class and finished the manuscript of *The Little Death* just a few days shy of my twenty-ninth birthday. After so many years I do not, of course, remember Paul's precise comments as I was working on the book; what survives in my memory is an overall impression of the acuity of his critiques and the generosity of his encouragement. The latter is important—I was very nervous about how he and my fellow students would receive my gay protagonist. But I needn't have worried because Paul took a sophisticated view of the subject matter and that set the tone. It helped, too, that I was young, cute and self-effacing. (When one of my fellow students, a retired military man, suggested I give Rios a signature drink, I replied, "Pink lady?" The class thought this was hilarious.) A number of Paul's other students were also really fine writers and I was not the only one who was eventually published. By and large, we gave each other's work attentive and respectful readings, so different than what I hear goes on in many MFA classes. But then, we were not in competition with each other. Paul had a mantra I have taken to heart that, for a writer, the only true ambition worth having is the ambition to write well.

True to his word, Paul attempted to use his contacts in New York to find a publisher for *The Little Death* but his efforts were fruitless.[5] Back in the 1980s, some publishers would still look at manuscripts submitted "over the transom," that is, by the writer directly without an agent. Over the course of the next year, I submitted *The Little Death* to 13 publishers. The book was rejected by every one of them. The common theme in the rejection letters was that, while the book was well-written, the editors could not see a readership for, as one of them put it, "material like this." No one had to explain to me what that was code for.

5 Paul and I remained friends even after I stopped coming to his class, but then I stopped drinking and this became an obstacle between us. Our long lunches at his favorite Italian restaurant on Melrose were much less fun when I started ordering mineral water instead of splitting our usual two bottles of wine. I lost touch with him directly but kept up with him through a couple of fellow students who continued on in his class and with whom I stayed friends. I heard he had money and marital problems and was increasingly irascible, but his classes remained fully subscribed. He died suddenly in late 1995 of a heart attack. He was 58.

9.

How Rios got his name. When I pulled out the handwritten pages of *The Little Death* to type them up to present to Paul, my lawyer protagonist was still nameless. When Matt Coles and I had been spinning our version of the story, we called him Nick but Nick was too breezy for the brooding figure who had begun to emerge from my pages. I needed a name that was solemn and memorable. But what?

The criminal division of the City's Attorney's office was on the fifth floor of City Hall South across Main Street from the iconic Los Angeles City Hall of *Dragnet*. The two buildings were connected by a skywalk I sometimes took to the Criminal Courts Building which was on the other side of City Hall. One afternoon on my way to court I noticed a bust on a pedestal at the City Hall end of the skywalk and stopped to take a look. The bust was of the bureaucrat for whom the skywalk had been named: Henry P. Rio. With a little tweaking, Henry Rios was born.

10.

The rejections of *The Little Death* were disappointing but I had written it as kind of a lark and finishing it felt like accomplishment enough. Now that I knew how to write fiction, I thought I would put *The Little Death* in a drawer and try my hand at a "serious" novel.

The Silverlake district was halfway between downtown where I worked and the Fairfax neighborhood where I lived. A friend of mine told me there was a gay bookstore, A Different Light, at the intersection of Santa Monica and Sunset Boulevards in a tatty, one-story building which looked not much different from the outside than the TV repair and discount shoe stores around it. Unlike the windowless pornographic bookstore across the street, however, A Different Light had plate glass windows and signage that announced its business purpose. Still, it was enough off the beaten track that foot traffic was minimal and most of its patrons were gay men like me who had heard of it via word of mouth. The store consisted of two big rectangular rooms lined with bookshelves and scattered with tables that displayed new releases. The carpet was worn and the walls needed paint but it looked lived-in rather than squalid; the shabby but cozy home of a confirmed bibliophile. This impression was heightened by the proprietor, a large, friendly, bearded man who wore flannel shirts and bore a passing resemblance to Walt Whitman in his later Good, Gray Poet days.

Richard Labonté, a native-born Canadian, came to Los Angeles specifically to open a gay bookstore. By the time I stumbled across it, he and the store were fast becoming institutions in Los Angeles's gay community. I showed up when Christopher Isherwood signed his last book to a crowd that extended outside the store and around the corner. Visiting gay writers from New York and San Francisco packed its tiny space and local playwright James Carroll Pickett curated an ongoing reading series for L.A. writers. In those days before the internet, when media representations of gays and lesbians were either nonexistent or pejorative, books were the one vehicle for the transmission of our stories and our lives as they actually were. Every gay man I knew had his half-shelf of the same gay novels, from New York writers like Andrew Holleran and Edmund White, San Francisco's Armistead Maupin and the Brandstetter books of Joe Hansen as well as the classics like Gore Vidal's *The City and the Pillar,* Isherwood's *A Single Man* and John Rechy's *City of Night.* We read and reread these volumes because they were the only cultural mirrors we had and even when we did not see our exact reflections, there was enough of a resemblance so that our lives felt validated. Words validated us, reminded us we were not alone and that, in the face of society's still relentless animus, our struggle to live authentic, open lives had a moral purpose. That, as Paul Goodman wrote in a poem, "We deviate but do not err."

Our appetite for books eventually spawned a number of small presses. A friend, who knew I'd been looking for a publisher, told me he'd read a book from one of these presses and it hadn't been half-bad. I stopped at A Different Light and asked Richard about this press, Alyson Publications. He directed me to maybe a half-dozen trade paperbacks. I read a few pages of each. Chuck was right, they weren't high art, but they weren't bad. I wrote down the company's address and submitted *The Little Death.* Within a couple of weeks I got a letter from an editor who told me he had been up all night reading the book and had strongly recommended that Sasha Alyson, the proprietor, publish it. On the heels of this letter came another letter, from Sasha, offering me a $600 advance and enclosing a contract. Even in 1985, $600 was not much money but I wasn't in it for the money. I was just happy that someone, anyone, wanted to put my book into print. I signed the contract and sent it back. I was going to be a published novelist!

II.

Sasha Alyson. In April 1986, Sasha Alyson flew to Los Angeles to attend my first book signing at A Different Light. (He must have had other business too since he was far too frugal to fly across the country for a single event.) The book had received unusually good reviews, mostly in the gay press, but also from a few establishment outlets. Most surprisingly, it had been politely reviewed by Newgate Callendar, the pseudonymous mystery reviewer for *The New York Times* who thought the book exuded a "calm sort of strength" and seemed relieved that "the homosexual elements [were] handled with dignity." I think it was the first time one of Sasha's books had been reviewed in the *Times;* I remember getting an excited call from my Alyson stablemate John Preston on the Sunday morning the review appeared. He read it to me and then dissected it in detail, concluding that, on balance, it was favorable.[6]

At that point I had only corresponded with Sasha and, in those pre-Google days, I had no way of discovering much about his background. I didn't even know what he looked like, although I assumed he would be tweedy, middle-aged and quite possibly a pipe smoker. The man I met at the airport, however, was only a couple of years older than me, sloppily dressed, with bleached

---

6 John was famous (or notorious) for bringing S&M erotica into the gay literary mainstream. Among the books he published with Alyson were the "Master" series: *In Search of a Master, I Once Had a Master, Love of a Master* and *Entertainment for a Master.* "What," I asked him, "no Brunch for a Master?" He was not amused. I have only seen photos of him in his leather regalia. Whenever I ran into him he was dressed like the headmaster of a seedy prep school for wayward boys—button-down shirt, crew-neck sweaters, khakis—but perhaps that was the point. He was a lively and entertaining gossip, particularly about other writers and all matters literary. He was more excited by the Times review than I was. He was a victim of the plague.

blond hair and a pale, knobby, pleasant face. A backpack was slung over one shoulder and in it he carried around a floppy-eared, stuffed dog who he introduced to me as Le Dogg. We went to lunch at a café in Beverly Hills where he removed Le Dogg from his backpack, sat in him a chair and asked that he be given a menu. (When the waiter came to take our order, Sasha said, apologetically, that Le Dogg had not found anything suitable to eat.)

Even after I stopped publishing with him, I saw Sasha at least once a year, on one coast or the other for the next decade. He was odd, for sure, but not inexplicably so. I soon figured out that Le Dogg was not an affectation but a prop he used to navigate social situations that made him uncomfortable (and almost every social situation did). In his publisher persona, he could be direct and forceful, but when he stepped out of that role, he was often monosyllabic. Born and raised in Ohio (under a different name, he christened himself Sasha Alyson after he left home), he was imbued with Midwestern modesty and unpretentiousness. Liquor loosened his tongue—he had a palate for good wine—and he could be dryly witty but no one except, perhaps, his (now former) boyfriend of many years got very close to him.

Sasha was given to unusual enthusiasms—in his Boston apartment, he kept a collection of unopened cereal boxes that he assured me would one day be extremely valuable. At one point, he discovered parchment paper and for months everything he cooked was wrapped in parchment and shoved into the oven; he even planned a parchment paper cookbook. I don't remember if he followed through on that project but he did carry out his plan to print a Le Dogg calendar. He was, I decided, one of life's observers, participating in the world only when it served his purposes and always on his own terms. Otherwise, he was wrapped up in a kind of solitude that I, for one, never entirely penetrated. I can't say that we ever had a truly personal conversation. Still, he was completely admirable, a person of great integrity, foresight and courage. With no more than a high school diploma—he thought college would be a waste of time—he created the most important independent gay press of its time and also founded Boston's gay newspaper, *Bay Windows*. When he started the press, he had no prior publishing experience, nor were there deep pockets in his family to support his venture. What he had was vision, intelligence and determination.

When AIDS struck, he corralled other publishers to jointly produce a book called *You Can Do Something About AIDS*, distributed free in bookstores, that ultimately reached 1.5 million copies in print. He was the first publisher to initiate a series of children's books, writing five of them himself. To publish gay-themed children's books at a time when gay men were still being widely demonized as pedophiles was a startlingly brave and prescient act. He took a lot of flak for it; his children's books were condemned, burned and banned. One of them, *Heather Has Two Mommies,* by Lesléa Newman has the distinction of being, according to The American Library Association, the eleventh most banned book in America. In all his professional activities, he seemed to be guided by a firm, interior conviction of what needed to be done.

After he sold the press, he operated a travel company that offered upscale adventures to gay men, like bicycle tours of the French wine country. Cleverly, Sasha had found a way to make money from three of his favorite pastimes: bicycling, traveling and drinking wine. A few years later, he sold that company and moved to Laos where he founded and as of this writing still runs a small press called Big Brother Mouse. His goal, he explains in an online article, is to promote literacy in Laos by creating books for its children in their own language. Sasha writes many of the books himself and gets them to children by means of transport that include elephants.

That Sasha, in his 60s, should be delivering children's books to remote villages in Laos by elephant seems at once wildly improbable and perfectly in character.

12.

Rereading *The Little Death* after its publication reminds me that I never intended it to begin a series. It was meant as a one-off, a way to teach myself how to write fiction, and an inversion of the noir fiction of the tough guy writers of the 30s, 40s and 50s, particularly Raymond Chandler. Chandler loomed large in my mind for a number of reasons. Like countless other readers, I was captivated by his inimitable style, a style as distinctive as

Faulkner's and a lot more fun to read. Then, too, Philip Marlowe was not only an outsider, but an outsider with whom a gay boy could particularly identify. Marlowe, for all his tough talk, was an honorable man who embodied the virtues that society purported to honor but rarely displayed—loyalty, courage, integrity—and, because of his status as a private eye, was the object of society's contempt. Nonetheless, despite their contempt for him, he was the person that the *gente decente* turned to in their times of trouble and to whom they revealed the squalid secrets that lay beneath the surface of respectable society. This gave him a ringside seat to society's hypocrisies.

Gee, I thought, *who does that remind me of? Oh, right, me.*

Like Marlowe, my inner experience of myself as a decent person was wildly at odds with society's characterization of gay men and the contempt in which it held us. This very contempt fueled my determination to be productive, honest and ethical; I would not give in to the society's hatred of gay men by fulfilling its stereotypes. Then too, like Marlowe, I was privy to society's hypocrisies, in my case, those affecting sexuality and sexual orientation. Gay men were feared as sexual predators who preyed on the weak, especially children, but as a prosecutor I knew that the vast majority of sexual predators—child molesters, rapists— were heterosexual men. Gay men were said to hate women but the battered women who showed up in my courtrooms had been beaten by their husbands and boyfriends. Moreover, it was male misogyny that oppressed women, not my sexual disposition toward other men.

Thus, I saw that the private eye in noir fiction could work as a metaphor for the position gay men occupied in straight culture.[7] (Of course, the connection would not have been so apparent had Joe Hansen not blazed that trail with his Brandstetter novels;

7 This idea of the private eye as social or political outsider gained traction in the 80s and 90s as African-American, Latino/a, feminist and lesbian writers turned to the mystery to tell some home truths about race, ethnicity and gender in America. They took characters who, in the classic noir novels, were marginal and stereotyped figures—the dame, the "colored" guy, the "spic"—and put them front and center. The Rios novels were part of a wave that included such fine writers as Walter Mosley, Sara Paretsky, Manuel Ramos and Katherine V. Forrest. It was excellent company to be in.

they provided my blueprint and my immediate inspiration.) Chandler intrigued me for another reason: Marlowe was ostensibly heterosexual but his most romantic relationship was with another man, Terry Lennox in *The Long Goodbye*.

It's difficult for a gay man to read the opening chapters of this novel and not conclude that Marlowe falls in love with Lennox. In the first chapter, Marlowe comes to Lennox's rescue after Lennox, falling down drunk, has been abandoned by his female companion. Lennox is strikingly described with his "young-looking face" and "bone white" hair; his first name is gender ambiguous. Marlowe takes him home, puts him to bed, and sobers him up. Here, Lennox plays the traditional role of damsel in distress—beautiful, helpless, mysterious—who inspired Marlowe's chivalric response. After Lennox departs, Marlowe cannot get him out his mind. "I'm supposed to be tough but there was something about the guy that got me." Which I read as: I'm supposed to be straight, but, yeah, I wanted to fuck him.

They renew their acquaintance after Marlowe comes to Lennox's rescue a second time and their relationship unfolds in the intimate dusk of a bar where they sit together at a booth drinking, at Lennox's insistence, gimlets (a ladies' drink if ever there was one), and talk around the subject of Lennox's mysterious past. One could easily imagine them as two closeted gay men glancing back and forth from their girly drinks into each other's eyes, talking in circles, bodies tensed, one trousered leg brushing up against another, each waiting for the other to make the first move. In their last scene at the bar, Marlowe snaps, "You talk too damn much. . . and it's too damn much about you. See you later." Translation: Goddammit, we both know what we want, stop jerking me around.

In the first chapter of *The Little Death* when Rios meets Hugh Paris I made explicit what seemed to me was implicit in *The Long Goodbye*: two men meet and fall instantly in love or lust or some noir combination of both. *The Long Goodbye* and Joe's novels gave me the warrant I needed to make this leap. I didn't think then, and don't think now, that it violated the code of noir; it simply extended it, taking it to one logical conclusion.

I was reticent about describing sex, however. When Paris comes to Rios's apartment, I get them to the bedroom door and then cut away. This was a deliberate choice. Too much gay fiction at the time seemed sex-sodden to me, gratuitously so, and I didn't see how inserting an explicit sex scene would advance the narrative. Besides, sex scenes are difficult to write without falling into pornographic clichés or silly euphemisms. Rereading the book has changed my view. The sexual intimacy Rios experiences with Hugh Paris, in light of Rios's isolation and loneliness, is one of the elements that drives him to investigate Hugh's murder. So, in revising *The Little Death* I have added a couple of sex scenes to flesh out (as it were) Rios's motivations.

There is also very little in the book about Rios's background, particularly his *latinidad*. Indeed, many white readers in 1986— before the seismic demographic changes that have made Latino/as an emerging majority in this country—may not even have known "Rios" is a Spanish surname. Again, I had my reasons for not placing Rios's ethnicity front and center.

The first is, as noted, that *The Little Death* was conceived of by me as a one-off experiment that queered the familiar tropes of the *roman noir*. I didn't see how an explicit exploration of Rios's ethnic background would fit. The second reason is that Rios's ethnicity *was* part of his character, if not the plot. His ethnicity emerges in subtle ways, although granted, this requires some knowledge on the reader's part about the Mexican-American/Chicano community in California.

I certainly knew that community and understood the implications of making my protagonist Latino. I knew a lawyer named Rios in California in the 1980s was in all likelihood Mexican-American, the son or grandson of immigrants, from a working-class or poor family, and likely the first person in his family to have obtained a higher education. He would have been one of a few hundred Latino/a lawyers in California and he would have spent most of his professional life among white lawyers where the pressures to conform to their codes and standards would have been intense.

In *The Little Death,* Rios's ethnicity and his background emerge in his character and the choices he makes. There is a gravity and melancholy about Rios that are characteristically Mexican. An archetypal representation of these qualities is Benito

Juarez, the great nineteenth century Mexican lawyer-president. Juarez was a man committed to the rule of law in a lawless time, defender of Mexican sovereignty against the French invasion that nearly succeeded in turning Mexico into a French client state. Juarez embodies that particular male Mexican gravity that arises from a deep sense of duty, obligation and sacrifice, a quality I witnessed firsthand in my grandfather, and which may be the one positive aspect of *machismo*. As for Rios's melancholy, Octavio Paz has written an entire book about that quality of Mexican character in his classic (if not entirely persuasive) meditation, *The Labyrinth of Solitude*. From the beginning, even before I knew there would other novels in the series, I saw Rios as typifying this kind of Mexican dignity, humility, sacrifice and solitude, tempered, of course, by the fact that he is also a product of American individualism.

Rios's background also informs his choices, as for example, his decision to practice criminal defense law and his rejection of Aaron Gold's offer to join Gold's white-shoe law firm. These are not the choices of a man from an entitled background but those of someone who embraces the marginal because he has direct experience of marginality.

13.

When I got back the publishing rights to *The Little Death* and decided to do a print edition, I saw this as an opportunity to go back and make some relatively minor revisions. I wanted to add passages that more clearly delineated Rios's ethnicity and background because, as those qualities became increasingly important in the subsequent books, some foreshadowing is in order. But what started as a revision of my first book became a re-imagining in light of everything that followed, not just the other books in the series, but the history of my communities, LGBT and Latino/a, in the thirty years since the publication of *The Little Death*. Ultimately, I used less than five percent of the published work and the changes seem so consequential to me that I wanted to signal them by giving the book a new name. *Lay Your Sleeping Head* comes from the first line of W.H. Auden's poem, "Lullaby," which is not only of the greatest poems in English, but which was written by one man to another. It seemed appropriate to what this book became in the rewriting.

It might seem to some readers that for me to go back and rewrite a book that has been in print for 30 years in light of the volumes that followed it is a kind of cheating. Maybe so. But the Rios books have turned out to be my life's work as a writer and from my perspective it remains unfinished. I agree with what Paul Valery wrote about literary work: "A work is never completed except by some accident such as weariness, satisfaction, the need to deliver, or death; for in relation to who or what is making it, it can only be one stage in a series of inner transformations."

In rewriting *The Little Death*, I have returned to a work temporarily interrupted by its publication and go deeper into it as part of my journey of inner transformation.

Michael Nava
San Francisco
May 2016

ACKNOWLEDGEMENTS

I began my literary life being published by Sasha Alyson, an independent publisher of great integrity, who ran Alyson Publications, the most important gay press of its time. After 30 years, I have gratefully returned to the world of independent presses with Kórima Press and its publisher, my friend Lorenzo Herrera y Lozano. Lorenzo embodies the same kind of integrity as Sasha did. Like Sasha with gay writers, Lorenzo's commitment to publishing queer Latino/a writers provides a forum for writers whose voices might not otherwise be heard. It has been a joy to work with him. I also want to thank my friend, the photographer and blogger, Michael Strickland for his close reading of the manuscript and for his beautiful image of the grieving angel. My appreciation also goes to photographer David Quintanilla for his image of the two lovers and to the models, Jorge Montero and Nelson Marin, who brought them to life. Lastly, my love and thanks to Joan Larkin, a woman and a poet of great humanity and wisdom, for letting me use her poems.

ABOUT MICHÆL NAVA

Michael Nava is the author of an acclaimed series of seven novels featuring gay, Latino criminal defense lawyer Henry Rios which won six Lambda Literary Awards. In 2000, he was awarded the Bill Whitehead Award for Lifetime Achievement in LGBT literature. The New York Times review of the last Rios novel called him "one of our best." His most recent novel, *The City of Palaces*, was published in 2014 by the University of Wisconsin Press. *The City of Palaces* was a finalist for the 2014 Lambda Literary Award for best gay novel and was awarded the 2014 International Latino Literary Award for best novel. This new novel, *Lay Your Sleeping Head*, a reimagining of the first Henry Rios novel published 30 years ago, is the first of a revised edition of the Rios novels to be published by Kórima Press.

OTHER KÓRIMA PRESS TITLES

Amorcito Maricón
      by Lorenzo Herrera y Lozano

The Beast of Times
      by Adelina Anthony

Brazos, Carry Me
      by Pablo Miguel Martínez

The Cha Cha Files: A Chapina Poética
      by Maya Chinchilla

Ditch Water: Poems
      by Joseph Delgado

Empanada: A Lesbiana Story en Probaditas
      by Anel I. Flores

Everybody's Bread
      by Claudia Rodriguez

Las Hociconas: Three Locas with Big Mouths and Even Bigger Brains
      by Adelina Anthony

Jotos del Barrio
      by Jesús Alonzo

The Possibilities of Mud
      by Joe Jiménez

Salvation on Mission Street
      by Cathy Arellano

Split
      by Denise Benavides

*Tragic Bitches: An Experiment in Queer Xicana
& Xicano Performance Poetry*
      by Adelina Anthony, Dino Foxx, and Lorenzo Herrera y Lozano

When the Glitter Fades
      by Dino Foxx

71741011R00165

Made in the USA
Middletown, DE
28 April 2018